Everything was completely under control

Kylie reassured herself as she knocked on Cole's door. They had business to conduct, so their lust would take a backseat. Work first, play later.

Then Cole opened the door and she melted like chocolate in a warm fist. "Hi," she whispered, ready to drop her briefcase and dive into him.

His face lit with joy, but he stepped back to let her in instead of grabbing her into his arms.

"Maybe we should rethink what we're doing," Cole said.

Oh, no. If he got sensible, she was sunk. She so needed another night with him, making love, feeling that release, not to mention discussing her projects. She had to reason with him.

"We're getting carried away, right? I know. But I have the solution. We work *first*." Kylie threw her briefcase on the table, struggling to get it open. She'd crammed so much into it, the clasp was stuck.

Suddenly it sprang open, spewing items: a file, a notepad, her toothbrush, her sexy lingerie and two packets of honey, similar to the ones they'd made sexy use of the other night.

Cole picked up one packet and a slow smile spread across his face. "You had something in mind?"

Dear Reader,

The perfect match. What a dream. Wouldn't we do anything to find that one person? Isn't that what matchmaking services—with their profiles—provide?

Of course, there's more to finding a lifelong love than can be recorded on a chart or a bubble test. There's that extra something…the heart and work and compromise of it….

That started me thinking about a character who isn't interested in any kind of match. Meet Kylie Falls. She's on her way to a big future in L.A. when she trips over Cole Sullivan. How inconvenient. Try as she might to keep things casual with Cole, she learns there's no such thing as *simply sex*.

I hope you enjoy this story…and that someone you love is reading a book beside you right now. Or else you're about to bump into him at the bookstore or the Laundromat or a Starbucks—he's out there, I know it.

Let me know what you think of the story, at dawn@dawnatkins.com. Visit my Web site for upcoming releases—www.dawnatkins.com.

Yours,

Dawn Atkins

Books by Dawn Atkins

SIMPLY SEX
Dawn Atkins

TORONTO • NEW YORK • LONDON
AMSTERDAM • PARIS • SYDNEY • HAMBURG
STOCKHOLM • ATHENS • TOKYO • MILAN • MADRID
PRAGUE • WARSAW • BUDAPEST • AUCKLAND

To David, my own perfect match,
and to my sister Diana—he's out there!

Acknowledgments
All my gratitude to Lynda Johncock-Henkel,
a real-life matchmaker who's brought happiness to many
Arizona couples. Lynda, keep the happily-ever-afters coming!

ISBN 0-373-79209-3

SIMPLY SEX

1

"YOU WON'T BELIEVE THIS, but the guy on line one just asked me to kiss his willy."

Kylie Falls and her sister Janie looked up at Janie's receptionist, standing wide-eyed in the doorway.

"He asked you to kiss his what?" Her sister's face went pale.

"His hoo-hoo…johnson…whatever, Janie. I'm *not* saying what *he* called it."

"What did you tell him?" Janie asked.

"I told him no, of course—heavens, what do you think? And now he wants a refund."

"A refund? Is he a client?" Janie's matchmaking service was one year old and struggling and she'd called Kylie with her PR expertise to help turn things around.

"God, no, he's not a client. He thinks we give phone sex."

"That's ridiculous." Janie picked up the handset and punched the flashing button. "Sir? I'm afraid you've confused Personal Touch with another kind of, um, touch. We arrange committed relationships and—excuse me?"

Color flooded Janie's face. Was the guy saying something mean or gross? Kylie stood, ready to tell the jerk where he could stick his wagging weenie, but Janie's words were calm.

"You've obviously read the wrong ad, sir. Hang on." She palmed the mouthpiece. "Grab the *Arizona Weekly,* Gail."

Gail fetched the free entertainment paper for the Phoenix metro area, folded to an inside page and handed it to her boss, her gypsy bracelets tinkling.

Janie examined the paper, then looked up at Kylie in dismay. "They put our number in the phone-sex ad!" She handed her the tabloid.

Sure enough, PT's number was also in a boxed ad with the headline "Let's Get Personal." An easy mistake for an overworked ad rep to make, but a disaster for her sister's business.

"What do I say to this guy?" Janie asked Kylie.

"I'll handle it." Gail grabbed the phone, pasted on a smile and spoke sweetly. "Sir, I'm afraid you've reached the wrong number, but this is your lucky day. Instead of anonymous encounters with unseen strangers, why not get the personal attention of the best matchmaker in the valley?"

Kylie stifled a laugh. Gail had been Janie's first client and was her biggest fan. There wasn't an unattached adult Gail didn't believe wouldn't benefit from "a happily ever after with The Personal Touch."

The guy must have said something harsh, because Gail slammed down the phone. "Be that way, Mr. Hoo-hoo. Your loss."

"I'm afraid you'll be fending off willy whackers all week," Janie said on a sigh. "Though that's the least of our problems." She turned her worried face to Kylie, her breathing labored. Janie's childhood asthma flared when she was under stress and circling the bankruptcy drain definitely caused stress.

"Take a slow breath, Janie," Kylie said softly, waiting

for the soft inhalation before she shifted into business mode. "We'll get a correction and a free extension, don't worry."

"Tell me what to demand," Gail said.

Kylie rattled off concessions and Gail jotted notes, then headed off to do battle with the classified department, earrings and bracelets jingling merrily.

"I'm just so glad you're here," Janie said. She came around her spindly antique desk to smother Kylie in a flappy-sleeved hug. "Thanks for not saying I told you so."

"There's no point in that." Kylie believed in moving on, not dwelling on mistakes. It was no secret she thought a matchmaking service was a waste of Janie's psychology degree and a risky place to invest her half of the trust their parents had provided, but she'd done some research and discovered Janie's customized approach filled a unique niche in the volatile dating-service market.

"I'm sorry to interfere with your plans." Janie had insisted on handling everything herself until this financial crisis hit. "What about your new job?"

"I'll ask for a later start date." When her sister had sent out her S.O.S., Kylie had been busy closing down K. Falls PR, since she was due to start work in two weeks at a top agency in L.A. She hated to disappoint Garrett McGrath, a titan in the business, who'd asked her to join his firm, but it couldn't be helped.

"What would I do without you?" Love and relief shone in Janie's eyes and she hugged Kylie again. "At least it's for a good cause. You're helping me save people years of flailing around in the singles sea. Doesn't that make you feel good?"

"It makes me feel seasick."

"You don't mean that. Why do you act so tough?"

"That's just me." And always had been. She'd been the strong one through all the moves of their childhood. Their father's food-service company sent him all over the country and Kylie's job at each new place was to ensure her shy, frail sister felt safe, secure and content wherever they landed—from Philadelphia to Fresno and all major cities in between. Kylie scouted the best routes to schools, scrounged up the playmates and playgrounds and planted the familiar garden.

"People make too much of romance," she said. "If they'd just focus on living full lives, they wouldn't need someone else to feel complete."

"It's not being incomplete. It's sharing your life with someone, being part of something bigger than yourself— a couple, then a family." Janie's pretty eyes glowed with mission.

Kylie admired her sister's commitment—she was dedicated to preventing others from making the romantic mistakes she'd made over the years—and her resilience. Her heart must feel like the last bruised apple in the gunnysack after her string of bad boyfriends, but she remained convinced love was worth it.

Kylie wished like hell that Janie would find a man good enough for her. Or stop wanting one so much.

"Trust me, Kylie. You *are* making a difference."

"Whatever." No sense getting all mushy. Clearheaded strategies were what they needed now. "So I'll get the Web site fixed, pitch some feature stories, work up a promotion, place a few ads, and barter a business plan from the guy who did mine."

"And cut costs, right?" Janie said.

"Yeah. You'd better drop the party hall lease—we can do inexpensive networking parties. What else can we lose?" She surveyed the office, lush with romance—lace curtains on the window, doilies on the fussy antiques, pink-striped wallpaper, red velvet chairs. "Stop buying those." She pointed at the vase of fresh roses under the window. Janie changed them every week.

"Roses warm the room and offer hope."

"Get some silk ones." She studied the Victorian-era secretary on which they rested. "And how about eBay for that?"

"I won't dismantle the welcome center. That's false economy."

"Maybe you're right." She was being too harsh perhaps. Maybe it was the saccharine Muzak overhead. "I Will Always Love You," blended into "You Look Wonderful Tonight," to be followed by "You're the One…" "My Only You…" "It Had to Be You."

Blech. A person could drown in that sea of syrup.

But why was she so cranky about it? She didn't begrudge anyone the search for love or schmaltz. She knew why. Lack of sex. Months and months and months of drought. If only she had a bed-buddy for the occasional booty call. Or the chutzpah to waltz into a watering hole and snag a hottie for one sweaty night. Lately, she'd been too busy to sleep with anyone.

She sighed. "So, I'm on it." It didn't seem as bad as Janie had made it sound on the phone. Three weeks, maybe, and all cookbook stuff. No need for creativity, her secret Achilles' heel. She'd zip in and zip out—a one-woman marketing SWAT team—and juggle her own plans, too. If all it took was hard work, she could handle it. She knew how to work.

There was that piercing fear that Garrett McGrath might rescind the incredible job offer or, worse, rethink his high opinion of her, but she'd deal with that. She had to. Janie was counting on her. Work over worry was the philosophy she shared with her father.

"So, that's it, right?" she asked, just to be sure.

A pink sunrise flared in Janie's cheeks.

Uh-oh. There was more. "What else?" she said, dread rising.

"There is one thing…." Janie reached into a drawer and handed over a sheaf of legal papers.

Kylie read over the first page of the packet and her heart sank. "You're being sued by a client?"

Janie nodded miserably. "I found him some wonderful Potentials, but he wants women completely inappropriate for his maturity and intellect."

"You mean he's a comb-over who wants a bimbo? Preferably stacked? Isn't the customer always right?"

"I find life mates, Kylie, not ego boosts. If a man wants a midlife crisis, he can buy a Mazda RX-8 or become a ski instructor. I cannot allow him to drag some poor young woman into his morale morass."

"Yes, I know." Janie had better standards than some of her clients, no question, and all the integrity in the world.

"I know you can fix this problem like that," Janie said, snapping her fingers so that her gauzy sleeves flapped like butterfly wings. She looked at Kylie the way she had as a child, standing at the door to a new school, squeezing her hand, smiling up at her. *I know you'll make things right for me.*

The knot in Kylie's stomach turned into a fist. What if she couldn't do it this time? "I'll do my best," she said.

A lawsuit was big. A few whiz-bang promotions wouldn't make a dent in that expense. Unless she found the right legal help in a hurry or somehow appeased the disgruntled client, her marketing SWAT swoop couldn't save Janie's business. She'd need more than creativity. She'd need a miracle.

THE PLACE WAS way too pink, Cole Sullivan thought uneasily as he sat in a plush chair waiting for Jane Falls. He'd chosen Personal Touch for its pragmatic approach—fingerprint and credit checks and a computerized personality inventory—but her rose-filled, doily-decorated office made him feel foolish, instead of practical. Hiring a matchmaker was like hiring a headhunter. He was saving time, prescreening for compatibility, just as he would in the search for a new law firm. Marriages were partnerships, after all.

Who was he kidding? This was no business decision. He was lonely. There was something of the treadmill to his life, a hollow ring to his days that he figured marriage would fix. That was practical, right? So he was practical *and* foolish. He guessed he belonged in this Pepto-Bismol fairyland, after all.

He sensed movement behind him and turned to find a woman walking—no, floating—his way. Glenda the Good Witch, minus the bobbing bubble, tiara and wand.

He had a fleeting fear that, in a syrupy voice, she'd command him to click his ruby wingtips together three times, except she held a no-nonsense clipboard and wore a serious expression. "Janie Falls," she said, reaching to shake his hand, her voice direct and syrup-free. "I'm happy to meet you in person, Cole."

"Likewise." Her handshake was as solid as her voice.

She was pretty, with wavy blond hair that hung down her back, but not his type, really, even if it were ethical to date one's matchmaker.

She glanced at her clipboard. "I see we have your Check Mate profile already in our database."

"Yes." He'd appreciated the after-hours convenience of taking the inventory online. It asked him to evaluate his temperament, conformity level, career ambition, affection needs and attitudes toward religion and finances—all issues Jane claimed were predictors of compatibility. Made sense.

"So, today we do your interview and your Close-Up. Have a seat." She gestured at the red velvet chair where he'd been sitting, then went to sit behind her desk.

The video he dreaded. He patted his pocket to be sure his prepared remarks were there. He was short on time, so maybe he could skip the interview. "The profile was pretty comprehensive. Could we just do the video?"

"The face-to-face provides subtle details, Cole, so that my intuition kicks in. I find that's how I make the best matches."

"I never argue with success." She claimed over a thousand clients and something like an eighty-percent match-up rate, convincing him to choose her service over several others. If more personal information brought the right woman into his life, he'd read his childhood diary to her. If he had one.

"So, tell me about your most recent relationship."

"It's been a while," he said, feeling himself go red.

"Was it serious?"

"No. Casual." Sheila had been irritated that they spent most of their brief hours together in bed. She liked the bed part, but wanted more time. Which he didn't have. "Because of my schedule." He'd hated disappointing her. And Cathy before her, who'd pick a fight if he didn't call her every day. In the end, he'd given up dating altogether. He couldn't stand the pressure.

"Have you ever been serious with a woman?"

"Not until now. In college everyone was casual. And I worked a lot. To help my parents and pay my way through law school."

"Tell me about your parents' relationship."

"They've always been very close."

"And is that what you want? What your parents have?"

"Absolutely. They're devoted to each other. To their careers, too. They're both high school teachers."

"But you went into law?"

"Yes. I enjoy the law. The puzzles, the complexity." He'd chosen challenging work. His parents had pounded into him the need to use his intellect in whatever career he chose. "I enjoy helping clients. Meeting their needs."

"You work very hard." It wasn't a question.

"Yes, I do." *Be the best, never quit.* His life blood.

"Tell me more about why that is."

He fiddled with the crease of his slacks, feeling sweat trickle inside his shirt. He wasn't much into self-analysis. But he babbled on about the prestige of his job, the satisfaction of hard work well done.

"And the money?" she prodded.

"Money matters, sure." He'd worked all his life— through high school, college and night law school. Those low-skill jobs had showed him how easy it was to lose economic ground and end up living hand-to-mouth like many of his co-workers were forced to. He had a way out and he vowed to make the most of it. He appreciated his good fortune more than his trust-funded colleagues, who'd gone straight from college to law school and never felt the pinch of poverty.

Even his parents, with master's degrees and thirty years of teaching experience, struggled to make ends meet. He never wanted that. In fact, he intended to make their lives easier as soon as he was in a stronger position at the firm.

Janie listened closely, writing an occasional note, honing in on him with her gaze, working him over with her intuition. God, he wanted this finished. He ran his finger under his collar.

"What about outside interests? What are your passions?"

Hell. He couldn't say *work* again. "I used to play baseball for a parks and rec league. I rode with a bicycle club. Also, photography. I won some prizes."

"But that's not recent?"

"I'm on a partner track."

"Sure," she said, but she pursed her lips in mild disapproval.

"I went skiing two weeks ago," he blurted, though it was for the firm and he'd mostly schmoozed with clients or worked in his room. He'd only managed one ski run.

"What leisure activities will you share with the woman in your life?"

"I thought we'd eat out, go to movies, plays, all that." That sounded lame. "Maybe hike?"

"Relationships take time, Cole," she said gently. "If you're not in a good place with your career…"

"I'm prepared to budget the time." Benjamin, Langford and Tuttleman could spare a few of the sixty hours a week he gave them so that he could advance the greater good—their mutual future.

"Spontaneous is better, Cole."

"Spontaneous?" Sweat dribbled down his temples. This was way more nerve-racking than he'd expected.

"Just relax, be yourself, and speak from the heart. Go!"

Oookay. "Yes. Well. I'm Cole. I'm an attorney—business law, specializing in mergers and acquisitions. Benjamin, Langford and Tuttleman, or 'BLT, hold the mayo,' we like to say." He laughed—which came out in a snort—and felt like an idiot. His cell phone chimed from his breast pocket. He lifted a hand. "One sec."

Janie shot him a look, but when he heard Rob Tuttleman's voice, he was glad he'd taken the call. Tuttleman wanted to meet with Cole and Trevor McKay, one of his competitors for partner, about an important case that had fallen through the cracks. A crucial break for Cole. "Terrific…looking forward to it," he said into the phone. "We can meet as soon as I get back in about…" He glanced at his watch, then at Jane, who looked stern. *Dates aren't billable hours.* "I'll buzz you when I get back."

He hung up, determined to hurry this along. "Sorry. Where was I?"

"Holding the mayo. Let's talk about you as a person, not a lawyer. Go."

"Let's see. I'm dependable…loyal…faithful. Hell, I sound like a St. Bernard. What else? I'm looking for a woman who wants to join her life with mine." That sounded hopelessly drippy.

The clink of jewelry signaled the arrival of the receptionist—Gail was her name, he thought—and he was relieved by the interruption.

"Sorry, but I have Harold Rheingold from *Inside Phoenix* on the line, Janie. It's about the article."

"Oh. I should take this." She looked apologetically at him.

"I can do the Close-Up," Gail said, bustling to the camera, her large bosom jostling for air behind a tight purple blazer.

Jane looked uncertainly at him.

"We'll be fine," he said, figuring the woman couldn't possibly have Jane Fall's intensity, sense of mission or intuition. He'd get Gail to cut it short.

Once Jane was gone, Gail pushed a pencil into her piled-up red hair and looked at him over half-glasses trimmed in rhinestones. "You're one lucky man to have Janie Falls on the case. She found my husband for me, you know."

"You were a client?"

"Nope. I was interviewing for the receptionist job and Wayne, the light of my life, was installing phones. Before he could say 'Can you hear me now?' Janie had matched us. And Wayne is the song in my heart, let me tell you. She'll find you yours."

"I hope so." He did. He craved a bond with one special person. Yeah, getting married would help his career, but what he really wanted was someone to grow old with. Someone to stand side by side with, facing life's challenges, enjoying its triumphs. A soul mate, corny as that sounded, though he'd never say that out loud to anyone.

Gail bent to study him through the viewfinder, making him feel like a bug under a microscope.

"I think I should explain what I'm looking for in a mate," he said to hurry her along. If they knew what he wanted, the women could self-select. He didn't want to disappoint anyone.

Gail tapped a finger to her lip. "Not sure that's compelling, but we can always edit it out. Okay…action!"

Action? They were in Hollywood now? "I'm hoping for someone comfortable enough in her career that she can be flexible about mine. There are social events and charity projects related to the firm, so she should enjoy that. She should also be an independent thinker, a self-starter and a team player."

"Hon, do you want her to marry you or work for you?"

"Oh. Sounded like a job description?" On the other hand, too many couples got caught up in chemistry and learned later their lives didn't mesh.

"You're not putting in an order at the Wife Factory. Try selling *her* on *you*."

"So I should explain that I'm—"

"Not the 'self-starter, team player' bit. Give me something tender and sensitive."

"Yes, but—"

"Even independent, self-starting team players want roses and poetry. I'll walk you through it, don't worry."

Gail swung into action, directing every aspect of his performance, from his body angle, facial expression and vocal quality to the words he used. She yelled "cut" and "action" until he had a headache, before finally declaring it a "wrap," and offering to show him the "rough cut."

He didn't have time. He was hopelessly late for the meeting with Tuttleman and McKay. Besides, he couldn't bear seeing what she'd gotten him to say. He'd blurted the Sunday-morning-and-the-*Times* fantasy *and* confessed his deepest hopes. What sensible woman wanted a sweaty, desperate lawyer blathering on about melding two lives into one?

He'd need a redo. With Jane, this time, not Gail Ford Coppola, who kept saying, "Go deeper, no, deeper, give me the inner Cole." He hoped to hell his computerized personality inventory netted him Potentials, because all the inner Cole would earn him was therapy.

2

"OF COURSE I'll come out for the retreat," Kylie said to Garrett McGrath, her future boss, swerving to miss a minivan. "And the account meetings are no problem." Her heart pounded high and tight from the near-accident and the stress of easing the impact of her delayed start date in L.A. Plus, if she didn't get the artwork on her front seat to the printer in ten minutes, her client's grand opening would be ruined.

"Just think of me as a satellite office for these few extra weeks," she said, wishing Garrett had waited just an hour to return her call. Who knows what other promises she'd make in her frantic effort to survive the drive and make him happy? She'd already promised two trips to L.A. and an entire weekend for the firm retreat.

"That sounds workable," Garrett said in the melodic drawl that had been the voice of America's cushiest toilet paper in the eighties. She'd mollified him, thank God, but how would she manage all he'd asked, along with closing out her own clients and rescuing Janie?

"We need your fresh voice in the room, Kylie."

Hearing those glorious words from the genius of Simon, McGrath and Bellows, she knew she'd do it if it killed her. She honked at a woman applying mascara at a green light, then barreled after her on the yellow.

She'd come to Garrett's attention by winning a national ad award for her campaign for an effective handgun-locking device. He'd searched her out and offered her the chance of a lifetime.

Saying yes had meant closing down her two-year-old agency, but the honor had been too great to reject. The professional validation was enormous and she hoped to learn tricks to compensate for her weaknesses. Besides, she told herself, with the prestige of a few years at S-Mickey-B, as the firm was affectionately known in the marketing world, she'd draw clients like flies when she reopened her practice later on. The month-to-month financial struggle had been more daunting than she'd expected. She wasn't that sure of herself.

"Just clear your conflict fast," Garrett said, "so we can have you all to ourselves." His words made her heart swell with pride and squeeze with pressure. Her already-knotted stomach turned inside out with all she had to do.

At least she'd made progress promoting Personal Touch over the past week, including scoring a profile at a trendy rag with the right demographic, but neither she nor Janie had yet gotten the suit-happy client on the phone. Soon she'd have to look at hiring an attorney. Big bucks they didn't have, dammit.

She shifted her gaze from the traffic to her dashboard clock. Seven minutes before Sun Print closed and her client, Dagwood Donuts, was out of luck.

"I'd like your thoughts on a campaign for Home Town Suites," Garrett continued at the leisurely pace of someone not braving murderous traffic with a cell phone pressed to her ear and a client's future on her passenger seat. "Maybe you can sketch some ideas when you have time."

Time? Time? She had no time. A Crystal Water truck screeched to a stop in front of her. "Damn!" She slammed on her brakes.

"Excuse me? Is that a problem?" Garrett said.

"I was swearing at traffic, not you, Mr. McGrath." A collision with the mountain of water before her seemed welcome at the moment. It was October, but the desert heat hung on like desperate fingertips on a ledge. Her suit was lightweight, but dark blue—chosen to reinforce her authority—and it was baking her alive.

She let Garrett rattle on about branding and niche marketing, while she wove through traffic like James Bond, praying any passing police would be too awed by her technique to ticket her. Wrapping up the conversation at last, leaving Garrett content and her overloaded, she scored a neighborhood shortcut and roared into a Sun Print parking spot just in time. She grabbed the artwork CD and raced inside.

Twenty minutes later, she exited, mission accomplished. Shaky with relief, she smiled at the dropping sun and slid behind the wheel, noticing she'd gotten ink on her fingers from admiring some freshly printed flyers—you had to compliment the pressmen. They were where the ink met the paper in her biz.

Glancing in the mirror, she saw her blouse collar had black fingerprints, too. Ruined. Along with the pricey panty hose she'd snagged along the way. Collateral damage was inevitable when you worked as hard as she did.

She was on the street headed home when her cell emitted the music she'd assigned Janie's calls. Unwilling to risk another accident, she zipped into the closest parking lot to call her back. Fleetingly, she noticed the marquee above her head: Totally Nude. All You Can Eat Businessman's Buffet. She'd parked at a strip club. Yuck. Middle-aged salesmen ogling boob jobs while they inhaled ambrosia salad and bean dip. Strip clubs seemed so desperate.

Of course, sexual frustration made her do strange things, too—pant over *Cosmo*'s naked chefs issue, devour erotic romance novels and think wicked thoughts about cucumbers. Masturbation was a pale second to the joys of a warm and willing man. Where was one when she needed him?

"I need your help ASAP," Janie said when she answered, her voice thin with tension.

"Take a slow breath, Janie Marie."

"I'm okay," she said, but she sounded like someone had wrapped a rubber band around her vocal cords.

"Breathe, Janie. Consider it a personal favor."

"Oh, for pity's sake." She huffed in a couple of irritated breaths. "There. Are you happy?"

"Yes, I am. Now what's up?"

"I need you to fill in on a date." Over the past few weeks, as problems mounted, Kylie had stood in for missing matches a number of times. There'd been a mistake on the Web site which had married couples appearing as available and Gail had double-booked a few people. Kylie's job was to be polite and genial and noncommittal and keep the client around until the right match could be made.

"What happened this time?"

"Gail got overly enthusiastic. Turns out the client's match is in London right now."

"I love Gail, but she's not much of a receptionist. She's never at her desk, for one thing."

"She's my entire sales force. Everywhere she goes she pitches Personal Touch."

"When the money turns around, hire a real reception-ist, okay? Let Gail do what she's good at full-time."

"Will you do the date?"

"Just tell the guy there's been a mistake."

"He's a lawyer. Unhappy lawyers file lawsuits. This is his first date with us and he's barely squeezing in the time. I'm afraid he'll bail. You're so good at smoothing. The woman in London is his perfect match."

Someone honked at her from behind. She looked in her rearview to see the guy motioning her forward. What the…? Then she spotted the low Jack-In-The-Box sign beside his car and realized she wasn't parked in the strip club lot. She was blocking the fast-food drive-thru lane next door.

"Just a sec," she said to Janie, then rolled forward to or-der a mint-chocolate-chip milkshake. Might as well get something out of the mistake, right? "Tell me about this guy," she said on a sigh.

"Thank you, thank you, Kylie! His name's Cole Sullivan and he's smart and serious and handsome. You'll love him."

"I'm going to apologize to him, not marry him, Janie," she said, reaching to take the milkshake from the clerk.

"You have twenty minutes to get there."

"Twenty minutes? It's tonight. Now?" In her alarm, she squeezed the cup and icy green sludge slid down her jacket and plopped onto her navy blue lap. "Shit, shit, shit."

"Don't swear at me. I won't ask you again. Jeez."

"I'm not swearing at you, Janie. I'm swearing at the mound of ice cream in my lap."

"The what?"

"Never mind." She dabbed at the mess with a wad of nap-kins and planned out her best route through rush-hour traf-fic. The things she did for love. Someone else's love, that is.

DEBORAH RAMSDALE was twenty minutes late, Cole realized, glancing at his watch. Not a good sign on a first date. She was an attorney—international law—so she knew the value of a minute. He couldn't help wondering if she'd seen his desperate video and changed her mind altogether.

He'd taken Gail's word that this lawyer was perfect for him, since he'd been unable to check out her video at Personal Touch. *Brunette with a breezy cut, medium height, a tad tense, but you'll fix that,* was how Gail had described the woman when she'd called him. Gail was a trip.

But the tense brunette with the breezy cut was getting later by the minute. Cole swallowed his disappointment. At noon he'd zipped out to buy a new casual shirt. The salesgirl at Neiman Marcus had declared it flattering against his skin, letting her fingers linger on his shoulders longer than was strictly necessary to check the fit.

He'd had hopes that Deborah would let her fingers linger, too. He'd cut out of the office an hour early to change into the shirt and black jeans and to do a quick pickup at his apartment, even changing his sheets, just in case they ended up at his place and things…progressed.

If she didn't show, he'd go home and work, he reasoned. With no date, he'd get more sleep and head into the office early Saturday morning. Larry Langford, the non-golfing partner, was usually there by eight, so he'd score some dedication points. Not so bad, after all.

Except his neighbor Betsy was bringing her dog Radar over in the morning. So, he'd bring the dog to the office with him. Betsy had assured him that Radar was cheerfully self-sufficient, but he didn't want to leave the poor thing alone in a strange apartment on the first day.

Convinced he'd been stood up, he rose to leave, then noticed a woman had just walked in. She searched the room, taking in each table, rejecting each in turn, until she caught sight of him and their gazes locked. For just a second, he thought he heard bells, but it was only a cash register ringing up a bar bill.

She shot him a relieved and radiant smile and headed his way, weaving quickly among the tables, catching all eyes—especially male—as she went. She looked…famous…important…and very pretty.

So this was Deborah. He hadn't counted on beauty, but he wasn't sorry. Wow.

She'd been held up at work, he concluded, since she wore a business suit over a great figure. Or maybe changing a tire, he amended when she got close enough for him to see black smudges on her cheek and collar. Then he noticed blotches of pale green on her jacket and skirt. A food fight perhaps?

"Cole?" Her smile overcame every shred of dishevelment. "So sorry I'm late. Traffic was bad and I was clear across town." Her eyes, a sparkling green, were the shiniest he'd ever seen, and he thought he saw a flicker of attraction. Jane was good. Talk about "potential."

"Deborah?" he said.

"No, but I'm here on her behalf." She made as if to sit, so he pulled out a chair. She scooted in so fast he was left holding thin air. A take-charge woman. He liked that. Except—

"You're not Deborah?" His soaring hope sank like a stone. He sat across from her.

"Let me explain. I'm Kylie Falls."

"Falls? Are you related to—?"

"Janie? Yes. We're sisters."

"You don't look alike." Janie was tall and blond, while this woman was petite with short, dark hair. Not medium, not brunette, and more intense than tense. She seemed to have gathered the loose energy around them, like reining in wild horses, turning them into a team in her hands.

"Deborah was called away to London, Cole. Gail will reschedule when Deborah returns and I just want to apologize on Janie's behalf for the mix-up and the delay."

A cell phone tinkled. She lifted a finger, smiled apologetically, then whipped the phone out and to her ear. "Candee?" She turned slightly away for privacy. "I made it, but barely. Watched them load it myself. It'll make the Sunday circulars and ValuPak drops... Mmm-hmm... That's why I get the big bucks. Send four-dozen Dagwood glazed for the crew at Sun Print, please. Thanks."

She smelled good, too, he noticed. Something light, not sweet. Sporty, he thought, was what the magazines called it. No wedding ring. *She's not Deborah*, he reminded himself.

"Gotta run. I'm at dinner... No, as a matter of fact, I'm not alone." She glanced at Cole, then dropped her gaze. "I do too have a life. Say goodbye, or I'll ruin yours."

She put the phone away and he couldn't help watching her breasts move beneath her jacket. "Sorry. My secretary. I had a last-minute thing to take care of." Catching him mid-ogle, she glanced down at herself. "I'm a mess."

He cringed at getting caught drooling, though she'd had the grace to pretend he was noting her grooming. Classy lady.

"Never drink and drive. Or at least, not a mint milkshake."

"You look fine," he said. *Good enough to eat.* He changed the subject. "Sounded like your secretary was surprised you weren't alone."

"I'm more or less a workaholic and Candee cuts me no slack."

"Me, too, but all attorneys are workaholics, so no one cuts anyone slack."

"And we know you carved out time for this date, Cole. Janie deeply regrets the error and we'd like to treat you to dinner."

"That's not necessary." He had a frozen pasta thing in his freezer and the Littlefield work in his briefcase.

"I insist."

The stubborn flicker in her eyes intrigued him and made him say, "Only if you'll join me."

"Of course." He could tell she'd half hoped he'd let her escape with just the bill. "Janie would never forgive me if I left and some beautiful woman snatched you up before Deborah gets back."

"That's not likely."

"Sure it is. You're a very attractive man." Sexual interest flared again in her face, sparking a pointless heat in him that he enjoyed immensely.

She looked at his empty martini glass. "Gin, vodka or something more elaborate?"

"Gin, neat, olives."

"Ah. A traditionalist."

The waiter appeared on cue and she ordered another for him and one for her before Cole could object.

Not that he wanted to. He intended to work when he got home, but how could he pass up the sting of gin while looking over a frosted glass into this woman's shiny eyes? "I'd arm wrestle you for the check, but something tells me I'd lose."

She jammed her elbow onto the table, braced for fore-

arm battle. "Want to try me?" Her tone held mischief and
challenge. *Go for it, big guy.*

"Too many men watching you. My ego couldn't take the
hit if you beat me."

"Come on." She seemed to think he was just flattering her.

"I'm not kidding. Every man in the room is sneaking
glances."

She blushed, which had the effect of making her eyes
look greener. "They can't believe I haven't been kicked out
as a transient." She brushed at her stained jacket.

"Trust me, that's no problem. But you do have a little…" He brushed at his cheek to show her where a smudge
remained.

She scrubbed the spot. "Gone?"

"Not quite." He reached out a finger, then thought better of it and dampened his napkin in his water glass to wipe
her cheek. Their eyes locked. Energy surged between them.

"Thanks." She dried what remained of the water with a
finger and they both took a shaky breath.

"So, Deborah's in London," he said, reminding himself
why they were smiling and breathing at each other.

"She'll be back in four weeks. On the fourth."

"A month?"

"Sounds long, I know. Maybe Janie could connect you
two by phone."

"I can wait. This was a dry run on making time for a social life and it hasn't exactly been easy." He regretted leaving work to buy a new shirt and changing sheets for
Deborah. Though he wasn't quite sorry about meeting
Kylie, even if it was a waste of time.

When their drinks arrived a second later, he raised his
glass. "Here's to a happy mistake."

"Absolutely." Her eyes gleamed more richly. She seemed relieved he wasn't angry about the mix-up, but there was delight there, too. She wasn't sorry, either.

He took a sip of the drink, relishing the chill, the burn, the smell of juniper and Kylie's eyes. "So," he said, setting down his glass, embarrassed that he couldn't take his eyes off her. "You work for Personal Touch?"

"Oh, no." She almost shuddered. "I have a PR and marketing business. I'm just helping Janie out with some promotions. And I want you to know this mistake is not typical."

"No need to apologize again. I'm paid up through the year." He touched her hand. The contact was electric and his entire being lit up. Ridiculous. He'd just met the woman. But he'd been celibate for a long time.

She took a harsh breath, so he knew the reaction had at least been mutual. "So, you enjoy the law?" she asked, clearly changing the subject.

"Very much. I'm in corporate law. Benjamin, Langford and Tuttleman. Mostly mergers and acquisitions." Then he caught himself, remembering his video ordeal. "I'm sure you don't want to hear about my work."

"Oh, yes I do. Talk to me about it." She wiggled into her chair, resituating herself as if she anticipated some thrilling tale of due-diligence derring-do.

Her breasts swelled under the ice cream–stained jacket, reminding him how hot she was, but he forced himself to talk about the all-important Littlefield case and was soon engrossed in the topic. She asked good questions and he found himself jotting down an idea or two she sparked in him.

Somewhere in there the waiter took their orders of steak and the restaurant's signature Caesar salad. Kylie selected a terrific pinot noir—a prime selection in *Wine Spectator,* he recalled—proving she had taste as well as intelligence and beauty.

He hoped Deborah Ramsdale was like her. He'd love evenings spent this way, with time zipping by, words flying, warmth and connection growing. Maybe his time would have been better spent working at home, but he didn't give a damn. It was more than the loosening effect of the second martini. He plain liked Kylie.

"So, you have your own PR firm," he said. "How did that happen?" He settled in to listen to her describe with animation and energy how she'd come to start K. Falls PR, who her clients were, what campaigns she'd created.

Then she told him she was closing it down and moving to L.A. in a month. He felt a punch of regret. As though he'd caught the tail end of something wonderful about to tear out of his world. The woman was a stand-in, here to apologize and buy his dinner. They would never see each other again.

"What's wrong?" Kylie stopped herself in the middle of gushing over the S-Mickey-B offer. Cole Sullivan was looking at her as if he'd lost his best friend all of a sudden.

"It's stupid," he said. "Just that you're leaving town. And I'm enjoying this…the dinner…and you."

He blushed the most adorable pink. The guy was a hottie, with a sturdy and graceful face, warm brown eyes ready to sparkle at the slightest pleasure and her favorite mouth—sensuous, but masculine. Lucky Deborah Ramsdale.

"Me, too," she said, flattered by his reaction. "I'm enjoying you, too." The thrill of attraction had every nerve tight and she liked the guy, felt as if she knew him far better than she actually did. He was a workaholic and a good listener, just like her. If she weren't leaving town, she'd want more dinners like this. Hell, she'd want more than that. She wanted him. That sexy mouth, those strong hands, those amused eyes drinking in her naked body.

Stop, stop. She was simply crazed with sexual frustration. The first attractive man she'd met in a while had her wiggling in her chair ready to meet him under the table for some mad groping.

"Tell me about this award you won," he said, sounding embarrassed by his admission. So, she told him about Lock-It and its success and how Garrett McGrath had searched her out and about why it made sense to put her company on hold while she built her success. She almost admitted her doubts about making it on her own, her sense that she lacked the brilliance required to really succeed.

He seemed deeply interested in her ideas. His comments were pertinent and insightful. He wasn't just waiting for a chance to talk again. And he kept smiling as if she delighted him.

And that turned her on. In a way, her reaction was odd. She deliberately hooked up with guys who were different from her—laid-back, easygoing, with jobs, not careers. Cole was very much like her—ambitious and driven—so she would expect to feel kinship, not passion.

But she was feeling more than comradely. The warm tickle between her thighs had become a steady throb. She crossed her legs to control it, feeling like a girl in the throes of a crush.

"More wine?" Cole lifted the bottle.

She nodded and when they both reached for her glass, their fingers brushed. Heat shot through her and she took in a violent gasp. Lord, what a weakling she was. "Hiccups," she lied, faking a second harsh intake of air. She watched him pour the last of the bottle into her glass, the light gleaming off the magenta liquid, and realized the sad truth: Dinner was over. They would part soon. Forever.

She sighed. She couldn't help it.

"What's up?" he asked, his tone as affectionate as a friend, his expression as attentive as a lover.

Lover. The word sent chills through her.

"Nothing," she managed. "I just haven't done this in a while. Gone to dinner with someone for fun." She squeezed her crossed thighs tight, trying to quell the relentless throb. She couldn't act on the feeling. Her purpose was to soothe Cole, not seduce him. It plainly wasn't healthy to go so long without physical release. Now she'd latched onto the first wonderful, interesting, smart, funny man she'd met.

Cole Sullivan was a find, though, no question. Any woman would react to him. She was human. She had needs.

"I know exactly what you mean," he said, his eyes twinkling with mischief, and she was pretty sure he shared the sexual frustration, too. "I'm Cole," he said somberly, "and I'm a workaholic."

"Hi, Cole," she said, but then she thought she should be serious for a second. "I don't think we should have to apologize for working hard. We have goals. You're fighting for partner. I'm pushing for recognition. When we're ready to kick back, we will, right?"

"Right." He grinned with relief. "Exactly. I'm glad you said that."

"Except you're looking for a wife, so you must intend to make some changes." She was curious why he'd paid a matchmaker when he was hot enough to attract plenty of women.

"Some changes, though I hope to find a woman at a point in her career that fits with where I am. Someone who's willing to help with the social duties that come with being a partner."

"Ah. You want a corporate wife." She hoped he wasn't expecting the adoring little woman, circa 1950, who would meet him at the door naked, wrapped in Saran Wrap, holding a Tom Collins mixed his way. Cole seemed better than that.

"You don't approve?"

"Some women are okay with that, I guess. My mother gave up an architectural business to go with my dad wherever he got transferred. She never complained, but I think she has regrets about sacrificing her career."

"I don't want a woman to give up her work for me, just make room for mine."

"That makes sense." It did, she guessed, for the right woman. She hoped Cole found her. Maybe it was Deborah, whom Janie had declared a perfect match.

But here he was with Kylie now and they were sipping the last of their wine and staring at each other in a silence thick with arousal. Maybe just a kiss. The idea roller-coastered through her and her stomach plunged.

"Enough about my marriage plans," Cole said softly, his flicking cheek muscle signaling the desire she read in his eyes. Her heart began to beat so fast she put a hand to her chest.

"Can I get you anything else?" the waiter asked wearily.

They both started at the interruption. They'd had dessert and coffee, paid their bill, and their table had been cleared long ago. They'd dragged this out impossibly long.

"No, no. We're fine," she said.

Cole sipped at his empty wineglass, putting up a pretense of still having something to consume. She was glad he seemed no more inclined to say goodbye than she was. Their connection felt condensed, as though they'd swallowed their friendship as a bullion cube instead of sipping cups and cups of broth.

"It's hard to believe you need Personal Touch," she said.

"I take it you don't approve of dating services."

She realized how he might take that. "It's not that. And Janie's the best. If you need help. But you don't seem…"

"Like a loser who has to pay someone to get him a date?"

"That didn't sound right." She blushed. "I just hate the taste of shoe leather, even flavored with mint and chocolate."

He chuckled lightly. "I figure I owed the love of my life the same energy I'd invest in a career search. I see Janie as my relationship headhunter. I don't have time to hit bars or parties, so I see this as a practical answer to a time-consuming problem."

"It's efficient, I guess." When he put it that way it made sense. "If I ever want to settle down, I might do the same thing." Janie had offered her services many times.

"So, no boyfriend?" His face went from pink to bright red.

"Not right now. I'm too busy. And it gets too…"

"Complicated?" When she nodded, he said, "I've been out of circulation for going on two years. Gets lonely."

"No kidding. I miss sex." She swallowed hard.

Cole laughed. "That's cutting to the chase."

"Why be subtle?" She flamed with a blush all the same.

"Good point. Sex can be a problem for workaholics. The last woman I saw wasn't happy that I only had time for, well, for—"

"Quickies?"

He grinned sheepishly.

"Boy, do I know what you mean. You have a nice evening—great sex—but you need sleep. Except the guy wants waffles and strawberries in the morning, then there's more sex and before long the weekend's lost. So you try to catch up working late all week, but he feels neglected."

"Exactly. It's a drag to disappoint someone."

"I keep hooking up with guys with a lot of spare time and they want to hang out, go to games or concerts or camping or sailing. What little free time I have I like to spend—" she leaned closer and whispered "—watching TV." She winked. "I'm a secret TV junkie."

"Me, too. Comedy Central is my favorite."

"Oh, I live on that station." The cable network featured stand-up comics, quirky sketch shows and humorous talk shows.

Cole grinned, delighted, she could tell. "I hustle all week so I can watch *Friday Night Stand-Up.*"

"Bingo," she said and laughed. He joined her, his eyes twinkling, then settling into something much hotter.

A silence fell. It was clear that neither wanted to leave, but the tables were all empty, the waiters were putting up chairs and somewhere someone vacuumed. Under the table, she felt as if her body were on fire.

"Why can't sex be simple?" she said softly, wanting very much to take this heat between them somewhere they could quench it. "Why can't it be a lovely physical encounter between two people who want each other?"

"And afterward they go about their lives," Cole said, his voice husky with emotion, his gaze level.

"Exactly."

"We should leave." Cole nodded at the waiters standing at the bar, shooting them go-home-now looks.

"We could go to my place and…talk."

"Yeah," Cole said slowly. "Let's talk."

They would do more than that, she knew, by the gleam in Cole's eye, her pulsing sex and the tension vibrating between them like a note held too long.

This was exactly what she needed—simple sex. A glorious hookup. For one night. Safe and easy. Except for one thing.

"What about Deborah?" she blurted. Would Cole's perfect match mind sharing him with her?

"Deborah's the future. This is now. Tonight."

"I'm so glad you feel that way," she said, relieved. And a little worried about herself.

It wasn't like her to jump into something like this. She had a plan, every hour laid out, timed to the minute. Tonight she needed sleep. She had major work tomorrow.

But she didn't care. Just like accidentally parking in the fast-food lane, she'd turn this mistake into a mint-chocolate shake. And *not* ruin a suit doing it.

3

WHAT THE HELL are you doing? Cole asked himself, accelerating to keep up with Kylie's pale blue Accord. She was zipping down the nearly empty streets as though they were in a car chase. He'd like to think she was hell-bent on getting her hands on him, but he was pretty sure her usual pace was breakneck.

They'd only met a few hours ago, but he felt as though he'd known her for years. Toward the end, they were finishing each other's sentences. They were surprisingly alike. They were even both big tippers. She'd scrutinized the gratuity he'd insisted on paying and it turned out they'd both done stints waiting tables and knew how hard the work was.

Now desire pounded through him like a heartbeat. He glanced up at the moon shining through his sunroof—big and round and so bright it looked fake. He wanted to howl at it like some randy beast. He squeezed the cool leather of his steering wheel and kept driving.

Somewhere in North Scottsdale, he caught the pale flash and bright blink that signaled Kylie had turned into a residential area. He followed, winding through a complex of red tile-roofed townhomes. He pulled into the empty space next to where Kylie parked and noticed the dashboard clock said midnight. It was very late and he had lots of brain work on the Littlefield file in the morning. This was all pretty hasty. Not like him at all. Maybe he should suggest an end to the night, he thought, climbing out of his car. They both needed sleep. She'd understand. Probably be glad.

But she'd leaped out of her car and was heading his way, gaze level, stride determined, and he knew he wasn't leaving until he'd held this amazing woman in his arms, kissed those lips, touched her everywhere he wanted to touch her.

She was here now. Tonight. How could he pass her up?

She came to him and, without a word, cupped his face in trembling palms, drew his mouth down and brushed her lips against his so softly it was barely a kiss, full of questions like her eyes in the moonlight when she pulled back and looked at him. *Do you want this? Should we do this?*

She obviously wasn't as casual about sex as she'd sounded in the restaurant. He was aware of her ribs stretching and subsiding under his palms with each uncertain breath. His cock, hard against her body, knew exactly what it wanted.

"What are your doubts?" he asked her.

"It's so late."

"I won't stay long. You'll still get sleep, I promise."

She smiled. "What if it gets complicated?"

"We won't let it. It will be—what did you call it?—a lovely physical encounter between two people who want each other."

"And only one night?"

"Not even that. Couple of hours."

"No expectations? No hurt feelings?"

"None and none," he said, running his tongue along the

edge of her ear, relishing her shiver and quiet murmur. She trembled in his arms.

"What about birth control?" She was struggling to speak. "I'm on the pill…are there health issues?"

"None for me."

"Me, either. Good."

She had the shiniest eyes he'd ever seen. He couldn't even figure the exact color for the gleam. Green, but some brown, too. Smart eyes. Sparkling and intense. And she wanted the same thing he did—sex. He felt a rush of freedom. He was a lucky man.

He slid his mouth over hers and she opened to him, surrendering, melting against him with a sigh. He kissed her deep, wanting in. And she met him with the same urgency.

Desire tightened in him. He shoved a hand between their bodies to flick open her jacket and get at her breast, running his thumb over its knotted tip under the blouse and her bra, moving fast, frantic.

She squirmed against him, then gripped him through his pants. He moaned into her mouth. They staggered a little. They were groping each other, moaning, gasping, knees buckling, acting as if they hadn't had sex in a long time.

Which they hadn't.

She broke off the kiss. "If we don't get inside, my neighbors will call the police…or start videotaping." She grabbed his hand and he let her tug him forward to her back door and into her kitchen. "Do you want coffee or a drink or some water?" she gasped, pulling at him.

"No. You?"

"God, no." She hurried them onward. He got an impression of granite counters, glass-fronted cabinets and smelled cinnamon, coffee and some summer fruit, musky and sweet.

Kylie led Cole down the hall toward her bedroom, feeling carnal and wild, just rushing to bed like this. Maybe they should talk a bit. She turned to speak, but Cole kissed her desperately, as if they'd traveled too far without contact, and her doubts slid from her mind like butter from a hot knife.

Cole took charge, nursed the lust, feeding it like a fire so that it swelled and roared between them. Hot chills raced up and down her body and her knees gave way. She needed something to lie on. The bed. If she could…just… make it…there.

She broke off the kiss and tugged him the few remaining feet to her bedroom and then to the bed.

Cole shoved her jacket off her shoulders and to the floor, then grabbed for her blouse buttons. Normally, she'd want to show off the lovely peach-lace bra and panties ensemble she wore, but not now. A primitive message pounded through her… *Clothes off…now. Lie on bed… now.* Through him, too, it seemed by the way his fingers shook and his breath came harsh and quick. He unclipped her bra, ripped it off and flung it to the floor, then cupped both breasts in his hot hands. The man wanted her so badly he'd practically torn her clothes to get at her. That made her feel powerful.

And weak with lust. She had to get horizontal. She leaned back to fall onto the bed. Cole caught her, though, and reached below her to toss open the bedspread, making pillows fly. One knocked the silk arrangement from the bureau, another made the lamp wobble. "Sorry," he said.

"I don't care." *Wreck the place…whatever.* The part of her that was careful and thorough and efficient and thrifty seemed to have drowned in desire. She fell to the bed and dragged Cole with her, yanking at his shirt, while he massaged her breasts and she squirmed under him.

In the end he had to unbutton his shirt for her. He tossed it into the darkness, tipping something over, but she didn't care. She had what she wanted—his naked chest hot against her breasts. He kissed her mouth again in that slow building way, then went lower to run his tongue across a sensitive nipple, one blessed bump at a time.

Oh, oh. Wow. She wanted more of this. More sucking, more licking, more kissing, more nudity. There were still so many *clothes,* she realized in despair. They'd kicked off their shoes in the earlier madness, but Cole still wore pants and they had her skirt, hose and panties to contend with.

Cole lifted her torso to get at her zipper, but it jammed. This was the one that got stuck.

"Just rip it," she gasped. "It's broken." Well, nearly. And it would be after this.

He looked at her, dark eyes lust hazy, making certain she meant what she'd said.

"Do it. Really." The faulty fastener stood between them and blessed nakedness.

Holding her gaze, Cole jerked the skirt with both hands. The zipper gave with a dangerous-sounding rip.

"Good," she said and his eyes flared.

He yanked her skirt off her body, dragging her stockings, too, deliberately using force. He was stripping her. As if nothing could keep his hands off her—not a polyester sure-lock zipper, not Hanes Her Way control top panty hose, not her satin panties, which would have to be cut off, but she did not want him away from her body for a single second. Even though she knew exactly where the scissors were.

He jerked her panties down—almost as satisfying as if he'd shredded them with his teeth—then studied her sex, slowing everything down.

She trembled under his attention, the pleasure in his gaze conquering her anxiety about the way her stomach retained fluid and tended to look bloated, no matter how many crunches she did.

He ran his fingers down her stomach and brushed her pubic hair, setting her newly on fire. She had to touch him, too, but he still wore pants. She went at his belt. He helped her and after a few fumbling seconds, she gripped the lovely length of him.

He moved into her palm, solid velvet. "That's good," he said, his dark eyes host to an electrical storm, lightning strikes of lust crackling in their depths.

He slid a finger gently into her cleft, along the side of her clitoris with perfect indirect pressure. Men sometimes rushed to get there and startled the poor thing. He coaxed her higher and tighter and she squirmed under him.

"I want you inside me," she whispered, longing for that full, tight, glorious sensation.

"I want you on top so I can watch," he said.

"Sounds like a plan." She loved how easily they'd declared what they wanted. She rose on her knees, aware of his anticipation, the appreciation in his gaze, and guided him into her slick interior.

He went deliciously deep, filling her to her cervix and she moaned, a long, desperate sound that didn't even embarrass her. Instead, she did a slow twist on his cock, pushed forward, then back, in an erotic rhythm that made him close his eyes with a groan.

When he opened them, they were on fire. He reached

for her breasts, so she bent forward to give them to him. "You're so beautiful...you feel so...good." He was fighting to speak, she could tell, struggling to reassure her, which was thoughtful.

When he sucked a nipple into his mouth, she could only make noises and half words, riding his shaft with frantic jerks. The sensation was exquisite—the tight, wet pull on her nipples, the full friction of his shaft moving in and out, brushing her swollen clitoris. It was wet and wiggly and wonderful and almost more pleasure than she could stand.

He gripped her hips and guided her faster, moaning, his eyes rolling back, though he was trying to maintain eye contact with her. She loved that she'd made him crazy, so that he jammed into her with all his might, banged her cervix with sweet force, dug into her hips with his fingers.

She felt him tighten like a stallion collecting its power for a jump, so she knew he was about to come. She increased her pace, wanting to push him over the edge, wanting the power of forcing him to climax.

But he stilled and looked up at her, holding her with his gaze while he deliberately pressed his thumb to her button.

"Oh, oh, oh." She stilled, then rose high and jammed downward, pierced by a new heat. She pivoted wildly on him and her climax tightened, ticked, ready to explode. Cole was in charge and she was surprised she didn't mind at all. In fact, it was a relief to just let go and let him do her, stroke her, push her over the edge.

She opened her eyes to look at him, to let him know how grateful she was, how surprised.

"Kylie." The way he said her name made something inside her give way. Like a breath she'd held too long, a muscle she'd tensed to the point of pain.

Her climax arrived, distracting her, and she cried out, rocking helplessly, lost in sensation, in release, in joy. At the same moment, he pulsed into her. Their climaxes collided like storm-brewed whitecaps that collapsed into a rolling wave that swelled, then lapsed into ebbing ripples of pure bliss.

Kylie fell onto Cole's chest, panting for air. "That was incredible," she said, feeling his heart pound against her ear.

"Incredible? Is that all?" His voice was husky with amazement and humor. "I think we violated the laws of physics in there somewhere."

"I think you're right." She snuggled into his chest, slid a leg between his, their mingled fluids making their bodies deliciously slippery.

He wrapped his arms across her back in a soft caress. She wiggled in, eager for a few moments of rest. "I really needed that," she said, the proof in the deep, pleasurable peace she felt. "I've been under a lot of strain lately."

"I can imagine. With closing out your business."

"I don't know that I've ever…" *Had sex this good. Felt this comfortable with a man.* Something about Cole tempted her to blurt intimate truths. She remembered how he'd said her name, the look on his face. *I've found you, Kylie. You belong to me. We belong to each other.* Worse, she'd liked it. She'd wanted to rest in his arms, let go of something. What? What was she holding on to so tightly?

"You don't know that you've ever…?" Cole repeated. She realized his fingers, which had been tickling her skin, had stilled.

"…been so ready," she finished lamely. She'd been thinking crazy thoughts.

He released a breath. Was he disappointed? Then he

chuckled. "Then let me say how lucky I feel to have been handy." He shifted so he lay on his side looking at her. She did the same. "That was impressive for a first time."

"It was, wasn't it? We were in perfect synch." It was so startling she almost felt like she'd dreamed it.

Feelings crossed his face like wind-blown clouds. *You amaze me. I want you again. What's going on here?*

She felt the same. And it scared her.

Cole's lips moved, about to say something too personal, she'd bet.

Please don't ruin this. We had a deal, she thought.

"I should let you get some sleep," he said matter-of-factly, relieving her of that worry. He shifted as if to get up.

She had to grin. She'd used that line herself to escape to her own bed. "Don't rush off on my account, Cole. We could go again in a bit."

She watched the idea register. *That would be great.* Followed quickly by, *Better not.* "I promised you just a couple of hours," he said and kissed her before leaning across her to squint at her clock. "One-thirty. You can be asleep by two, and get five hours of sleep before seven."

"Lie here at least until your heart stops pounding. I don't want you to pass out in my driveway."

"Sounds nice." He smiled down at her, his eyes crinkling with pleasure, his breath soft on her face. In the late-night blackness, his face seemed familiar, like someone she'd looked up at in the dark for years.

He rolled onto his back and pulled her onto his chest, wiggling into the mattress. "This feels good." He made it sound like a guilty pleasure. Which was exactly what it was.

She cozied onto his chest, feeling more relaxed than she'd felt in months. A man like Cole could be a joy to have around. They were as compatible in bed as they'd been in conversation. She could get used to this.

Again, that odd pain speared her. Sadness. Loss. Where did that come from? Then she remembered. She'd been five and they were moving away from her best friend Patti. It hadn't been the first move, just the first that hurt. And the last.

That final day she and Patti had played all day. All their favorite games, breakfast through dinner at Kylie's, joined at the hip, giggling hysterically at everything, squeezing out all the fun they could to the very last minute. Then Patti's mother came to pick her up. They'd looked at each other and burst into tears. *Please don't go,* Patti had cried desperately, her face scrunched with pain. *I can't stand you to go.*

Kylie had felt so lost and helpless in the face of her friend's agony, which mirrored her own, that she felt a sharp pop inside her, like the sound of the garden beans she snapped for her mother. *Don't let it in, don't let it hurt.* That had been the lesson. Kylie had learned it well.

She must be stressed if she was drumming up childhood hurts while lying in a delicious postcoital doze with a lovely man who'd loaned her his body for these few glorious hours.

She kissed his cheek and nestled in, but her tension was back. What if he fell asleep and stayed all night? She had work to do. They'd made a deal.

In the morning when she woke, though, Cole was gone. Relief rushed through her. The knocked-over silk flowers were back on her bureau, her bedspread folded at the foot of the bed, the scattered pillows placed neatly on the bedside chair, and she smelled French roast in the air. He'd made coffee, bless his heart.

And written her a note, she saw when she padded to the kitchen. *Thanks for a lovely encounter. Good luck in L.A., Cole.*

What a thoughtful guy. She liked his handwriting, with its heavy, even strokes. They reminded her of—her gaze snagged on the grocery list she'd clipped to her refrigerator—her own handwriting. They wrote the same.

She felt a sharp jab in her side. She *missed* him, for heaven's sake. So silly. Probably due to the fact that she was moving away, which had unsettled her in secret ways, she'd bet.

She would miss Janie, for sure, though she'd been too busy with K. Falls PR to spend much time with her sister. Janie had been consumed by Personal Touch, too, for that matter. Kylie would miss her business, too. Candee, her assistant, a part-time student, planned to go to school full-time, so she would be fine when Kylie closed her doors. But Kylie would miss her and her clients, her office, the work itself.

Pointless nostalgia. She had a plan and a purpose and she would stick with it. The great sex had just caught her off guard, softened her defenses. She poured coffee and sipped the musky brew—Cole liked his coffee strong, too—and grabbed a pint of low-fat yogurt for energy. She had to get busy.

Her mind wandered to the night before.

That was impressive for a first time. Oh, yeah. She remembered his fingers on her body and an electric chill raced through her. If only he were still here.

Eh, eh, eh. Be sensible, girl. She prided herself on that. Going to L.A. was sensible, too. Cole had agreed with her. He'd put it perfectly: *You have to make short-term sacrifices for long-term gains.* Just a few words from him had boosted her confidence in her decision. Cole understood ambition and hard work, making plans and implementing them.

The flickering doubts that licked at her had to be the uncertainty of starting over somewhere new, along with the fear of screwing up at S-Mickey-B. The stakes there were high. Janie, with her psych degree, would be proud of Kylie's insight.

Now about Kylie sleeping with Cole…Janie would not be pleased. It was pretty outrageous and Kylie would not leak a word of it. She'd been a stand-in date several times. But none of the other guys had been like Cole.

Her mind wandered to a memory of him looking up into her eyes while he touched her sex, and she shivered. That had been delicious. She'd have to send Janie some fresh roses as a secret thank-you for the gift she'd accidentally given her—great sex with a fabulous man and no complications.

Well, except for this tickling wish to see him again. Would he call? Did he remember her firm's name? He could always call Janie and ask for her number. But that would tip her sister off—a bad idea. Maybe she should call him first. What was the name of his firm?

Stop it. She'd had a rejuvenating one-night stand, and that was enough.

Benjamin, Langford and Tuttleman. She remembered. Damn.

4

JANIE GALLOPED around her office, spritzing air freshener like a mad woman skywriting in scent. Her last client, Tony of Tony's Import Auto Repair, had trailed the aroma of gasoline, and she needed the perfect atmosphere for the magazine writer due any minute. His story would rescue her company, she hoped, so the place had to smell like success. Or at least not like a garage.

She took a deep sniff. Still a tang of metal. Candles! Candles would fix it! In seconds, she'd arranged a rose-cinnamon pillar and three lilac-rosemary votives in an attractive clump on the far corner of her desk.

The first two wooden matches snapped in half and the next two burned out, but the fifth worked and soon four golden flames glowed in red and lilac pools of wax. She brushed the match stubs into the wastepaper basket, then waved the *Arizona Weekly* over the candles to spread the aroma before dropping the newspaper into the trash, too— it was a competing publication, after all.

The candles' scent radiated outward, but too slowly, so she grabbed the stepladder out of her supply closet and climbed it to mist the AC vent with freshener.

A tap at the door to her left made her jump down, but before she reached the knob, the door flew open, reveal-

ing her visitor—a man holding a notepad, a camera over
his shoulder. Definitely the reporter from *Inside Phoenix*.

"Sorry to bust in," he said. "There was no one out front."

Gail chose the worst times to disappear. At least when
she returned she generally brought in a new client or two.

"No problem. I'm Janie Falls." She switched the spray
to her other hand and reached to shake his.

"Seth Taylor." He had a nice grip and startling blue eyes
that gave her an up-and-down just this side of decent,
which sent a charge straight through her.

He was handsome, with a cocky smile, longish hair and
the beginnings of golden stubble emerging from a strong
jaw. Why did he have to be hot? She needed full focus to
give him the best possible impression of Personal Touch.

"Have a seat," she said, managing to sound gracious.
She motioned toward the guest chair beside her desk.

He headed there with a lazy grace, his washed-out jeans
cupping his behind like friendly hands. He sat and rested
a foot in worn athletic shoes across his other thigh. Con-
fident, carelessly groomed and sexy as hell. In short, he was
just her type. He reminded her of Jason, the firefighter
who'd headed for Alaska when things got comfortable between them.

She'd declared a moratorium on dead-end relationships
for as long as it took to get Personal Touch in good shape
and until she was emotionally mature enough for the real
thing. She had no idea how long that might take.

Her reaction to the reporter was just a vestige of the old
urge. An automatic physical response. Nothing she could
do about that. She headed for her desk, determined to show
no crack in her armor.

Just as she passed him, the reporter said, "Uh, Jane?"

She turned.

"You might want to…" He motioned at her behind.

At first, she was offended at his nerve until she saw that her slip was on full display. The back of her gauze skirt had brushed up when she jumped off the ladder, no doubt. She shoved it down, blushing.

"Purple's your color," he said with an easy smile. *No need to freak. We're good.*

"Thank you," she said primly. So much for her armor, she thought, watching Seth flip back a page on his steno pad with long, strong fingers. She had a thing for men's hands. Certain men. Certain hands.

She forced her eyes up to his face and swallowed across a dry throat. "Are you single, Seth?" *Please be married, please be gay, please be leaving for the Arctic.*

"Am I single? Yeah, but—" Her question had startled him. Great. That put her more in charge.

"Good, because I thought the best way to show you how Personal Touch works is to give you a dry run of a client's experience. Just a sample."

"That's not necessary. Your press kit is very complete."

"We'll compress the time, don't worry. We'll do a Personality Profile inventory, I'll interview you, show you some Potentials in one of our quarterly magazines, and—"

"Thanks anyway. I just have a few questions and I need to take your picture."

"But if you want to capture the Personal Touch atmosphere…" Speaking of which, the air had begun to reek of something burning. Something besides candles.

She glanced to the far side of her desk, where a wisp of black smoke rose above the wastepaper basket. Heck, oh dear, she'd started a fire!

The paper towel Tony had tossed in the trash must have contained oil. Her discarded matches and the newspaper were heat and fuel. She lunged for the basket, intending to run it to the bathroom, but her movement made the fire lick at her loose sleeve. The gauze lit up like tissue paper.

Seth was there so fast she hardly had time to panic. He grabbed the trash out of her hand, upending it, then whipped off his jacket to smother her flaming sleeve. After that, he bent to pound out the embers with the bottom of the basket while she examined her arm under the flash-fried fabric.

He rose. "Are you hurt?"

"Only my pride."

He acknowledged her joke, but he gripped her wrist and turned her arm to examine it for himself. "Maybe ice it."

It stung a little, but she was too mortified to dwell on that. She pulled out of his grip, shook her tattered sleeve into place, aware of how close he stood. "It was stupid to run. Thanks for saving me."

"No problem." He shot her a wry smile. "When a woman's on fire, I'm always ready to kill the flame." Did he have to be self-deprecating, too? The needle of her bad-boy meter shot into the red zone.

They both bent to scoop the charred debris back into the trash. The combination of candles and burned paper made her office smell like a burning gift shop, but beneath the stink she picked up Seth's mix of soap—Irish Spring?—coconut shampoo and worn leather. Her favorite smells on a man.

Seth plopped the basket over the burn marks that now marred her pastel-flowered Oriental rug. "Good as new."

"For now, I guess."

They both rose, standing close together. His blue eyes

twinkled with amusement. "You were saying something about atmosphere?"

She grimaced. "How about if you wipe this from your mind?" She waved her arms as if to clear the smoke and the memory.

At that moment, Gail burst in the room. "Did that reporter ever get here?" She caught sight of him. "Oh, good. I was at the Macy's sweater sale and got to talking. You'll be happy to know that the women's wear sales staff includes two divorcées, a widow and three women with Singles-Bar Burnout. Expect appointments this week."

"That's great, Gail. Thanks."

Gail scrunched her nose. "Bad incense, hon. Smells like burning tires and candy apples."

"I had a little incident." She lifted her sleeve, which looked like it belonged on a pirate, postpillage.

"Criminy Christmas, Janie, be careful." She turned to Seth. "She was so nervous about you coming."

"You were nervous?" Seth asked her. More twinkling.

"No. I—"

"Extremely," Gail inserted. "This story is vital to us."

"Uh, Gail, we don't want to tie Seth up." *But can I offer you a gag?* "Will you hold my calls?" Janie attempted an eyebrow move meant to convey a plea for cooperation.

"Hold your calls?" Gail blinked. Janie wanted Personal Touch to seem thriving but they hadn't even had the usual quota of wrong-number perverts since Seth had arrived. Finally, Gail caught on. "Oh, you bet. I'll do my best to keep those calls at bay. It's not easy, let me tell you. It's wild out here on the switchboard." If anything was worth doing, Gail believed in overdoing it.

After she'd gone, Janie smiled at Seth. "Gail's very enthusiastic. She was my first client, you know."

"Oh, yeah?" Seth listened politely while she explained how she'd matched Gail and her husband, but took no notes.

"Maybe that would be a good sidebar?"

"Maybe."

"I don't mean to tell you how to do your job." Was she irritating him? He hadn't responded to any of her ideas so far. Her skin itched from tension, and the spots where the fire had touched her arm stung like crazy. "So, how did you envision capturing Personal Touch for your readers?"

"Envision?" He smirked, but kindly. "I don't know if I intended anything so lofty, but how about a photo of you?" He lifted his camera.

"You're a photographer, too?"

"When I have to be." He didn't seem too happy about it.

"Okay. Where do you want me?"

His eyes sparkled at her words. *You really want to know?* Then he surveyed her office. "Man, it's pink in here. Looks like a dollhouse."

"I chose this look to reassure our clients. The flowers, the soft colors and the lace convey the idea that dreams can come true."

"You check that theory with men? Looks pretty girlie to me."

"Men want romance, too, Seth. Along with logic. And that's why Personal Touch is unique. We mix the pragmatic with the romantic."

"Sure. I get it." But he thought she was dishing out a sales pitch and he didn't buy a word. "So, back to the photo."

"How about here?" She rushed to the table under the lace-curtained window, where a vase of fresh pink roses rested. Kylie, who'd declared live flowers too expensive, had inexplicably sent her a dozen dewy blooms.

Seth considered the scene. "Kind of a cliché, but why not?" He moved closer and snapped a quick shot, studying it for a sec in the viewfinder. "Looks great."

"Did I blink? I don't think I was smiling."

"See for yourself." He turned the digital camera for her to look in the viewfinder. In the photo she looked startled and nervous and wore a faint smile.

"Pretty eyes, nice smile, see?" he said, and she was too swamped by the crinkles around his eyes, his scent, and his strong fingers clutching the camera to object. "Just a few questions and I'll get out of your hair." He started toward his chair.

"But I want you to take all the time you need. The computerized personality profile would take just ten minutes. That's your angle, by the way. I have a trademark on the software, which is unique to the industry."

He turned to stare at her, his impatience palpable, though he was clearly trying to appear relaxed.

"I know your time is valuable…."

He studied her while the antique clock behind her desk clicked off five seconds. "I give," he said finally. "Show me your software." His tone was teasing and low, the way he'd ask a lover to reveal something even softer.

There was a zing of connection between them. Gratifying, but not good.

"It'll be quick, I promise," she said, swallowing past the knot in her throat. She went to her desk and clicked open a fresh Mate Check computer file. Seth stood behind her and looked over her shoulder, his gaze warm on her skin, that lovely mix of coconut and leather filling her head.

Keeping her voice steady, she described the six areas of compatibility and opened the first set of questions, her fingers a little shaky on the mouse. "So, how would you describe your temperament, Seth?"

He didn't answer immediately.

"How about...?" She checked the box for *I'm usually easygoing, but when I'm angry, I blow.* She was being generous. He struck her as irritable and a bit gloomy.

"Close enough."

She guessed at three more questions.

He nodded. "Okay. What if I lied?"

"Like any good psychological test, this one includes questions designed to detect inconsistencies. And the profile is only part of the Personal Touch process."

"I get it. All very scientific." He returned to his chair, evidently finished. "And you also make videos, right? Close-Ups? I've looked at your Web site. What else?" He prepared to write.

"There are networking parties, of course, and—"

"The magazine. Can I see one of those?"

She found the summer *Book of Possibles* and handed it to him.

He flipped through it, scanning the pages. "My favorite things are calico cats," he read from one listing, "and the smell of the desert after a rain." He shook his head, then flipped forward. "I can't wait to swirl snifters of brandy with you in front of a roaring fire in my custom-built Prescott cabin." He looked at her. *Do you buy this?*

"The magazine piques interest, Seth. I handpick the matches based on my analysis of all the data I gather."

"And you're a good judge of character?" He returned the magazine to her, holding her gaze.

"No one's infallible, but I must be doing something right, since my success rate is—"

"Eighty percent, yeah, I read that. Impressive for a year-old business."

"We think so." Now they were getting somewhere. At least he'd done some advance reading.

He made a note, then raised his eyes. "So, describe your average client."

"I have no *average* clients. Each and every one is special." She smiled, pleased at her line, though Seth didn't react.

"But we're talking professionals, right? CEOs, doctors, lawyers. People rich enough to pay your fees?"

"I charge the same as less-customized services, Seth, and I have teachers and builders and bankers and secretaries, too." Her reasonable fees were partly why she was in financial doo-doo. "My clients find that if they tally their expenditures on dead-end dating, personal ads and bar-hopping, Personal Touch saves them money."

"Sure," he said, a half smile lifting his lips.

"Many of my competitors merely serve as a video library. Clients view tapes until their eyes glaze and they give up in despair. We share only the videos of the top Potentials, hand selected by me."

"For the 'personal touch.' Got it."

The distance in his eyes told her she was sounding like an infomercial again and her heart sank.

"So, what do you do with the homely guy who wants a stacked blonde? Or the gold digger looking for a sugar daddy?"

"I ask them to look beneath the surface to what really matters."

"I bet they love that." His eyes twinkled at her, inviting her to let him in on something juicy.

"Externals are minor when you're looking for a soul mate."

"But you do credit and fingerprint checks, right? So externals must mean something."

"As a measure of client integrity, yes. And at first people do look at the superficial. I mean, no one walks into a dating service looking for someone poor, fat or ugly."

"That's a good one." He smiled and scribbled.

"I meant to say that you can't judge a person by appearance or checkbook." That had come out wrong. Her stomach tensed and her chest tightened.

"Poor, fat or ugly. Much better. Trust me."

"But that sounds harsh and judgmental. Please don't use that."

"It'll be fine." He winked.

Her uneasiness intensified.

"So how do you keep out the married guys looking to cheat?"

"We certify marital status, of course, but most people mean well. That's a myth, by the way, that—"

"What about sexual predators? How do you protect your clients from the ones who don't have criminal records?"

Ice water began to trickle down her back. The reporter who'd moseyed in so casually, pretending he had just a few quick questions was now digging at her, his clear eyes sharp as shards of blue glass.

"I interview each person, as I said. We, of course, advise caution during the first few dates—meet in a public place, make sure a friend knows where you are, don't share full names. Good sense precautions. We've had no problems, Seth."

"Not so far." He made a note. "I read that three-fourths of dating services fold in a year. How are your finances?"

"Excuse me?" The ice trickle became a stream rushing along her veins. She didn't want to talk about the money troubles or the lawsuit or any of the glitches Kylie was helping her with.

"Is this story vital, like your secretary said, because you're in debt?"

She fought for calm. "We need an unusually high number of clients because of our very customized service. A positive story in your magazine will spread the word."

"So, you're short on clients?"

"We're growing."

"But not fast enough?" His eyes honed in, tracking her, a predator ready to pounce on any weakness.

"What are you getting at, Seth? Am I on trial here?"

He smiled, attempting to disarm her. "Sorry. I wouldn't be a good reporter if I didn't mix it up a little. Throw a few hardballs in with the soft tosses. Consider me the voice of a skeptical client. Convince me."

"I'm doing my best." What was he after here anyway?

"Look, you seem sincere, Jane, but desperate people are easy prey for the unscrupulous. I see it all the time."

"My clients aren't desperate, Seth. They are attractive, intelligent, successful men and women who want to save time and heartache in their search for a mate."

But hunting for a wife would be a desperate act for Seth, she could tell. She'd bet he had a conformity score in the basement and a low need for affection. He was the kind of guy who felt trapped if you asked him what time he'd be over for dinner.

In other words, her kind of guy.

Highly sexed, though, and she didn't need a Mate Check score to tell her that. She felt it in her being.

When the sex was new, he would want her every minute. That's how Liam had been. And Jason, who said he *burned* for her. *Burned*. Pretty romantic for a firefighter. Derrick wrote her poetry. It was all incredibly seductive. Except the minute she gave in and fell in love, they couldn't get away fast enough. Liam to Peru for his thesis. Jason to fight fires in Alaska and Derrick…any other city where they could use a bass player.

"What about you, Jane? Are you single?" He tilted his head at a friendly angle, abruptly changing tacks.

"Currently, yes." She'd prepared an answer to the obvious question of why, if she knew so much about relationships, she wasn't in one. "Right now my focus is on growing Personal Touch. When I'm ready, I'll use my Mate Check system to connect with someone who's right for me."

"Makes sense. Sure." His gaze settled on her face for a moment with electric interest. *Who would be right for you?* She could feel him wonder that. *And how would it be?* Sparks snapped and popped. Oh, dear.

"Can I show you anything more?" she breathed.

"Show me…?" Seth broke the gaze, cleared his throat, as if he hadn't intended to reveal his reaction. "I think I've got what I need." He pushed to his feet and held out his hand. "Thanks."

She stood and they shook. Such a warm hand. Warmer than he allowed his eyes to get. "Can I at least take you on a tour? Show you the video room, run a Close-Up or two?"

"I'll call if I have more questions."

Which he wouldn't, she could tell. "You will contact the clients in my press kit? Interview them?"

"Possibly." He smiled at her, done and wanting out.

"Can I see the story before you finalize it? To at least make sure my quotes are right?" If he used the "fat, ugly or poor" comment, she'd die.

"I'm a journalist, Jane. I don't take dictation." His eyes became blue ice for just a second. She'd insulted him, she realized in despair. He forced a smile. "Story will be out in three weeks. I'll make sure you get advance copies of the magazine. Can I use your john?"

"Sure, sure." She led him to the lobby and stopped at Gail's desk to point down the hall. "On your left."

"I most certainly will not tell you what I'm wearing," Gail said into the phone. Seth immediately honed in. So did she.

"Yes, that's very bad," Gail continued. "You *should* be punished. Oh, ick. Not if you *like* it."

"Gail!" Janie tilted her head at Seth.

Gail mouthed, *Sorry.*

Seth laughed. "Kink calls? Now that's what I call customized service."

"Our ad got mixed up with a sex line. It's straightened out now, but you wouldn't believe how long people hang on to those weeklies."

"Interesting." He eyed her closely, curious and questioning. He didn't believe her?

"It's true, really."

"Sure. By the way, I'd lose the dancing hearts on your Web site. Kind of goofy."

"Oh, that's being changed." She went hot with embarrassment. Kylie was fixing the childish Web site. The Web designer had been inexperienced—and just fifteen. She hoped Seth hadn't looked until after the "just married" list had been removed from the "New to the *Book of the Possibles*" section.

He sauntered off toward the restroom.

"And the phone sex is really a mistake!" she called to him.

"How did it go?" Gail whispered when he was out of sight.

"Terrible. He zoned in on the bad stuff. Stalkers and gold diggers and our finances. And that phone call, for all I know. He doesn't have a feel for us at all."

"So invite him to the skating party." Gail thrust the Skate World flyer at her. "He can interview clients. Maybe he'll even meet someone."

"Are you kidding? He's a Stubborn Single, no question."

"Maybe he's just a Scared Single, did you think of that? Recovering from a broken heart? At least invite him."

"Maybe." She couldn't imagine Seth Taylor on skates. "Oh, listen, Cole Sullivan called."

"Why? Was he mad about the mistake?"

"He sounded strange. I couldn't tell what he wanted."

"Strange? He sounded strange? That's bad. Lawyers who sound strange are considering a lawsuit."

"More dreamy, I guess. Dazed. Maybe we should have Deborah Ramsdale call him. You know, give him something to cling to?"

"Good idea. Get her number in London from her office—Leland and Associates." She became aware that Seth was at her elbow. She shot him a gracious smile. "Thanks for coming, Seth. I just…I hope you will call with any questions."

"Come to our mixer," Gail said, thrusting a flyer into his chest. "Thursday…seven…Skate World…Scottsdale."

He looked at the flyer, then at Janie. "Skate World?"

"It's a networking party. On wheels. You could interview clients in an easy, informal setting. Doesn't that sound like fun?" She sounded like a camp counselor coaxing a homesick kid to enjoy himself.

"I'll think about it." He folded the flyer in fourths and tucked it into his jacket pocket, where the dry cleaner would discover it some months later. No way would he show.

He turned for the door.

"Call me?" she urged him as he passed out the door, taking her hopes with him. "With any questions at all! Any! At all!"

She turned back to find Gail staring at her, eyes wide. "My God, you want him," she said.

"I do not." She sighed. "Do you think he could tell?"

"Probably not." Gail was lying for her benefit.

"I can just feel he's going to write a terrible story. He thinks we're a racket or a joke." She looked down at her arm, where charred shreds of gauze dangled to her wrist. The whole interview had gone up in flames like her sleeve.

"Maybe express your concerns to Mr. Rheingold."

"I don't know…." The mere suggestion she get to see her quotes had riled Seth. If she complained about him, he'd be furious. Plus, the publisher might not be sympathetic.

"Maybe he'll come to the party," Gail said, then looked at her closely. "Maybe he's interested in you, too."

She fought the stupid little thrill that idea gave her. "Maybe I'll invite him again." She had to do something. Her fate was in the hands of a smart-ass reporter who made her melt. She was hopeless.

5

SETH STOWED his camera and notepad in separate jacket pockets and climbed onto his bike, hating this lame assignment. Better than the new water park on the west side, he guessed, his other choice. Water parks in the desert…the ultimate irony.

He'd come to Arizona because he wanted out of Florida and liked the desert, and chose Phoenix on the recommendation of friends from journalism school. Investigative beats were drying up all over the country, but a shake-up at the daily—*Arizona Republic*—meant a possible news opening.

In the meantime, his uncle had invited him to join his magazine staff. Think pieces and news analysis. That was the plan until a key writer on the barebones staff had quit, so now Seth was writing puff pieces driven by advertising. The budget was so stripped they couldn't afford a freelance photographer for his stories.

Taking a snap of Jane Falls had been a pleasure, of course—she was easy on the eyes—but he was no photojournalist. His tools were words, not pictures.

He kicked into gear and roared off, weaving between cars, grateful for the breeze. October in Arizona could bake you to dust if you didn't keep moving. He loved the desert—so stark that spring wildflowers and cactus blossoms seemed exotic gifts from God. The mountains here were geologically raw, speaking to him of endless possibilities. He liked that, needed that, feeling at a crossroads himself.

Which was why he enjoyed hanging with his uncle's stepkids. He'd taken them fishing the past couple of weekends. His uncle considered them smart-assed and lazy, but they were eighteen and nineteen and wide-open to life. They were interested in journalism, so that had perked Seth up.

As he turned east toward his apartment, he cooked up a lead for his story: *Jane Falls, owner of Personal Touch Matchmaking Service, meets clients with a handshake as warm as her mission—to find Phoenix's singles their perfect match. Speaking of warm and matches…watch out or she might just set you on fire.*

But this wasn't a humor piece. And Jane seemed sincere, though that could be faked, he knew from his investigative work for the *Miami Trib.*

He'd interviewed sociopaths who, with tears in their eyes, claimed to be saving helpless seniors from hordes of roaches with scented water spray and caulking. The human capacity for self-deception amazed him. Truth was the ultimate reward.

He pictured Jane Falls. Her eyes were an unusual blue—almost purple—and round as a doll's with thick, curved lashes. *Arresting.* That was the word for her eyes. In all its meanings. They could stop you cold, make you hold up your hands in surrender. *Ya got me.* He smiled at the image. And she was so damned earnest. You'd think she could change the world.

Where was the edge to the story? The conflict? The angle? Maybe he could expand the piece to cover other dating services, including the scams he'd read about in his research.

There'd been that odd exchange he'd picked up on coming out of the john. Something about a mistake with a lawyer client named Sullivan. Cole Sullivan. And a woman in London—Deborah something…Ramsay? Ramsdale. Yeah. From Leland & Associates. Law firm? CPA? Maybe he'd look up Sullivan with the bar association and find out what had gone wrong.

And what about the sex call? Jane had jumped in with both feet to explain that away. Was there more to the story? He'd check. Anything to spice up the piece, which could send a diabetic into sugar shock if he wrote it the way she'd presented it.

What the hell color were her eyes? Lilac maybe? Or some flower color—periwinkle. Sweet, but with a definite bite. And a mouth so puffy you wanted to kiss it just to see if it could be that soft.

He'd let his interest show. Not smart, but, hell, he was human, and he'd been alone for a while. She smelled damn good and there was something about her and those big lilac eyes. Stupid.

Even if she weren't a story source, he wasn't interested. He hadn't even had the energy for a tumble since Cindi. And Cindi had been a mistake, anyway, because of Ana. He wasn't sure what it would take to get over Ana. She was all tangled up with losing the book deal and it just plain hurt too much to think about.

Meanwhile, Jane Falls had invited him to watch lonely schmucks parade around on roller skates. He wanted the truth, not to expose human beings' tender underbelly. And the underbelly was never more tender than in matters of love. He knew that cold.

He swung into his apartment lot, parked, ripped off his helmet and pushed the hair off his sweaty forehead. He needed a haircut. One of these days. Inside, he checked messages for a word about the *Republic*. Nothing.

Maybe he'd call the TV station that had been blasting teasers about a new investigative team—Eye Out For You. There was something brewing at a local security company he could pitch and look into. Irregularities with hiring, a sexual harassment complaint.

Maybe later. He tossed his helmet on the sofa and plopped into the lounger, clicking on the TV. He'd watched a lot of daytime tube since he got to town a month ago. Just getting story ideas, he told himself, his gut tight with guilt.

Who was he kidding? He'd been sluggish, maybe depressed, after losing the book sale. And Ana. Always Ana.

He had a right to feel bruised. He'd done most of the work on the Pulitzer-winning series on the pest-control industry, but the paper had pushed Ana into the limelight, wanting to celebrate the only woman on the five-reporter team. The other guys were assholes about it, but Seth hadn't minded. Ana had worked hard.

Then she started believing the hype. Plus, their relationship went south. He quit the paper with much fanfare to work on a book about investigative reporting and had interest from two agents and a publisher…until they learned that Ana's similar title was already in progress at another house, rendering his redundant. She'd known his plans, dammit, and gone ahead anyway, beat him to his dream.

That, on top of the months-earlier breakup, made him want out and away. Out of the state and miles from the scene of his stupidity. He'd actually laid money down on a house for her, wanted to settle in, grow roots. He should have known better. Should have known Ana better. And himself.

Where was the damn remote? He found it between the cushions of the sofa—generic beige like the rest of his rented furniture. This was just a brief stint in Limbo Land. He'd rent a better place once he got a job he wanted.

For now, he had a story to write. And Jane Falls wanted him to go to a skating party. God. When he'd folded that flyer into his pocket, her face had just sunk and he'd felt straight-armed in the chest. He'd bet her boyfriends were putty in her hands. No man would want to put hurt in those lilac eyes, send that sweet mouth into a frown.

Nice hair, too. Blond, wavy. Long enough to tickle your face when she made love on top.

Cut it out.

For all her airy-fairy style, she was stubborn, too. A butterfly with a spring-loaded spine. And she'd inserted some practical considerations into her goofy business. Interesting contradiction: romantic dreamer and pragmatic entrepreneur. Maybe he had given her short shrift.

The woman had set herself on fire within five minutes of his arrival. Imagine what she'd do at a roller rink.

KYLIE'S BREASTS settled into Cole's hands, a soft, warm weight in his palms. He pressed his tongue to the warm bumpy velvet of their tips. She moaned. He thrust into her, gripping her hips while she pivoted wildly on his shaft. They rocked in a timeless rhythm. Like dancing, but better—perfectly timed. Rushing and riding, closer and closer to the edge of the cliff and over the—

"Is that right, Cole?"

Right? What? Cole started out of his daydream of Kylie to the awkward awareness that he'd missed Rob Tuttleman's question. They were meeting on the Littlefield project—Tuttleman, he and Trevor McKay—and he'd faded into a memory.

Complete with hard-on.

Shit. He couldn't show weakness to either man, so he shifted the bulge to a less painful position and faked an answer. "I believe so. Yes."

Trevor, to his left, made a sound.

"I'm glad to hear that, Cole," Tuttleman said. "Trevor said three weeks was too short, but I said if you worked as a team, you could manage. I'm glad you agree with me."

Shit again. He'd privately agreed with Trevor to push for six weeks. Trevor would think he was kissing ass.

"We'll do whatever it takes," Trevor said smoothly—the younger man was far better at brown-nosing than Cole.

"That's why I chose you two," Tuttleman said. The man played people against each other by praising them privately, Cole knew, and it worked brilliantly. Associates, secretaries, bookkeepers and paralegals alike slaved away on extra projects or worked endless overtime to prove themselves worthy of Tuttleman's trust.

Cole and Trevor had been singled out for this expedited project over the other single male associate, and Trisha Larner, who was married, which definitely put them ahead on the partner track. Trisha trailed because she was a woman—the glass ceiling sucked. For Mace Cornwell it was because he missed regular weekends over women and wind—he was an avid hang glider.

"Stop by my office after this and we'll divide the research," Trevor said to Cole, seizing leadership, since Cole's dazed state had made him slow on the uptake. "Rough weekend?"

"Not at all," Cole said, rallying. "I came in on Sunday, too, as a matter of fact." He'd had to make up for his late start Saturday after the Kylie experience.

"You were here on Sunday?" Tuttleman asked Cole.

Sunday work was a bit unusual. Impress-the-boss was a stupid game, but Cole would play it until he was in a position to change the rules—once he'd achieved some stature as a partner. And if he couldn't shape things to better suit his values, he'd start his own firm with like-minded colleagues.

"Most of the day, yes," he said. No phones and no interruptions meant for productive hours. He'd been the only one in the place.

"You bring a dog with you, by chance?"

"Uh, yes. I'm watching a neighbor's dog. Why?" Dread filled him.

"Well, it left something outside my office door, which I discovered this morning. On my shoe."

"Oh. Sorry. I kept him in my office, but I did come out to the kitchen to make coffee. He must have...um, gotten confused." Cole's face went hot and he caught Trevor's smirk.

"Have someone in reception cancel my complaint about the cleaning crew then. And don't let it happen again."

"Sure. Of course." He wouldn't be surprised if the dog hadn't done it on purpose. Radar had resisted all Cole's efforts to establish rapport, ducking away from a pat with an indignant shake and a glare: *Hands off, pal. I have a life.*

He'd gotten *confused* on Cole's kitchen floor, entryway and the floor of his bedroom. And now the beast had nixed his workaholic points via dog-doo on Tuttleman's loafers.

As soon as the meeting ended, Cole headed to the restroom to splash water on his face. In the mirror, he caught sight of the fading love bite Kylie had left and tugged his collar up to cover it. It was a silly thing, but he liked having a reminder of how very hot those hours with her had been.

The sex had been incredible. They had been so in synch, so hot, but he was uneasily aware there was more to his reaction than that. He liked Kylie. Her quick wit, her energy, her directness, the way she finished his sentences, but more than that, the way she'd looked at him while making love— as though she was lost and he was the one to find her.

What was wrong with him? He sounded the way he had in that sappy Close-Up. He made a mental note to tell Jane to erase the gooey part.

He and Kylie had had great sex that they both had needed, and now they'd moved on. But he sure liked her. They hadn't really said goodbye. Maybe he'd call her, see if she'd gotten caught up with her work over the weekend. K. Falls PR was her company, right?

But he wanted more than that. And what was the point? They had a deal. One night. A second night could never be that good.

But maybe she wanted to see him, too. Perhaps she'd said something to her sister. He should at least thank Jane, right? He had piles of work to do and Trevor was prepared to duel to the death for partner. He needed full focus. He should stick to work. Absolutely. No time for childish phone calls....

Jane wasn't in, it turned out, and Gail kept going on and on about Deborah Ramsdale, so he figured it was all for the best. His foolish impulse had been wrong. He would forget all about Kylie.

His intercom buzzed. It seemed there was a reporter on the line for him. Seth Taylor…working on a story about Personal Touch.

"How did you get my number?" he said to the guy as soon as he could get a word in. He glanced up to make sure no one could overhear him through his open office door. Hiring a matchmaker would sound desperate to people around here, no matter how practical it was.

"The receptionist mentioned your name while I was there—something about a mistake? So, I looked you up. Would you mind telling me about your experiences with the agency?"

"Not for publication, thank you." The last thing he needed was his name in a story.

"I need an honest evaluation from a client whose name I didn't get from the company. To be fair. You can understand that. And you'd be anonymous, of course."

The guy wanted dirt, Cole could tell, and that raised his hackles. Jane Falls had integrity and compassion. And an incredible sister…

Forget that. The date with Kylie had to stay a secret. That was probably the mistake the guy had overheard Gail mention. "I'll answer your questions, as long as you don't use my name." He had to help Janie. She'd given him a date with an incredible woman and the best sex of his life. Even if it had been a mistake.

"PERSONAL TOUCH, how can I help you?" Janie managed to sound serene, despite the fact she was answering phones for the again-AWOL Gail. No way did it take two hours to get your teeth cleaned.

"Personal *touch,* huh?" the caller said in the husky register she recognized after a half-dozen sex calls this morning. "How about your personal *touch* on my personal—?"

She cringed at the body part he'd named, but before she could correct his error, another line rang. "Hold, please."

"Oh, I *am* holding. So tight."

Gross. Just when she thought the perverts had fixed the number in their grubby Rolodexes, a new batch started in asking to be rubbed, stroked, spanked or licked. She was tempted to screen, but her policy was to greet everyone who called. It was too easy for a client to lose his or her nerve as it was.

Before long, she had Mr. I-Need-a-Spanking on hold and was refusing to describe her underwear to Sir I'm-Wearing-a-Silk-Thong. Then the third line rang. Gail better bring in the dentist, hygienist and the entire waiting room after this.

"Please hold," she said to Sir Panties, who undoubtedly already was. "Personal Touch, how may I help you?" she said to the third caller.

"It's Gail. Sorry, but my car wouldn't start. The good news is that a nice man just offered to jump-start me. He's divorced and lonely, and I told him—"

"Just get here, Gail, please." Gail amiably refused to talk dirty to anyone and saw her mission to be convincing the confused, lonely callers to join Personal Touch and the perverted ones to get help from a therapist on the list she'd taped to her desk. Fed up, Janie punched one of the pervert lines and said, "I'm not interested in your underwear, I will not spank you and I refuse to touch Mr. Big."

A tentative male voice said, "Jane?"

Damn. The pervert had hung up and the new caller knew her. "I'm sorry. I thought you were a per— Never mind."

Lord. She did not belong on the switchboard until this problem was solved.

"It's Cole Sullivan, Janie."

"Oh, Cole. I'm sorry. Our number got mixed up with a sex line. Let me get rid of this guy." The blinking light went blank. Mr. Silk Thong must have "held" long enough to meet his needs and hung up for a cigarette.

She went back to Cole. "Again, I'm so sorry. How can I help you?"

"I thought you should know that a reporter called me. A Seth Taylor? From *Inside Phoenix* magazine."

"He called you?" How did he even know about Cole? Her heart leaped in her throat.

"He overheard you and Gail talking about me, I guess, and wanted my impressions. He seemed to expect me to complain. I didn't though."

She remembered that Seth had appeared at the tail end of her conversation with Gail. He must have eavesdropped first. Now she really did have to call the publisher to complain. This was frightening. "If you don't mind my asking, what did you say?"

"That I'd delayed my use of your services, but that I'd been pleased so far. I didn't much like his attitude."

"Thank you so much, Cole. I've been worried about that reporter. And you're right—he is looking for problems. You've saved the day, I think. Please let me rebate six months of your dues. As a thank-you and to apologize for the inconvenience."

"That's not necessary. As a matter of fact, I'd like to thank you for—"

"It *is* necessary. We so appreciate your patience about the mistake with Deborah. We're so eager to—"

"I had a great time." Cole cut her off. "With Kylie, I mean."

"I'm glad to hear that." Kylie could be charming. Thank goodness she'd charmed Cole or Seth would have had terrible ammunition against her. She had to get off the phone to call the magazine.

"Your sister is…an interesting person."

"Yes, she is." He sounded dazed. The skin on the back of her neck began to tingle. "Again, we appreciate your flexibility. We thought if Deborah called you from London—"

"I hope I didn't bore her."

"Bore Deborah?"

"Kylie."

"I'm sure you didn't." Uh-oh. Cole was hanging on to the topic entirely too long. "The main thing is that *you* had a good time."

"I did. Very good. Great. Please tell Kylie."

"Sure," she said, thinking that was a very bad idea.

"Is something wrong?" Cole asked.

"Not really. It's just that it's a sore subject—me dragging Kylie on a date when she's so busy—so I'd rather not bring it up." That was decent cover.

"Oh, right. I see."

"She does a lot for me—too much, really. It's a sister thing."

"Sure. But if the subject arises, tell her I enjoyed her… it…the dinner." Oh, brother. Oh, no. Deborah had better call him ASAP. If not sooner.

She hung up from Cole, still uneasy, and called Harvey Rheingold, who promised to fix the problem, leaving her not quite certain what that meant. Then Kylie walked in, looking—uh-oh—dreamy. Kylie meandered toward Janie's desk, a file folder in her hand. Meandered? Kylie marched or strode or charged. "The roses look nice," she said wistfully, surveying the expensive bouquet she herself had sent. She turned eyes as glazed as Krispy Kreme doughnuts to Janie. The flowers had arrived the morning after the mistake date.

Warning goose bumps shot down Janie's arms. On the phone, Cole had sounded the way Kylie looked. What had happened between them?

"They're lovely, Kylie. What made you send them?"

Kylie's face turned as pink as the flowers, confirming Janie's fears. Kylie rarely blushed. "The real thing is warmer…more…I don't know. And the smell is fabulous. You left out how good the smell is."

"True." Luckily, the trash fire smell from yesterday had faded. Janie had no intention of mentioning that to her sister. It was bad enough she had to explain that the magazine story had gone awry. How could she have given that smart-ass skeptic Seth Taylor the benefit of the doubt? Distraction by attraction, dammit.

"So, what brings you in?" she asked, wondering what she should say about Cole.

"I thought I'd show you what I've done so far." She sat on the chair beside Janie's desk and handed her a folder.

Janie flipped through pages she'd already seen, while Kylie absently described the upcoming radio promotion, the Web site correction and the business plan trade-out she'd achieved. She'd done a remarkable amount of work over the two weeks since they started the project.

"You showed me all this Sunday, Kylie," she said gently. "Is there something new?"

"Oh, right." Kylie blushed. Again.

Janie had to be sure it was Cole who had derailed her

sister. "Cole Sullivan called me today…because the reporter for *Inside Phoenix* contacted him with concerns."

"He did? Cole called?"

Damn. Kylie had skipped over the reporter part altogether. Something was definitely up. "Luckily, he said good things about us to the *reporter,* who was *digging for dirt.* I got Mr. Rheingold's promise that he'll fix it, whatever that means."

"Mr. Rheingold?" Kylie absorbed the news slowly. "The reporter was digging for dirt?" She sat forward, anxious now.

"Yes, but I'm handling it, so don't worry. You're already doing so much for me."

"Good. Did Cole, um, have a nice time?" Oh, dear. If her sister wasn't leaping to make calls or demanding Janie breathe into a paper bag, she was really enthralled.

"He had a great time." Janie sighed.

"Good. I was afraid I bored him." Kylie's face flared pinker than the roses and she shoved her hair around both ears. "We talked and…talked."

Holy Hannah. Had they made out? Surely not slept together?

"So, on the magazine story…do you think I should give Cole some pointers. In case the reporter calls again?"

Janie leveled a look at her. "What are you doing, Kylie?" If Cole got sidetracked by an infatuation, it could throw off his reaction to Deborah, who tended to be a bit high-strung. "I appreciate your filling in on the date, but Cole's anxious to meet Deborah now, remember?"

"I just want to touch base with him…about the reporter and all."

"We don't want anything to distract him from his perfect match, do we?"

"Of course not." Kylie blushed furiously.

"All right," Janie said, copying down Cole's numbers and handing them over. "Just to touch base." She had to trust Kylie to do the right thing. Kylie and Cole were both sensible people. But since when had lust been sensible?

"Thanks," Kylie said, grinning far too broadly, looking far too pink. She bolted for the door.

"You forgot something." Janie held up the folder.

"Right." Kylie came back to retrieve it. "I don't know what's wrong with me."

Janie had a pretty good idea and didn't want to think about it. "Though you didn't ask, I still haven't gotten Marlon Brandon on the line." If she couldn't talk with her disgruntled client, there was no way to settle out of court.

"Oh, right." Kylie blinked, seeming to pull herself back to work mode. "Sounds like I'd better find an attorney."

"Give me a few more days. I'll try working through his receptionist. She likes me. If we can save legal fees…"

"Sure. Keep me posted."

"I will." The issues were piling up—phone-sex calls, a screwed-up magazine story, a lawsuit no closer to being settled and her sister so lust-dazed she could complicate a match made in heaven.

Janie sighed and looked toward her window. At least she still had roses, even if they'd been sent for the wrong reason. As she watched, two petals shivered to the tabletop.

Nothing was perfect. Not even roses.

6

"THAT WAS NO *crack* this case fell through," Cole said to Trevor, stunned by the towers of Littlefield file boxes around them at his table. "More like the Grand Canyon. There's no environmental impact, three missed filing dates and no tax records."

"Tuttleman wants it done, so we'll do it," Trevor said, then shot him a calculating look. "Unless you're not up to it...?"

"Oh, I'm up to it." Cole wouldn't drip from so much as a paper cut around this Armani-clad shark.

"That makes one of us." Trevor sounded surprisingly vulnerable and looked a little pale today, now that Cole focused on him. "I've got the Bowman buyout, the Valley Rentals sale and a flight attendant with a ticket to Bali and a body that makes men walk into walls." He sighed. "Sucky timing."

"My bad on the deadline." Trevor had had the class not to bring that up since his blunder.

"What the hell. Doing the impossible racks up the partner points. I'll get my Palm Pilot and we can book meetings." He headed off without his customary swagger.

The pressure got to young turks, too. Because of his late start on law school, Cole at thirty-three was older than most of his partner-bound colleagues. He considered commiserating with the guy, but that would be self-indulgent. They'd both known the game when they signed on. You gave it all you had, sacrificed everything and it came back to you tenfold in stature, income and security.

Cole couldn't wait to get there, fulfill his dream and his parents' pride in him. He planned to fund something extravagant for their retirement—a condo in La Jolla or maybe Hawaii. If he could ever convince either of them that their students would survive when they left the classroom for some well-deserved rest, that is.

He, on the other hand, had to push hard. Rest wasn't an option. There were other approaches, he supposed. Like Trisha's. She'd bought him lunch the other day to ask for his help covering crucial meetings so she could accompany her husband on a business trip.

Cole had readily agreed, flattered by her trust in him. *You've got your head on straight,* she'd told him, a reference to his advanced age, he assumed. She was midtwenties, but seemed wiser than her years—feet flat on the ground and no nonsense. She didn't even sound bitter about being passed up for the Littlefield plum.

I love the law, but my life is more than that. He admired her for making the best of a bad situation.

Trisha was smart and fast, able to quickly cull critical details from a file. She was a better writer and more organized than he. If he ever opened his own practice, he'd want Trisha with him, if she were interested.

But that was way down the line.

First, he had to make partner. And that meant turning the Littlefield case around fast. Getting married would help his cause, too, he'd concluded after a recent golf game, where he'd teamed with Rob Tuttleman against two guys from the law firm where Tuttleman had failed to make partner.

Over celebratory brews—they'd won big—Tuttleman had waxed nostalgic. "I thought all it took was hard work and brilliance," he'd said of his failure. "But the partners wanted stability, and, frankly, debt. A mortgage, country club dues, orthodontia. Maybe they were right, because I didn't get serious about billables until I married Sandra. Maybe it was chicken and egg, but it worked. Word to the wise, Sullivan," he'd said with a slow wink, tossing back the last of his third "'tini," as he called them. "Word to the wise."

So, a wife would be a good asset. But that wasn't the main thing. He thought about Trisha's face when she talked about her husband. She practically glowed with love. This brilliant lawyer, this self-sufficient woman *needed* her husband to be happy. And it was obvious he felt the same about her.

Cole wanted that. Hungered for it, if he were honest. He wanted someone who understood him, knew what he faced, what he wanted, could say what he had to hear to turn wrong things right.

Someone like Kylie.

Stop it. Even if she wasn't moving to L.A., Kylie had no interest in settling down. She'd practically sneered *corporate wife*. She had no interest in compromise when it came to her career and he didn't blame her.

Now Deborah Ramsdale was ready to settle down. And she'd be back in less than a month. He took her profile out of his briefcase and skimmed it. *Career has been top priority*, she'd written, *but plan to limit travel and adjust hours to accommodate a relationship and, eventually, a family.*

Exactly what he wanted. He looked at her photo. She was attractive, though appearance wasn't as important as personality. Her eyes held a glint of ambition, which he liked. Kylie had more than a glint. She had a beam, a klieg light, an Olympic torch of drive. She was going places as hard and fast as she could. She made love that way, too.

He had to stop lapsing into thoughts of her. Her busy body, shiny eyes and full-faced smile had shimmered just below the surface of his awareness ever since that night, like a reflection in a pond.

Forget Kylie. Back to Deborah, who had minors in philosophy and art history, which meant she'd do well in his social milieu. He looked forward to insightful discussions over Sunday bagels thick with cream cheese and buttery omelets—make that lite cream cheese and Eggbeaters, since she'd surely be a cholesterol watcher.

He liked that they shared careers. And BL&T would be glad to connect with such a prominent firm. With luck, he and Deborah would be engaged before the firm's Christmas party. The partner decision would be announced just after the first of the year. It all clicked into place, like an exclusive country club that had invited him to join before he'd even considered applying.

He returned her profile to his briefcase, then opened his computer calendar for Trevor's return. The Deborah date was a yellow square for last Friday. He'd met Kylie instead.

What a wonder she'd been as a lover, rocking on his shaft and crying out like no man had ever made her feel so good.

Shit. An erection. In his serious office with its serious diplomas, sober law books and elegant paintings, he had a serious boner.

Trevor walked in. Of course. At least Cole's desk hid his crotch. He scooted his chair farther in just to be sure.

"You all right?" Trevor asked.

"Sure. Just…thinking." And aching.

They booked three meetings and were searching for a fourth when the secretary spoke through the intercom. "Cole…Kylie on line two."

His heart and penis jumped like both wanted out. "Kylie? I'll take it."

He'd sounded like an idiot, obviously, because Trevor looked him over. "Kylie huh? Is she cute as a button?"

"Look for something Friday," he said, ignoring the jab, and shifted the monitor so Trevor could check out his calendar.

Cole picked up the phone and turned his chair away. "How the hell are you?" he said, going for a conversational backslap to keep Trevor off the trail.

"Cole?" There was a pause, a sharp inhale, then a relieved exhale. "I get it. Someone's there. I can call back."

"No, no, not at all. Can you hang on?" He turned to see what Trevor had found.

"I'll cancel racquetball and we can meet over lunch," Trevor said, winking. Then he left, whistling, as if he'd just learned the secret to Cole's demise. Or seen beneath his desk. Maybe both.

"I can call back." Kylie's voice was faint.

"No, no. It's good to hear your voice." He softened his tone to match the intimacy he felt. "I'm alone now."

"Oh. Good." There was breathy expectation in her tone, but she seemed to catch herself and her next words were businesslike. "Janie mentioned a reporter contacted you. I'm calling to be sure you're comfortable if he should call again."

This was a business call. Damn. "I had only good things to say. I doubt he'll try me again."

"Janie told me you had a good time." Her intimate tone sent an arrow of lust straight through him.

"I had a *great* time."

"Me, too. Very." Silence. They inhaled and exhaled at the same time. And again. Two people didn't breathe at each other over the phone unless they were thirteen and clueless. Or they'd had great sex and didn't know what to do about it.

"I can't stop thinking about that night," she said—fast, as if the words had jumped from her throat.

He laughed, so relieved he wanted to shout. "Me, either. I've been daydreaming at the worst possible times."

"I've been staring at this marketing plan for an hour without making a keystroke. So I just gave up and called." Her voice had a sweet wobble. Of desire, relief and pleasure.

"No sense suffering alone." How could his body be hard as a rock and soft as butter at the same time? His surroundings blurred and he was aware only of Kylie's low voice in his ear, imagining her lips pressed against the mouthpiece on her end.

"I guess we both needed that night," she said wistfully. Oh, hell, she was wrapping it up now.

"I guess so." *I want more. I want you. Now.* The words pushed into his throat, but he swallowed them back down.

"Yeah." Pause. "Well." Another pause. "So, when is…Deborah…getting back?"

"Three weeks."

"Oh."

"Three weeks and three days actually."

She breathed at him. He breathed back.

Plenty of time. He pushed back the inappropriate thought, but it jumped right up again.

"I should let you get back to work." She sighed.

She was right. He'd be taking tons of work home tonight and he didn't dare stay late or Radar would express his opinion somewhere. "Hell, I work too much," he blurted.

"Me, too," she said quickly. "I took an advance job for my boss-to-be, can you believe it?"

"I volunteered for a tight deadline on a big case."

"Why do we do this to ourselves?"

"Because people count on us and we come through. Simple."

"Exactly. It's worse because my local accounts are heating up and I really love working on them. I feel like I've started to build something. I had to turn down two new clients yesterday."

"Because you're leaving it probably makes what you have seem all the more precious."

"I'm sure that's true. Though I can see that I could definitely build if I wanted to. Maybe I'm making too much of it."

"It's perfectly normal to have doubts," he said, happy to reassure her. "And when you're ready to build your business again, there will be new opportunities."

"Exactly. Maybe the fact that I'm moving on makes me seem more successful to others. All I know is that I'm working my butt off to the bitter end."

"You have to maintain high standards."

"God, it's nice to talk to someone who understands. My sister accuses me of not having a life."

"Your sister and your secretary, right?"

"Oh, yeah. They're both on my case all the time."

"Your work is your life right now."

"Exactly. Thank you."

"For me, too. Which makes it a problem that I'm taking care of my neighbor's dog while she's out of town. Whenever I get home too late, he lets me know with a little doggie deposit."

"Oh, ick. Poop or pee?"

"Poop. Cleans up quick, no residue."

"At least that. I couldn't take the guilt of owning a pet. Looking into those woeful eyes every morning when I left and getting that desperate welcome when I returned. My only guilt now is not getting enough exercise."

"Not enough *exercise?*" He deliberately loaded the word, meaning sex. How could he help it?

"Not even close," she said in a way that told him she knew exactly what he'd meant. "It's so good for you, too. Exercise releases the endorphins that are vital to concentration and productivity and feelings of well-being." She spoke seductively, as if she were describing a sex act in intimate detail.

"Well-being. You bet." His cock rose to hopeful attention.

"But we're too busy to get some, right? Exercise, I mean." She sighed in what sounded like hopeless frustration.

"Your marketing plan won't write itself."

"And your deadline's ticking ever closer."

They breathed at each other for a few seconds, the heat building across the miles and wires.

"Maybe we could take care of it…over the phone," Kylie said finally, huskily, sounding surprised at herself.

"You think?" His prick did a little happy dance.

"We'd be saving travel time."

"You're good," he said. He looked up. The secretary

whose desk faced the glass panel at the side of his door was gone to the doctor, but it was only four and the place was full of people. Maybe if they were quick about it. This was Kylie, for God's sake, whose very name gave him an erection. They'd be quick. "Hang on." He lunged to his door and locked it, returning to the phone that held the hottest woman he'd ever known. "I'm back."

"I've never done this before," she said breathlessly.

"Me, either. But I like the sound of it." Just her voice in his ear would be enough to send him over the top, he was embarrassed to realize.

"Where do we start? Maybe with what we're wearing? I have on a green suit and a white silk blouse."

"Silk is good. I like white. Bright green suit?" He closed his eyes, focused on her voice, pictured her body, full breasts pushing out of the bright green—

"Olive-green."

"Hmm." Olive-green. He could see it now and he put his hand on himself to shift his erection where he could get at it. "Is there cleavage?"

"Sorry. High collar."

"Mmm. I'm picturing cleavage." That mint-stained blouse with the inky collar. Yeah. And her chest heaving with uneven breaths…

"Good point. We should use our imaginations. Okay… my skirt has a slit up the side…that goes clear…up… to my…ass." Her slow-as-syrup words were as arousing as the picture she was painting in his head.

"Mmm. Panty hose? Say no."

"No panty hose. No panties, either." The idea seemed to arouse her and her breath went harsh. He tightened his grip on himself, pretending it was her hand on him.

"Just you," he breathed. "Where you're so soft?"

"Mmm. Yesss."

"Are you touching yourself, Kylie?" He was rocking into his palm, wishing to hell he dared to unzip.

"And pretending it's you, yeah. Your finger. In me."

He pictured her squirming in her chair like she'd wiggled on his shaft the other night and in so many daydreams. At this rate, he wouldn't last thirty seconds. "It's me, all right," he said, concentrating on her, "and I'm shoving your skirt out of the way to see how wet you are…."

"I'm very wet…because of you."

"I want to taste you now." He rubbed himself faster, prickling with lust, gripping the phone with his other hand. "I'm on my knees now, holding your thighs apart…."

"Holding me open? Oh, yes. I love that."

"Now I'm licking you." His vision dimmed. He wanted to be doing exactly that.

She gasped. "Oh, your tongue is right there. I'm wiggling so much…it's too much…you won't stop…I can't stop…it's too strong…I'm…coming…help me…."

And then there were frantic breaths and a cry and he only hoped no one was anywhere near her desk, because the sounds were unmistakable. He surged against his zipper, but managed to hold back somehow, wanting to hear what she would say.

"That was good," she breathed, sounding barely collected. "Did you…?"

"Not yet."

"This is no time to be a gentleman, Cole. Ladies don't have to be first." She laughed softly. "Okay, I'm walking over to you now…I'm behind your desk…"

Yes, he could picture her. He tightened his grip.

"I'm shoving your chair back so I can get at you…I'm on my knees…putting you in my mouth…."

"Oh, yeah." He loved the picture of her bending to him, her pretty lips round, opening, sliding onto him, wet and warm.

"You taste salty and warm and…so good. Mmm."

Laughter and talk rose in the hall outside his office.

"Stop," he ground out. "There are people…" Damn.

"I can wait a bit."

"It's too busy now." Trevor or Tuttleman could pop in midstroke.

"I guess associates on a partner track can't go around with wet splotches on their slacks," she said sadly. "But I can't leave you like that…all swollen…and hard…and sore." She dragged out the words like Nurse Feel Good asking where it hurt. "It's cruel…almost dangerous…you could hurt yourself."

"Good point. I sure as hell can't walk now."

"Whose place can we get to faster?" She spoke in such a practical tone, he was caught off guard.

"I'm forty minutes from mine, thirty from yours." Blood pounded in his head—and everywhere else.

"My place it is."

"Are you sure?" What was he saying? He had a ton of work.

"If you take the Fifty-One, you can make it in twenty-five."

"Twenty if I speed. I'm there."

He shoved a bunch of work into his briefcase and disappeared down the back stairs so no one saw him leave before five. He refused to have second thoughts. They'd be fast and he'd be home in time for Radar's potty break, clearheaded, relaxed and full of energy. This was smart, forward-thinking…

Insane. He was doing it anyway.

7

THE INSTANT she got inside her town house, Kylie ditched her underwear, so she'd be as naked beneath her suit as she'd told Cole she was in their phone fantasy. He'd be here any second, so she only had time to brush her teeth. Hands shaking, she jiggled paste on her toothbrush. *This is crazy.*

Even working nonstop she could barely keep up with Personal Touch and her final client work, not to mention the S-Mickey-B Home Town Suites project she'd agreed to work on from Phoenix.

But you have to have him.

She did. She was wound tight and ticking, coiled to spring, loaded to explode, but only on contact with Cole. She had to do something about that, didn't she?

Didn't they say you should manage energy, not time, and if you restored your energy, you got more work out of each moment? Right? Right? *Oh, shut up.* No way was she sending Cole away, no matter what the time management gurus said.

She caught sight of herself in the mirror. Her flushed face, glazed eyes and toothpaste-foamed mouth made her look completely mad. She *was* mad.

But when the doorbell rang a second later, her entire body sang with joy. She rinsed, slammed her toothbrush into its holder and raced to let him in.

There he stood in her home, button-down shirt open at the collar, tie hanging, hair mussed, panting as though he'd run all the way. His eyes looked so desperate for her that her knees turned to water.

She noticed a briefcase dangling from one hand. "You brought work?"

"In case we take a break." He threw it down and yanked her into his arms in a way that told her it would be a long while before they breathed, let alone took a break. His tongue went deep, digging in, demanding she give herself to him. At the same time, he tugged at her blazer.

The button flew off, clicking onto the entry tile somewhere. "Sorry," he said into her mouth.

"It was loose."

He braced her against the door, seized her breasts through her blouse, as if he had to have her now. She was dizzy with desire, alive with the thrill of his urgency.

He shoved his hand under her skirt and found her naked. "Yes." He trembled at the discovery. "I could hardly see to drive thinking of you like this, waiting for me to—" He ran his thumb down the swollen length of her.

She gasped and sagged against the door.

He attacked her mouth again, still stroking her.

She begged in desperate murmurs for more.

He slid two fingers inside, digging in to snag her G spot.

"Oh…oh…ohohoh." She pushed back against the door, her legs too rubbery to hold her up. She felt like she was on one of those carnival rides that slapped you against the wall and spun you and spun you and spun you. "That feels…so…good…so…oh, oh…"

She hooked a leg across his backside to open herself more fully to his fingers. "What about you?" she moaned, wanting to make him feel good, too, but not coordinated enough to do more than stay upright and experience this.

"Later. I want you to come for me." He did something magical with his thumb while his fingers squeezed that glorious ridge behind her pubic bone.

Prickles shot across her skin, pushed by waves of heat and desire until she thought she might pass out.

Cole braced her more firmly against the door, reaching under her skirt with his other hand to cup her bottom, which increased the pull on her sex.

In seconds, she was shot through with the thrill of climax—a slow bullet of ecstasy, passing through her steadily, endlessly, taking its time, while Cole held her in hot hands, giving her a pure pleasure that would…not… stop.

She fell against him, completely overcome, seeing double, then not seeing at all. He'd made love to her barely inside her door, his briefcase at their feet, but it had been as incredible as all night between satin sheets.

She felt his unspent lust like a gathering storm between them. He moved fast, unzipping himself, shoving his pants to the floor, lifting her and adjusting his position to enter her, sliding immediately deep. His groan was rich with relief.

She wrapped her legs around his waist, which tore the side seams of her skirt. Another suit damaged, but she didn't care. Cole wanted her so much he was taking her against the door, his pants around his ankles, completely out of control. She gloried in the wild recklessness of the moment.

Cole pulled out and thrust again hard, bracing her with his hands, pumping in, holding her in place, making her feel every inch of him.

She didn't expect another climax, but it loomed, spurred

by the hunger in Cole's face, the power in his stroke, the way he held her safely all the while.

Moans and cries and gasps filled the air, she couldn't tell their voices apart. They blended in a lusty symphony.

Then Cole sped up, pumping so rapidly, she couldn't believe it didn't hurt. But it seemed like they were one body, perfectly connected, perfectly in tune. As if the curve of his crown, the swell of his shaft had been made to fit her exactly. They moved in perfect synch, a smooth rush to the peak and then over together.

She felt each spasm of his release as a gift. *Here and here. From me to you.* She clutched him with her internal muscles and gave of herself. *For you, Cole. For you.*

And then his mouth landed on hers and they kissed for soft, lush seconds. Still holding her, Cole kicked off his pants, shoved off his shoes and managed to carry her to her bedroom, where they crashed onto her bed together—her on her back, Cole looking down at her.

She'd just had two orgasms with most of her clothes on. She placed her palms against Cole's chest. His heart thudded behind the thick, starched fabric of his shirt.

"We're still dressed," Cole said, a twinkle of amusement in his dark eyes. "I can't believe you went to work without underwear."

"I didn't. I whipped them off before you got here."

"Good girl," he said, kissing her again. "And you took time to brush your teeth." He licked the corner of her mouth, then seemed to sample the taste. "Hmm? Thompson's Ultimate Fluoride?"

"How can you tell?"

"It's what I use. Mouthwash, fluoride and whitening all in one little dab."

"So efficient."

"Exactly." That little flicker of connection made her feel ridiculously happy.

Cole smiled, feeling it, too, no doubt. He sat up and unbuttoned his shirt, then tossed it to a chair, his muscles fanning out beautifully as he moved. God, he was hot. So what if she should be working? This was such a thrill, an incredible experience she was lucky to enjoy.

She removed her own clothes and tossed them to the floor—who cared about wrinkles and dry cleaning…so not like her—then spread her limbs in a snow angel in the sheets. When was the last time she'd felt so loose and easy? Summers in high school, maybe, when she'd wake with nothing to do but read, swim and listen to her favorite music. Those were the days, when her time was her own. When had she gotten so busy and why?

"You look comfortable," Cole said, watching her, his gaze possessive. *Mine, all mine.*

"Oh, I am. I don't want to move."

"All the endorphins, huh?" He lowered his mouth to kiss her breasts, each in turn, lifting his head to look at her in between.

"Oh, yeah."

"So you feel more productive?" he teased, running his tongue over her nipples, one at a time. "Better able to concentrate?"

She wiggled under him, pivoting her hips, wanting him again. "Mmm. Soooo productive." They should get up now and work. He had his briefcase, after all. But she was getting aroused all over again and it felt too good. Who knew when she'd have an opportunity like this again?

"Hungry?" he breathed against her breast.

"Oh, yeah. Hunnnngry." She dragged out the word, wrapping her legs around his back, sliding her sex against him for some delicious friction.

He chuckled. "I mean for food." He kept up his nipple action, sucking this time, while rubbing her sex with a slow finger.

"We can…get…delivery," she managed to say. "Menus… in…kitchen." She closed her eyes and soaked in the glory of his fingers and tongue working her over, making her knot up and go limp at the same time.

"I'll go," he breathed against her chest, then ceased his lovely torture. "You don't move."

"I can't," she moaned. "I'm a noodle."

"Don't tempt me, I'm already starving." He kissed her mouth and pushed off the bed, returning seconds later with a take-out menu, his wallet and something small between thumb and forefinger. "Jacket button," he said, placing it on the bureau. "So it doesn't get lost."

"You are the most thoughtful man."

"I thought maybe Mexican?" He held out the menu he'd selected—the best deep-fat-fried-everything place in town.

"My favorite place."

"I love Mexican food, but I don't know this restaurant."

"It's the best. But there's nothing healthy on the menu."

"Ah, but this is a special occasion. Plus, look at all the exercise we're getting." He fished a credit card out of his wallet and handed it to her, then reached across her body for the phone from the nightstand. "You call. I'll pay." He kissed her neck, shifting his body over her until his erection rested snugly between her legs. "Order whatever comes to mind," he murmured, kissing along her collarbone.

She clicked in the number. The take-out clerk had just

asked, "What would you like?" when Cole began to trail kisses down her body. He was going down on her.

Oh, that. I want that. "Two orders of…fl-au-au-tas." Tightly wound corn tortillas with guacamole garnish seemed appropriately suggestive. "Huh?" she asked, her hearing foggy. Cole's fingers were ticking her skin while he kissed her stomach. "Beans? Yes…rice…sure…uh-huh… Oh, yes on the *hot* sauce."

He kissed her thighs, then blew softly between them and she ordered chile *relleno*—a pepper stuffed with hot liquid…which perfectly described her body below the waist.

Then his fingers spread her and his tongue found her, tasting her as if she were a delicious hors d'oeuvres. Feeling frantic, she ordered more hot and juicy items, her vision going gray. He dabbed her again and again, until she felt as though she would dissolve like *pan dulce* in milk.

Somehow she managed to read off Cole's credit card number, then tossed the phone away. "I sounded like I was slipping into a coma," she said to him. "The paramedics could be here before the food. Oh, oh, oh."

"I'll save you," he breathed, increasing the stroke of his incredibly skilled tongue, settling in between her thighs.

She locked her knees against his temples and rode him, faster and faster, her skin prickling with heat, her clit tightening with the pending release.

Then it hit, hard and strong, a glorious surge of pleasure. Just as the feeling faded, Cole inserted a finger into her and pulled down while pressing the tip of his tongue on her spot. To her amazement, she climaxed again, quick and intense. She would have flown off the bed, except Cole held her firmly until the sweet, quivery end of it.

"How did you…?" she gasped out. "Where did you…? You should write a book."

He chuckled as he kissed his way up her body, drying his face against her as he went in a way that felt luxurious and juicy and so sexy. He reached her mouth and kissed her, giving her a little of her own light musk. "Glad you enjoyed it."

"Enjoyed it? I was paralyzed. You should get a patent, teach workshops, start a movement, something."

"I've done some reading."

"No! You *studied?*"

"If you want to be good at something, study the experts." He winked at her.

"Give me your reading list or I'll never keep up."

He chuckled. "It's not the book, Kylie. It's you. It's being with you." He looked thoughtful. "I'm not usually so… on."

"Me, either." It was as if they could read each other's minds and bodies. "I feel lucky," she said, running her fingers through his hair. And a little puzzled. "Maybe it's because we're each headed somewhere—you're looking to get married and I'm making a big career switch—and we're nervous about it."

"Meaning…?"

"Meaning there's tension. And that intensifies pleasure." And made it hard to let go. She wanted to burrow into his body for hours, maybe days.

"Possible," he said, sounding not so sure. "You're saying we're the right people meeting at the right time."

"Exactly. And speaking of time…we've got ten minutes until the food gets here. I do my best work on deadline." She slid down his body, holding his gaze.

"Let 'em leave it at the door," Cole said, his voice rough with desire, the anticipation in his hot-coffee eyes making her want to give him the best head ever.

WHY THE HELL had he brought his briefcase? Cole wasn't moving one inch from Kylie's sweet mouth until she was done with him. And what she was doing right now made him hope that moment never came.

She tightened her lips over the head of his cock, did something extraordinary with her tongue, while her one hand stroked the lower half of his shaft in a tight rhythm that made it tough to keep from exploding into her. He shortened his thrusts, wanting to slow it down, but she moved faster, making him crazy. He wanted to touch her, too, but she teased the hot spot under his crown with the tip of her tongue and he felt pole-axed in place.

If he'd ever had sex this good, he didn't remember it.

Her free hand reached up to stroke his chest and he lifted her fingers to his mouth so he could run his tongue into the space between her index and middle fingers.

She quaked in response, then shifted to lock her thighs around his leg and madly work herself against him. He sucked and licked her fingers, which he'd be doing to her sex if he had the wherewithal to move or even remember his own name.

She rocked harder and he quickened the thrusts of his cock into her mouth. His balls tightened, preparing for release. He got ready to pull out, not sure how she felt about him coming in her mouth.

She sucked harder, bearing down with her lips and the back of her throat. *Do it. I want it.* She coaxed him to the brink and over and he bucked into her sweet mouth, while she held him—all his need funneled into that spurt of hot liquid that Kylie seemed to want every drop of. He couldn't imagine anything sexier or more tender.

Right people, right time, right? he thought as she slid up his body, smiling at him. She glanced at her clock. "Mmm. Nice appetizer. And with a minute to spare."

He smiled back and cupped her face. This was more than a happy collision of need and tension. He wanted more time with this amazing woman. More sex, of course, but more talk, too. He wanted to know all her secrets and tell her his.

How unfortunate, what with her leaving town and him needing a wife. Right people, *wrong* time, he concluded. "You're incredible," he said.

"I'd better be. You're a couple of orgasms behind. Luckily, we have all night to catch you up."

He wanted to say something about this not being a race, but he was too busy thinking, *Yahoo, she said all night,* and then the doorbell rang.

"I'll get it," Kylie said, pushing off the bed, flying into the bathroom, zooming out in a shiny red robe. "Run us a bath and we'll eat in the tub," she called as she skimmed by. "Bubble stuff's under the sink."

"Eat in the tub?"

"Multitasking!" Her light laughter carried back to him.

He flopped onto the pillow and found himself smiling like an idiot. It would be smarter to eat at the table, where they could work. There was Radar to think of, so he really couldn't stay all night…

Kylie laughed at something the delivery guy said and the sound cut through him with such power he started to shake. He had to stay. The universe was telling him to take this chance. It was a special occasion, right? He'd make up the work time somehow.

Kylie's bathroom was orderly and simple—a modest number of lotions and perfumes on a single glass shelf, hair dryer and curling iron on hooks and a separate shower stall. On the window ledge beyond the roomy tub rested a couple of photos in frames and a spiky plant—aloe vera, he thought it was. The window looked out on a terrace of plastic lawn furniture ringed by empty wooden flower boxes.

He located the bath stuff under the sink, still shrink-wrapped and bearing a bow. Baths must be special occasions, since she hadn't cracked the dusty gift basket. He poured a capful of "Tranquility Garden" bubble bath under the tap and adjusted the temperature to just shy of scalding.

The tub was steamy and brimming with bubbles by the time Kylie entered with a tray that held an open take-out box piled high with food. The aroma of onions, garlic and fried dough mingled with the flowery scent, jamming the tiny room with pleasurable aromas.

Kylie set the tray on the closed toilet lid and whipped off her robe. They faced each other and lowered themselves into the hot water. Her naked body made him lose his appetite for anything but her and she stared at his erection, bobbing above the foam. His need for her was embarrassingly obvious.

"I feel the same way," she said, her eyes glazed. She leaned forward to hold him, then let go with apparent regret. "One too many tasks. Let's save it for dessert. I got sopaipillas with honey, too."

"Honey? Sounds delicious."

She smiled and situated the groaning tray of lard-drenched glory between them, handing him a fork. There were enchiladas, chile *rellenos,* flautas, beans, rice, tacos and a couple of chimichangas. He looked from the food to her face. "Quite a feast."

"You had me so crazed I just kept ordering."

"So we have leftovers." He smiled. "Even better."

"Good point," she said, leaning forward to kiss him, the porcelain squeaking against her back. "I have the best freezer bags." She beamed and dug in. They ate in silence for a while, smiling at each other, trading bites, until she leaned back with a sigh. "Isn't this great? We're full and warm, inside and out. I never take baths. Or kick back much."

"Me, either," he said, the sinking awareness of all the work he wasn't doing making him wonder if he'd lost his mind completely. As long as he had Kylie in his sights he didn't seem to care about everything that mattered to him.

Her gaze drifted away, out the window. "Isn't that a sad sight? I put in boxes for a garden when I first moved here. I had this wonderful layout—flowers and vegetables in a color blend that would roll through the seasons like a shifting rainbow."

"What happened?"

"I managed one planting. The dry stalks made me feel so guilty that I ripped it all out. Now all I've got is this guy." She leaned forward to run a finger along a stalk of the aloe vera on the ledge. "He can survive on the humidity from my shower." She sounded so sad.

"You'll make time for a garden once you settle in L.A."

"I hope so. Growing up, I always helped my mom plant the garden. For comfort. The house would be different, the climate, the people, even the bugs, but the begonias stayed the same."

She shifted her gaze to one of the small photos beside the plant. "Janie really liked our gardens."

"That the two of you?" he asked, nodding at the picture, which showed them as toddlers in duck-shaped floats in a pool, Kylie with her arm tight around Janie, who grinned, cheerful in her sister's chokehold.

"Looks like I'm killing her, huh?" She picked up the photo and studied it, a trail of bubbles sliding down her arm.

"She doesn't seem to mind."

"I worried about her. She got sick a lot. Asthma, bronchitis…respiratory stuff. She was shy, too, and the moves freaked her out. My dad's job took us everywhere. I tried to make things easier for her in each new place." She put the photo back, still looking at it.

Her devotion to her sister was as palpable as the steam in the room. Until now, she'd struck him as emotionally guarded, but now her face was soft with love. Perhaps she felt safe with him. He hoped so. "And you still watch out for her?"

"When I can." Tension tightened her eyes.

He remembered what Janie had said about the stand-in date. "She's afraid she's imposing on you."

"She said that to you?"

"Not in so many words. She felt bad about making you meet me for the date."

"Oh that. Yeah. She feels guilty for taking me from my work. I just hope I can do what she needs…." She studied him thoughtfully for a moment. "Maybe I could get your opinion on something?"

"Anything."

"Janie's being sued by a disgruntled client. It's ridiculous, really. Janie refused to match him with a blond set of breasts on legs."

"And the guy's not exactly Adonis?"

"Exactly. Fifty-nine, comb-over, major paunch. His name's Marlon Bran*don*. Can you believe that? Not Bran*do,* as Janie keeps pointing out. Maybe the confusion gives him illusions of grandeur. Janie, bless her heart, insists on finding him a *suitable* match. So, even though Mr. Brandon would be delighted with a bimbo gold digger, Janie won't arrange it, and now he's claiming fraud and misrepresentation."

"Sounds frivolous to me."

"No kidding. We've been trying to get him to meet with us to work out a settlement, but he's stalling, so I'm afraid we need legal help. Is there some mediation service we should try?"

"That works if both sides are willing to compromise. Maybe I can help. Do some research, meet with the guy's attorney?"

"I can't ask you to do that, Cole. I just wanted your advice."

"I want to help. Really."

"But you're busy. We'll be fine."

"I can fit in a couple of meetings."

"I shouldn't have said anything."

"I won't do more than I can afford to."

She studied him, assessing his intent, hope and relief flickering in her eyes.

"If you say no, I'll just talk to Janie."

"You're serious?"

"Absolutely."

She put the food tray on the bathroom floor and threw her body across his for a hug, her breasts warm and heavy on his chest. She looked up at him. "I insist we pay you."

"I want your body, not your money." He took her bottom in both hands and squeezed until she moved against him, sloshing water over the side of the tub with a splash. "I think we just ruined the leftovers," he murmured.

"Who cares? Sopaipillas and honey are in the kitchen." She slid her legs between his and reached for him.

"Sounds delicious." Like the hot, wet woman lying on top of him.

Best of all, he now had a legitimate reason to spend more time with her. Time he didn't have and work he couldn't afford. But he was happier than he remembered being in years.

SETH HEADED to his uncle's office as requested and found him on the phone. "I'll fix this…don't you worry…absolutely…no problem." Seth should take the guy fishing. He looked harried and sweaty, appeasing some cranky advertiser, no doubt.

Then Seth noticed the book in the middle of his desk. *Buffaloed by Bugs* by Ana Ferris. Probably why Harry had called Seth in here. Harry must have read the acknowledgement page where she'd thanked Seth for his help, along with the team. That burned. He'd practically mentored the woman and she'd thanked him like one of the little people. Harry had no way to know it would be salt in the wound.

His uncle hung up the phone, then surprised him with a glare instead of a smile. "What the hell did you do, Seth? That was Jane Falls. Practically apoplectic."

"I was doing my job, Harry."

"By being—how did she put it?—'at best disinterested, at worst hostile.'"

"I wasn't hostile," Seth mumbled, though he knew his questions had alarmed her.

"This is a profile, not an exposé. A sweet little feature about a unique dating service."

"I just asked some questions. Followed up some leads. Practiced good journalism."

"Don't get arrogant on me, Seth. You're my sister's son and I want to help you, but you've got a chip on your shoulder the size of a Tuscan tile." Seth had taken the job as a favor to Harry, not the other way around, but there was brusque affection behind the words, so he saw no reason to point that out.

"Go to her damned skate party," Harry said wearily. "Take notes on whatever the hell she tells you. Make her happy. And write a nice little piece."

"Okay, okay," Seth said. He had no energy for a fight.

"Thanks for taking my stepsons fishing," Harry mumbled, clearly making nice after the abuse. "Those two never string more than two lines together at dinner and they were giving a regular harangue about the importance of journalism."

"They're smart kids." Their enthusiasm for his chosen career had reminded Seth of his old fire. They'd been good for him, too. "Just figuring out what they want to be."

"I wish they'd hurry the hell up, while they're on my dime—college is pricey." Harry's mouth lifted in a grumpy grin. Then he shot a look at Seth.

"If revenues pick up, I'll hire a feature writer and you can do the analysis we talked about." His gaze fell on the book in the middle of his desk. "Oh, and this came in for review. I saw you were mentioned. Want it?" He tilted it at him.

"I have my own copy, thanks." Ana had sent it with a gushy note, as if nothing terrible had passed between them.

"Figure out what's bugging you," Harry said, waving Ana's book at him, "and don't take it out on Jane Falls." He tossed the book onto a stack of volumes on his credenza, photo up.

"Right." Looking at Ana's picture just now, Seth saw clear as day what was eating at him. Not the stolen book sale, not her undeserved fame. It was losing her.

He'd been such a wimp about it—schmuck of the century. The minute he fell head over heels, she'd lost interest. The heat of new sex had cooled, the thrill of working together faded, and Ana just plain didn't like his personality. *You're too gloomy. Too cynical.*

He thought of himself as pragmatic and realistic. Like Ana, for that matter, who was a pretty brutal critic herself. The opposite of Jane Falls, who skipped through life looking on the bright side so hard she'd miss the cliff for the glare.

Of course, Janie wasn't all airy-fairy goodness. She was like an aged scotch—smooth, but with a kick that hit you in the back of the head after you thought you were out of range.

She'd tried to get him bumped from the story, too. That took brass balls. Guts, anyway. And now his uncle was making him go to her goofball skating party tonight and make nice. What a pain in the ass.

He grinned all the way home.

8

THAT EVENING, Seth braced himself on the rental counter and checked out the Skate World rink action. Couples only, judging by the sappy music. Tattered squares of light from the beat-up disco ball spun everywhere for a dizzying effect, flashing over the rink, the people on wheels and the low barrier that protected the audience from rogue skaters.

Accomplished pairs did spins or skated backward around the inner circle, while the fringes were packed with newbie couples, flopping up and down, grabbing each other for balance. Many sported Day-Glo pink name tags with the Personal Touch logo. Lord. They had to wear name badges? Announce their desperation to the world?

He felt like an uneasy voyeur. If his friends at the *Trib* could see him now… Every reporter got lame assignments, just not usually after a Pulitzer. He'd be back on track soon enough, though, when something else came through for him.

He wasn't taking out his frustration on Jane Falls, no matter what his uncle said. He didn't regret checking with Cole Sullivan. The man had been cagey, praising a service he supposedly hadn't used yet. A dating scam would be exactly the kind of consumer fraud piece TV 7 wanted for Eye Out For You. For now it was a puff piece for his uncle.

"Seth! Hi!"

The sharp call made him look up. Jane Falls wobbled straight across the rink, forcing annoyed skaters to zigzag to keep from hitting her. She was several feet away from the edge of the rink when she teetered violently, about to fall.

He dashed out to catch her and one of her wildly flailing arms whapped him in the face.

"Sorry, sorry," she said, holding herself up by grabbing his arm, then rubbing his cheek to make it better. So much for knight-at-the-roller-rink. Her fingers felt fine on his face. Skaters rolled by on either side. He was hyperaware of how near she was and how pretty she was and how great she smelled.

"You thought you had to save me again?" She smiled.

He shrugged and felt himself blush—*blush,* for God's sake.

A pilot light of interest hissed to life in her lilac eyes.

Leave it alone, he told himself.

A skater barreled toward them. "Let's get you out of range," he said, taking her arm and guiding her to the Astroturf edge of the rink. He couldn't help noticing the way her stretchy top squeezed her breasts upward and bared her stomach. Her pants were tight, too, and low on her hips. He'd been better off with that fluffy dress that left the details of her shape to his imagination.

At the barrier, he released her.

"Harold explained that I'd misunderstood your purpose in calling Cole Sullivan," she said, locking gazes. "You only wanted unsolicited testimonials. Correct?" The woman was no fool. She was offering him a get-out-of-the-dog-house-free card. Very smart.

An odd heat swelled between his shoulder blades, like

a space heater throbbing to life on a cold winter morning. "Cole Sullivan thinks you're great."

"Of course he does. I am great. And I'm happy you came tonight." Her big eyes just lit up. "We have time to skate before we gather at our tables to network." She motioned at the rental counter. "I'll wait for you."

"You want me to skate? I don't think so."

"It's easier than it looks. Come on."

"I know, but—" *Go to her damn skating party.* He started to object, but her eyes took on that icy bite and before he knew it he'd donned a pair of size elevens. He was vouchering this to *Inside Phoenix,* that was for damn sure.

Skates on, he stood, feeling like a jerk.

Then Jane squatted and began messing with his laces, making it worse. "If they dangle, you'll trip," she explained, glancing up at him, then back down. He felt better when he noticed he could see the top of her panties, which said *Saturday* in whimsical script.

She stood and smiled at him. "Much better."

"Except today is Thursday."

"And…?" She looked puzzled.

"Your panties say *Saturday.*" He winked.

She went pink, then winked right back at him. "At Personal Touch, every day is Saturday."

He could almost like the woman.

"Now don't be nervous," she said, linking arms with him as if he were a lost child looking for his mom. "I won't let you fall."

It tickled him that someone as shaky on skates as she was thought she was going to help him. Plus, he liked her body tight against his, so he let her lead him onto the killing rink, determined to have some fun with her.

Janie fought to focus on helping Seth skate instead of melting at how wonderful he felt beside her, his arm linked with hers, their sides touching. So what if he'd seen her underwear? Again. So what if attraction rumbled between them like an idling motorcycle engine? Again.

She would not flub this second chance. She'd hoped that Harold Rheingold would send a new reporter, but Seth didn't seem to hold a grudge about her tattling on him. No matter what, he would leave Skate World with a positive impression, Saturday underwear be damned.

She stopped at the rink entrance, her lungs tight. Skating was a fun first-date activity, but she was a terrible skater. Her tailbone already ached from several smackdowns. No matter. She had to help him. She unlinked arms and grabbed Seth's big, warm hand and shot him an encouraging smile. "Hang on tight. We'll go slow at first and when you get your balance, try it on your own."

"I'll manage somehow." He winked, then squeezed her fingers as if to comfort her. Hiding his anxiety under macho. The male ego could be so fragile.

The instant they rolled onto the rink, Janie saw she was in trouble. She needed both arms free for balance and one hand was glued to Seth's. She wobbled wildly, tensed to hit the concrete, muscles clenched, eyes squinted.

Except Seth tugged her tight against his body and pushed off fast.

She squealed. "Not so...fast!" Falling at high speed would hurt like hell. Except they weren't falling. They were gliding smoothly forward. Seth was in complete control. She'd been had.

"Why didn't you tell me you knew how to skate?"

"Because you were so cute helping me." He grinned at

her, the all-knowing bad boy at his best. He cuddled her close. "Here's the drill. Lean forward and use a long, smooth stride. Trying to stand straight keeps you off balance. You're like a bear on a ball."

"Like a bear? Couldn't I be something thin and graceful? Like a ballerina?"

"Just lean forward and you can be anything you want."

She did and found herself rolling forward more easily. She glanced up to catch him smiling down at her.

"There you go. You're a gazelle."

She was unnervingly close to him, tucked against his body, his arm securely across her back, his cheek stubble tickling her temple. It felt good. Too good. She could like this guy.

She just didn't dare.

They made a breezy run around the rink and then another and another, her confidence in her skills growing with each circle. She forgot for a few moments that Seth was doing an all-important story on her and she had to impress him with her professionalism and integrity and just had fun, one half of a skating couple spinning in lovely circles together, the breeze fresh in her face, Seth's powerful strides guiding her smaller ones, the two of them a team. And Seth looked down at her with a grin. "You're doing great, Jane," he said.

She was foolishly thrilled by his praise. "This is fun."

"Yeah. It is. I haven't done this in years." He looked almost cheerful, more carefree than she'd seen him during their interview. Maybe he wasn't so gloomy, after all. Maybe he just needed someone to cheer him up a little.

She hadn't felt easy in her skin with a man in a long time. Maybe never, now that she thought about it. Her stomach usually jumped, her muscles tensed for trouble and her breathing, often a problem, got shallow and uncertain. That made it exciting, of course, and the sex hot. But just now, spinning on wheels in Seth's arms, she felt free and her breath came easy, air swelling each little lung sac until she thought her ribs might crack. She felt like laughing. She felt happy.

Probably because she risked nothing with Seth. They would know each other for a few more hours then go their separate ways, hopefully after a positive story appeared in his magazine.

What if there was more?

That was no way to think at all.

She caught sight of the clock on the wall and realized they were late for the party. Her guests were all at the designated tables waiting for her. "We'd better head over for the icebreaker," she said to him, nodding at the group.

"Icebreaker? I thought the point was to not break anything. Least of all ice."

"An icebreaker is a game. A way to meet people."

"Oh, yeah. I did one of those at a baby shower for a reporter at my paper once."

"*You* were at a baby shower? That couldn't be good."

"It didn't last long, believe me. After I started reading *National Enquirer* stories about alien babies and bizarre births, they booted me out. Didn't even get any cake."

"You are bad."

"Thank you."

"I hope you'll behave yourself with my guests. Please don't ask if they're gold diggers or sexual predators, okay?" She pretended to be joking, but she was a little worried. She'd informed the group he was coming and told them to be honest about their experiences, but to feel free not to comment on any personal questions he might ask.

"I'll be good." He crossed his heart with his free hand. "I always am when it counts." His sincerity struck her like the shock of static from a carpet.

"I'll bet you are," she breathed, rubbery with abrupt lust, which made it hard to stay upright on wheels.

"Mmm," he said, fighting the urge to continue the flirtation, she could tell. He looked at her in a way that made her feel as though she couldn't keep a secret from him if she tried. He seemed to want to take her all in, learn everything about her and then some. It was…unnerving and in her unsettled state, she stumbled over the edge of the Astroturf.

Seth caught her arm, squeezing it with masculine sureness. "Got you."

Oh, he could get her, all right. In another place, another time, another life. She smiled uncertainly, then turned her attention to her guests. "Everyone, this is Seth Taylor. Seth, this is everyone."

The networking hour went smoothly. The rhythm was right and people were cheerful, chatty and lively. The five prospective clients who were checking out her service through the free party even signed contracts. The formal activities over, the couples headed out for more skating and Janie lowered her bruised bottom onto a bench for a relieved rest.

Until Seth approached, which sent her heart into double-time. She realized with dismay that it had nothing to do with the story and everything to do with the man.

"Got lots of great quotes," he said, waving his notepad as he sat beside her. He'd surprised her by effortlessly easing into talking with her clients as they shared pizza and beer. She'd picked up snatches of conversations laced with generous praise for Personal Touch. Hooray and thank goodness.

"I'm glad."

He smiled at her and she glanced away, unnerved by the familiarity she felt when he was near. She felt him slowly shift his gaze away from her to the rink. They watched in silence for a moment.

"Looks like you scored with those two." He nodded at a seated couple laughing a few feet away.

She shook her head. "Nope. They're Transitioners. This is his first date after a divorce and she just got dumped from a long-term relationship. They'll keep each other company until the hurt wears off, but that's about it."

"Really? You're sure?"

"Now those two are in good shape." She pointed at two of her clients bobbing and jerking awkwardly past them on skates.

"They look miserable."

"No, no. On those two that's ecstasy. She's a research librarian and he teaches history at ASU. They were too shy to meet one-on-one, so I invited them here to provide a distraction." The couple burst out laughing and hugged each other for balance, proving her point.

"Very smart," Seth said, nodding at her.

"You sound surprised."

"I'm not. I just didn't think…"

"That I knew what I was doing?"

"Not that." Pretty close, though, she could tell. He held her gaze. "Maybe I didn't give you the consideration you deserved."

Electricity crackled again. The personal and the professional kept getting mixed up with him. Her heart jumped and seemed to fight her lungs for space in her chest. *Stop this, right now,* she told herself. *Get back to the story.* Which was all that mattered here.

"Thank you, then. And thanks for coming." She tore her gaze back to the rink and swallowed.

"You must love it when a match works."

"It's thrilling, really. The ultimate joy is attending a wedding."

"That happen a lot?" He was taking notes now, which helped settle her down.

"Several times so far. One couple promised to name their baby after me. A little girl, who's due in February. I introduced them to each other at a Valentine's Day mixer."

The memory gave her a jolt of pleasure. Her recent worries had made her forget the joys of her mission. She turned to Seth, wanting him to understand. "That's why I do this. To help people find their happiness in each other. It means everything to me." She realized she'd sounded too sentimental. "I tend to get carried away."

"I respect that." He regarded her closely and she could almost see his opinion shift, deepen and lock into some place solid and safe. "I do."

He respected her? Joy. And he wanted her. She saw that, too. This was awful, all this double meaning going on. For a second, dizzy with confusion, she wanted this over. The story would turn out now. Seth respected her, he'd gotten good quotes, he understood. Now he should go. Take off those surprisingly sexy shoe skates and mosey out of her life.

She closed her eyes, gathering her strength.

"So, what's the story there?"

She opened her eyes, relieved to find Seth not staring at her demanding to understand what was going on between them, but nodding out at the rink at Samantha, a client, who was whipping by, arms swinging purposefully, eyes glued to the rink.

"She's been taking two circuits for everyone else's one for the last fifteen minutes," he observed.

"Samantha is a Nervous Thirty."

He chuckled. "Nervous because of her biological clock?"

She nodded. "Exacerbated by Singles-Bar Burnout. Nothing makes you feel older and less attractive than the club scene. All those twentysomethings with no flab, no wrinkles and all the energy in the world. When you're thirty, singles bars are a source of deep despair."

Seth laughed. She loved when he laughed. The sound was low and slow and sweet. Like he'd been surprised by something rare and wonderful he couldn't resist. "The only time she even spoke to a guy was to ask him to pass the pizza or get out of her path."

"The men here seem like losers to her. It's partly the who-wants-to-be-in-a-club-that-would-have-me-as-a-member phenomenon, but also the singles-bar mentality. Once she stops thinking of herself and the men she's meeting as selections from the butcher case, where the goal is to get the best cut, she'll begin to value them for who they really are. First impressions aren't always fair."

"Hmm."

"Like your first impression of Personal Touch, for example. I hope that's fixed now?"

He hesitated and that ice water feeling flooded her veins.

"Would a bribe help?" she joked miserably.

He released a delicious laugh that melted her doubts. "No, but how about we go for a beer after this? I have a few questions still. There's a microbrew pub down the street."

"A beer? Oh, sure." Her heart pounded against her ribs. More questions *for the story,* she reminded herself, but her toes curled in her skates and she could hardly draw a breath.

An hour later, she parked beside Seth's motorcycle—a sleek café racer. It figured he'd drive the bad-boy vehicle of choice. He guided her into the bar with a light hand at the small of her back and her whole body went ridiculously soft in response. *Get a grip, girl.*

The blasting rock and loud chatter were a relief, since the ambiance was far from romantic, but they had to lean close to be heard over the din.

"So, why matchmaking, Jane?" Seth asked, his eyes twinkling at her.

A good question, but hard to answer when her nose was filled with his great leather-spice-man scent. This close, she spotted a darling beauty mark high on his cheekbone and noticed secret swirls of navy in his clear blue eyes.

She managed to provide her practiced answer. "I'm honored to be part of the most important decision people ever make."

"No, really," he said, his voice low, digging in. "Why you? Why this?" *Tell me all.*

No way would she destroy her credibility with her sad tale of bad beaus. "Look around." She gestured out at the jam-packed bar. "All these people are looking for love."

"I'd say they're looking for sex."

"Some settle for that, it's true. And bars tend to attract Stubborn Singles—people who refuse to settle down. Many of my clients have had their hearts broken by them."

"So these Stubborn Singles are dangerous?" He was teasing her.

"They can be tricky. The worst ones don't realize that's what they are. They seem available—and think they are—but as soon as someone falls for them, they break it off. There's always a reason—she was too clingy or too aggressive or too quiet or too chatty...." She realized he'd asked her a question. She leaned closer. "Hmm?"

"Is this the voice of experience?"

She dropped back, desperate to hide her secret. "I've dated a Stubborn Single or two, sure." She took a swallow of beer to keep him from catching on.

But it was no use.

"That influence you to become a matchmaker? Your own heartbreak?"

She couldn't answer that. "I have a psychology degree and I believe relationships are the crucible where personality theories are tested." Could she be any more intellectual?

"I see." He didn't buy it.

"I've learned even more from my clients. Many suffer from relationship fatigue. They've been hurt over and over by people who are wrong for them. One client marks off depression days on his calendar when he senses a breakup on the way."

"That's pathetic."

"No, it's realistic. Others get superstitious. One client wears her granny panties when she wants to meet a guy, figuring they're the last pair she'd want a man to see her in, so of course she'll score."

"Good-luck granny panties? Cute." He wrote that down, then looked up. "You paint a pretty grim picture. How do you stay so cheerful with your every-day-is-Saturday underwear, Janie?"

Janie. He'd called her Janie. She got goose bumps. Like a swooning fool. "I guess I'm an optimist. I believe that if you uncover and analyze key personality factors, you can narrow the search down to people with whom you're truly compatible."

"But compatibility isn't enough." The words came out flat and she saw a flicker of pain in Seth's face, which surprised her. It seemed to surprise him, too.

"You've been there?" she risked asking.

He gave her a quick nod, then lifted his stein as their waitress breezed by. "Can I get another? You...?" he asked Janie.

She shook her head no. "Do you want to talk about it?" She kept her tone carefully neutral, wanting to help, and way too curious about him.

Do you want to talk about it? Seth looked at Janie, who was smiling warmly at him, a shrink patting her couch. Normally, he'd rather pass a kidney stone. But she looked so earnest, blinking those big eyes at him, that he wanted to tell her. *Wanted to.* Good God. Maybe all that love-match talk at the skating rink had gotten to him.

No way would he tell her about Ana. The Cindi thing was almost funny, so he'd go with that. "I was seeing this real estate agent back in Miami. We'd had a stupid fight, and I wanted to apologize, so I took some flowers to her—hokey, I know, but what the hell. I wanted to surprise her at an open house. I did. With her broker. Testing out the acoustics in the master bedroom."

"Oh, no. How terrible."

"Not to mention a violation of agent ethics."

"That would upset anyone, Seth."

He'd normally bristle at the sympathy, but she looked so easy about it. *Bummer. How can I help?* He found he felt...better. Not that the incident had affected him that strongly, really.

"We'd have broken up soon enough," he said. "She thought I was boring. All I did was talk about journalism." And think about Ana, which had been the real problem.

"But she's not the woman you mean—where it didn't work out?" she probed. "Despite how compatible you seemed?"

Dammit. "No, but, hey, that's way over. Ana. That was her name." What the hell? He was spilling his guts all over Janie's couch, after all.

"Try not to give up, Seth."

"Give up?"

"On finding someone special and having it work out. Eventually, I mean. I know you haven't asked for my advice, but I talk to so many people who get hurt and give up altogether. It's easy to think it will never work, that it's not worth the trouble. But it is. I know it. I don't know you well, but I think you have a lot to offer, a lot of love to give, and—"

Her eyes gleamed with faith in him and he liked it and that was weird, so he did what he'd wanted to do since he met her. He kissed her. And those lips were exactly as soft as they looked.

She made a sound, then broke off the kiss, her eyes wide and shiny as wet marbles, the pupils huge and black in the gold light of the bar. "Why did you do that?"

"I couldn't resist."

"But you're writing a story about me." She looked worried and frantic. And hot for him.

To which he couldn't help responding. "Not for long."

"For long enough." She sat back against the booth.

She was right, of course. All that you-have-love-to-give sympathy had just gotten to him. Along with being so close to her for so long. "You're right. Sorry."

"You just got carried away."

"Right. It was a bad idea." But he didn't quite care. He wanted to get lost for hours in her lovely eyes, in her incredible body, naked and warm and wet. Ah, wet. He loved wet. He hadn't felt this way in a long time, as though he needed her in his arms to feel all right with the world.

"Very bad," she said on a shaky breath, wanting him, too, he could see. "My point was not to give up and, well, if you'd like, I'd be glad to work up a profile, set you up with some Potentials and—"

He kissed her again. He couldn't help it.

She broke off again. "Write the story. I should go." She scrambled out of the booth.

"Sure," he said, standing, aware suddenly that he was damned lonely. Looking into this woman's face, lonely seemed the worst condition in the world.

"I'll be fine. Stay here. Finish your beer. Call if you have questions. Good night." She backed away, watching him as if she feared he'd pounce.

He just might. He knew by the pinch in his gut, the bubble of adrenaline in his chest, the hot sweat springing out on his skin, that this wasn't the end of the story. Not by a long shot.

9

"THIS IS A perfect time to talk," Kylie told Cole, even though the line two button winked a frantic red at her. She never left people on hold, but her first-responder instincts had been dulled by Cole.

"I was putting honey in my tea and had to call," he said so huskily she fairly throbbed in response.

"Honey? Oh." Last evening—Mexican night, as she'd lovingly dubbed it—they'd drizzled honey on their sopai-pillas…and elsewhere and she was still sticky in hard-to-reach places. *Honey, oh.*

The blinking light slowed to a languorous wink. *Take your time,* it seemed to be saying.

All wrong, she knew, but who cared? Mexican night had been spectacular. After "dessert," they'd rushed to Cole's place because of his doggie guest, where they'd made love until dawn.

Which had made for a brain-fogged day she was barely surviving. It had been a wildly out-of-character night. And it was over. So why was she neglecting a call? It was likely someone from S-Mickey-B with the specifics about the retreat and upcoming meetings. Blink, blink, wink.

"So, what do you *need?*" Cole asked in the same husky register he'd used last night.

"No, what do *you* need?" she replied in her sultriest tone, closing her eyes against the flashing line. She could spare a moment for a quickie on the phone, couldn't she? "I mean, you called me."

"But I'm returning your call, Kylie," he said, amusement in his voice.

"Oh, right." She sat up straight. She *had* called Cole. It was about the lawsuit. "Marlon Brandon called Janie back and she convinced him and his attorney to meet with us next week. So, I was thinking you and I should get together and go over our strategy."

"Strategy, huh? How about my place?"

"Your place?" He'd got right to her secret wish—to combine business with pleasure. What could be more glorious? She was hanging by the last frayed fiber on the knot of her work ethic, but what the hell?

"Yeah. Because Radar gets lonely and we might run... long."

"We don't want Radar to get lonely on your rug."

"Can you be here by seven? Or earlier, if you need more time."

How about now? "Seven will be great." That gave her three more hours in her office, after which she'd load her briefcase so that after the sex break that came *after* the lawsuit work she could do more on the Home Town Suites campaign.

She hung up from Cole and grabbed the call. Sure enough, it was an account rep named Gina from S-Mickey-B with details on the retreat and the account meeting next Thursday and Friday. Garrett had snapped up Gina last year, very much like he was doing with Kylie, so Gina had some words of advice and even offered her guest room until Kylie found a place she liked.

By the time Kylie hung up, she was feeling tense, but excited. Her future was just around the corner. She'd earned some relaxation with Cole, right? What could be better than healthy sex with a sunset clause? Cole needed it, too, with the pressure he was under.

This would enhance their productivity. *Really,* she told her sensible side, slumped listlessly in the corner mumbling about deadlines and workload and lost hours. Wasn't she bringing work in her briefcase?

Maybe she'd swing by her place for a change of clothes. Just to be comfortable.

Oh, shut up.

WORK FIRST, SEX LATER, Cole reminded himself, tucking in the corner of the satin sheets he'd bought on the way home from work. They were so slippery, he and Kylie might slide right off the bed. He couldn't wait to give it a try. *After* they'd worked, of course. Radar gave him a look: *You are pathetic.*

"Like you should talk," he said to the dog, perched on the pillow at the head of the bed, king of all he surveyed. The minute Radar had laid eyes on Kylie, he'd melted onto his back for a tummy rub, head lolling in ecstasy, giving Cole the eye: *This is how it's done, pal.*

Now the dog sneezed his disgust with Cole, hopped to the floor and trotted out to the entryway to wait for Kylie.

Cole flopped onto the bed, disgusted with himself. He knew damn well they'd make love all night and tomorrow he'd wear the same sleep-deprived look he'd worn today— like Trevor after a flight attendant weekend, except Trevor had the chops for wild nights. Cole was rusty. Not that he'd been very wild in the first place.

Now he itched—no, *ached*—to get Kylie in his arms. He could see spending more time with her. Lots more time. Time that neither of them had. Time to talk about their days, their work, their plans, their dreams, every little thing they cared about. And stuff they didn't.

His phone rang. He had a moment of panic that she'd realized her mistake and called to cancel. If either of them came to their senses, it'd be all over. He grabbed the phone. "Hello?"

"Is this Cole Sullivan?" The female voice wasn't Kylie's and it crackled as if from a bad connection.

"Yes?"

"Well, hello. This is Deborah Ramsdale. Have I caught you at a bad moment?"

"Deborah? Oh. Not at all." Except for the fact that a woman was on her way to have sex with him. He jerked upright, flooded with guilty surprise.

"Jane Falls suggested I contact you, since I won't be back until the fourth of next month. To get the formalities out of the way? I know phones can be impersonal, but she insisted it would help?" The question in her sentences made her seem sweeter than her stern photograph.

"That's a great idea," he said, carrying the phone into the living room. This would fix her more firmly in his mind.

"I'm glad you agree. I have to say I was delighted with your bio. We have so much in common."

"I liked yours, too." Luckily, she hadn't seen his video. He still needed to have Jane erase the mortifying junk Gail had dredged out of him at the end.

After an awkward silence, they both spoke at once.

"So, corporate law?"

"You're in international—?"

"Sorry."

"Me, too. Sorry."

She laughed. "Yes. I'm in international law, but I'm reducing my travel to make time for a social life. You know how that is. You can work so hard that you lose track of yourself."

"Believe me, I understand."

"Of course you do. I read your file. And you read mine." More silence. "So, you enjoy your work?"

"Very much. You?"

"Yes." Another pause. "At first I thought, 'A matchmaker? Isn't that desperate?' But the Personal Touch approach seemed so matter-of-fact and, well, realistic."

"And efficient."

"Exactly. No wasted time. And when Janie gave me your personality scores, I was impressed." Paper rattled. "I mean we match completely in sociability…some variation in conformity, but we're exact duplicates on financial views. Temperaments are a little different—I'm a little more volatile than you—but that's workable, don't you think?"

"I guess. Sure." She was studying their scores?

Radar yipped sharply.

"Is that a dog?" she said. "You didn't mention you had a dog." A flicker of suspicion rose in her voice.

"I'm dog-sitting my neighbor's terrier for a few days."

"Oh." She seemed to relax. "That's kind of you."

"Actually, it seemed like good practice for building balance in my life. Taking him for walks, getting home at a reasonable time so he won't be lonely…" He thought about mentioning the Poop Warning System, or PWS, as Kylie called it, but somehow he didn't think Deborah would appreciate it. Not yet, anyway. He'd have to know her better. Did she have a sense of humor? Too soon to tell. "Sounds lame, I know."

"No, no. That's excellent. Just…excellent." She laughed. "I'm repeating myself. I guess I'm a little nervous. But I thought, seize the day. If we can't get along long-distance, what's the point of meeting in person?"

"Good point."

She released a breath and so did he.

"And dog-sitting is charming. I'm charmed, Cole." His name on her lips was pleasant. When Kylie said it, flames licked his insides.

Forget Kylie. Deborah was racking up long-distance fees just to get to know him right now. He needed to picture her, so he whipped her profile out of his briefcase, and flipped to her photo. With her voice in his ear, she looked warmer to him. The phone call was a good idea. *Thank you, Janie.*

"So why international law?" he asked.

While Deborah explained her lifelong interest in travel, her affinity for foreign languages and her fascination with law, he carefully tore out her photo, folded back the edges and tucked it into his wallet, just as if she were already in his life. A good idea all around.

"The best thing about Personal Touch is that we don't have to play games," she said after a bit. "We can lay our cards on the table. Isn't that a relief?" Her edgy tone told him she'd been burned—lied to, left hanging or cheated on. Ouch.

"Right," he answered after a pause. Was sleeping with her stand-in playing games? Lord. He and Deborah hadn't even *started* anything yet. And the thing with Kylie had just…happened. He swallowed hard.

"Dating can be so childish, don't you think? Will he call again, did he really like me, all that?"

He understood that part of it, at least. "Absolutely." Was that a knock at the door? Kylie? No, across the hall. Whew.

"Cole?" Deborah said.

"Hmm? What do I...?" He retraced Deborah's last words. "Oh, yes. T. Cook's is terrific. Great food. When you get into town, maybe we'll have dinner there one night."

"How about making a reservation for Saturday, the day after I get back? Say seven? They fill so fast."

"Right, sure. I'll do that."

"I don't mean to push, but do it soon, won't you? It would be a perfect place for our first date and I'd hate to be disappointed."

"No problem."

"This is exciting. We're all set. And I'm glad I called, Cole. I feel so much better. You seem real to me now."

And she seemed real to him. No longer just a photo in a profile, words in a bio. Hell, he had *dinner plans* with her. Meanwhile, Kylie would bound in here any minute. Sweat sprang out on his body.

Deborah surprised him with a yawn. "Sorry. It's late here. How about if you call me tomorrow and we can talk about how our day went?" She sounded hopeful...and hardly pushy at all.

He took down her cell number—and her schedule—and they hung up. They'd spoken, at least, and he liked her. He hadn't exactly felt a connection, but it was too soon for that. Except with Kylie it had been instant. Like fingers twined. Long-lost lovers.

Forget Kylie. Think of Deborah. He'd better snap to on the T. Cook reservation. Jeez. But he liked women who went straight after what they wanted. *Women like Kylie.*

He couldn't stop thinking of her for one blessed minute? He clutched his head in his hands, elbows on his knees, then caught sight of Radar who actually looked as though he felt sorry for Cole. He was really losing it if he could imagine sympathy from a creature probably plotting the next place to deposit his opinion.

"Maybe I'll just tell Kylie what happened," he said to the dog. "Maybe we'll just work and she'll leave."

Radar emitted a sharp snort—he thought Cole was full of it—and trotted to the door where he barked. His hypersensitive ears had heard Kylie's car. Cole raced after him, not sure which of them was more excited to see the woman whose steps rang on the stairs.

KYLIE MARCHED up Cole's stairs to his landing and checked her watch. Exactly seven. On time. She patted her briefcase, which she'd jammed with work, and tugged at her jacket—she'd stayed in a business suit, since they had business to conduct—and knocked briskly on the door. She waited with her feet together, both hands holding her briefcase in front like a shield or a chastity belt, tense and determined. They would work first, play later. Everything was completely under control.

Then Cole opened the door and she melted like chocolate in a warm fist. "Hi," she whispered, letting her briefcase hang from one hand at her side.

His face lit with joy, but he struggled with some emotion and stepped back instead of grabbing her into his arms.

She moved inside.

"Listen, I've been thinking," Cole said. "Maybe we should rethink what we're doing."

Oh, no. If he got sensible, she was sunk. She so needed another night with him, making love, feeling that release, not to mention some time to discuss her projects and get his insights. She had to reason with him.

"We're getting carried away, right? I know. But I have the solution. We work *first*." She rushed for the kitchen table, ignoring Radar, who almost tripped her trying to get a tummy scratch, and threw her briefcase onto the table. She started on the clasp, aware that Cole was approaching slowly, not entirely convinced.

She fought the button—she'd jammed the case so full she'd had to sit on it to latch it—sensing Cole was about to object. "The meeting should go fine as long as we appeal to Brandon's ego," she said, digging at the latch. "He's stung, humiliated, which is why he hasn't been willing to talk to us. What we must do is reinforce his dignity by letting him think he's doing Janie a personal favor by accepting her services—" Her briefcase sprang open, spewing the top items: a file, a notepad, clothes, her toothbrush and two packets of honey she'd tossed in at the last second.

Cole picked one up and a slow smile replaced his worry like sun conquering clouds. "You had something in mind?"

"For after…?" She loved this look on his face—lust and delight and mischief. *Oh, Cole.* She wanted him so much. For this one night. She lunged into his arms to kiss him.

He gripped her so hard it almost hurt and kissed her back as if she were about to leave forever. Which she was…kind of. Tomorrow she headed to L.A. for the retreat. And they had to stop sometime soon. Didn't they? The idea made her feel empty, as if she were losing something enormous—a home, her best friend Patti. Oh, hell. Way too sentimental.

Cole broke off the kiss, still holding her. "I'm concerned about Deborah," he said, looking pained and guilty.

"You are? Oh." She felt a nasty rush of jealousy, which she squelched. "Of course you are. But she's not here yet, is she? And we have this perfect storm of need and opportunity right now. She's not back for two more weeks?"

"And four days." But he still looked guilty and she couldn't stand that. This was supposed to be fun and easy, not painful or hard. She had to suggest the right thing.

"Okay…" She took a shaky breath for courage. "If you need to get mentally ready for her, then we should stop. Just call it quits. We've had a great time. Any more is overkill."

"It has been great," he said wistfully, running the back of his hand along her cheek. "Very great. Incredibly great."

"So, let's plan some strategy and I'll leave." She grabbed the honey out of his fingers and threw it into her briefcase. That was that. She tossed in her shorts and top and the other spilled items, except the notepad, a pen and the Marlon Brandon folder. She felt hot and nervous and tense. *Don't let me go. Make me stay.* The thought alarmed her.

"Kylie," he said.

She jerked up her gaze, relief at the ready, but he was only holding out the black-lace panties she'd packed for a sexy little thrill.

"Oh, yeah." She shoved them in the case, aware that Cole watched like a dieter ogling an éclair, and closed the lid with a sharp click. "So, sound like a plan?"

He swallowed, shifted his weight, then said, "Probably best." He sat at the table.

She sat, too, and picked up her pen. She looked down at

her tablet, where she'd jotted a few notes already and settled in as best she could. "As I said, we should stroke his ego—"

"Don't say *stroke*," Cole interrupted.

Her eyes shot to his, which burned with emotion. He tried to smile at his joke, but didn't manage it. Instead he took a ragged breath and held her gaze, the tension between them ticking like an erotic time bomb about to blow.

"Okay, *massage* his ego?" she tried to joke back.

"Not that, either." He stared at her, eyes hot and hungry. "If this is the last time we're going to be together, Kylie, I don't want to spend it working." He reached for her hands, gripping them hard. His were shaking terribly.

"Me, either," she whispered, squeezing back. "The meeting's not till Tuesday, and I already have some preliminary ideas. We could talk when I get back from L.A. on Sunday morning and—"

But Cole lunged over the table and stopped her with a kiss, maneuvering his way around the table to her, pulling her to her feet so abruptly her chair crashed to the floor behind her. Radar gave a startled yelp at the sound.

"One more night," he said, swinging her into his arms like some kind of he-man. Her heels slid off her feet and clunked to the floor.

"Just one," she said, so relieved she didn't care if it was wrong or bad or meant she was in emotional trouble. She had another night with Cole and that was all that mattered.

"We can work afterward," he said, justifying this to himself and her, she knew.

"Absolutely." Who knows? Maybe they would work. She didn't even care.

She woke at 3:00 a.m. to the lush glory of satin sheets covering her front and aroused man cupping her back.

They'd fallen asleep, a no-no, but they'd talked a little strategy just before drifting off.

And they had accomplished a little something work related. Around eleven, they'd left the bed to try to make some notes on the meeting, but Cole noticed the Home Town Suites folder and insisted she show him her storyboards.

She had, loving the expression on his face, laughing at the fact she was putting on a presentation stark naked. He'd been impressed. "Fresh angle," he'd said and absolutely meant her pitch, not her bare body. "They don't know what they're getting, these S-Mickey-B people." She'd felt so reassured by his words. Then she showed him the wrap-up marketing plan for Lock-It. The company was exploring new products that she wouldn't be around to work on and she found herself near tears.

Cole had pulled her into his arms and reassured her. "Of course you're sad. You're leaving the company you started. That's hard. But you have a plan. You're moving ahead. Change makes everyone shaky—even incredibly strong, sexy, determined, sexy, independent, sexy women."

He was right, of course. And he had a plan, too. Deborah was out there waiting to bring it to fruition. Deborah or another woman like her. A corporate-wife-in-the-wings. Which also made Kylie sad. So she suggested food and they created a gigantic quesadilla stuffed with peppers and mushrooms and tomatoes and three kinds of cheese and fed it to each other while they watched the stand-up marathon on Comedy Central.

It was such a lovely pleasure to laugh with Cole—just let go and relax, lean over to lick dribbles of cheese off his chin, smear her grease-slick lips against his, like some old married couple who did this every night.

So of course they'd broken the all-night rule. Special occasion. Their last night, right? And it was so cozy in Cole's bed now, twined in a sensual cocoon, legs overlapped, their bodies slick, Cole's breath warm against her ear, his body a lovely human chair in which she reclined.

She was wide-awake now, though, so maybe she should go home and work. Seize the moment, get ahead, or at least catch up.

As if he'd read her mind, Cole slid his hands up to cup her breasts. *Don't go.*

"Mmm," she said, sliding her backside against the lovely length of him, her fleeting urge to work popping like a floral-scented bubble in their Mexican-night tub. Maybe she'd stick around a little longer….

Radar sighed and she heard the clink of dog tags, followed by a thump. He'd read her mind and jumped off the bed to avoid all the thrashing around.

Cole's mouth found her ear. "You stayed all night." He sounded so relieved that she just smiled, refusing to feel guilty. It was three in the morning. Not even Kylie worked that late…or early.

Then Cole pushed into her from behind, slowly and deliciously, his way made easy by the juices of all the love they'd made together. "Honey, I'm home," he murmured.

"I thought you'd never get here," she murmured back, loving how he filled her up and made her ache.

"You're slick and soft," he whispered, his breath warm on her skin, his length sturdy and demanding.

"And you're hard and in so deep."

"Mmm." He reached under her and around to cup one breast, then over her with his other hand to touch her clit, sending a sleepy thrill along her nerves.

In the dark, her sleep-heavy muscles were lax and slow. "I feel like I'm dreaming," she said.

He tightened his grip, keeping her snug and close. "I never want to wake up."

"Never." That was just sex talk, she knew, and she wanted his mouth, so she shifted so they could kiss. Now all of her was connected and busy—mouth, breast, backside, sex and clit. Her brain, too, was full of thoughts of Cole's body, his careful attention, his tireless touch.

Lust poured through her in thick, needy waves. He played her body to its natural crescendo, making her rock and writhe. He pushed steadily in and out, holding on, keeping them together, controlling the pace until they lunged together into a climax, thrusting hard, crying out, ending with a long sigh that lapsed into a lovely cuddle.

"Was it a good dream?" he asked softly.

"The best ever." She reached up to cup his cheek and felt his smile with her fingers. A smile she knew matched her own in the dark. So relaxed, so easy, so wonderful. So temporary.

They had to stop. She would be in L.A. until Sunday morning and Cole had Deborah on his mind. Kylie got a sharp, hollow pain like an unexpected drop on a roller coaster. *I want to go on.*

She was being silly, of course. The late-night dream feeling had taken over. This intensity couldn't last. It was like finding a hot new ice-cream flavor. She'd gone through a toffee-praline phase back when she was such a frenetic exerciser weight didn't stick. Every other night it was a praline waffle cone dripping with sweet honey flavor.

Then one day the flavor tasted cloying, grainy, boring. She moved on to double-fudge brownie, quickly switching to pink bubble gum, then lemon sorbet. Never again would she ruin something wonderful by keeping at it too long.

Better to quit Cole while the honey-brickle flavor was still golden on her tongue.

Besides, he was too much like her for anything long-term to work. She'd get bored. Him, too, no doubt. Boredom meant going dull and dead—in her life and in her work. They'd needed each other for now, at this time and place in their lives. This couldn't last. Nothing ever did. That was the point—to stay open and ready for the next good thing. And she had plenty of them to come.

They just didn't seem to matter right now in this cozy bed with this remarkable man breathing so comfortably near her ear, holding her in a way that made her feel so…safe. Life could never be this easy. This was a trick. Pure proof she'd be better off gone. This was all too confusing and she had too much to do to allow herself to be confused.

10

"SETH!" JANIE jumped up from her desk. She'd been day-dreaming about the kiss, reliving the thrill of his sudden assault on her mouth, the glory and wonder of it, and now here he stood in her doorway as if she'd conjured him out of her fantasy.

He'd come bearing gifts, too—a paper-wrapped bouquet of blood-red roses and a ragged-leaved, three-foot banana plant in a plastic pot bearing a clearance tag.

"I need more photos…have more questions," he mumbled, clearly cooking up an excuse. He lifted the plant. "I thought this would be good for the burned spot." He moved the wastebasket and put the pot in its place.

"How nice of you."

"And I thought you could use new flow—" He stopped when he noticed the fresh batch of white roses on the table. Cole had sent them. She figured it was a thank-you for getting Deborah to call him. "All stocked up, I see."

"They're from a client, Seth, not a man. Well, a man, but it's a business thank-you. They don't mean anything like—" She felt herself flush.

"Maybe take these home then." He thrust them at her, embarrassed, too, his shaking hands making the paper crackle and the leaves flutter. She remembered the "hokey" gesture with his ex-girlfriend. Maybe he was hokey at heart. She liked that.

"You can never have too many roses," she said, inhaling the fresh scent. "Mmm. I'll put them in water."

She hurried off for a vase from her office closet, then to the table to arrange the flowers, where she fumbled and trembled under his close attention.

"So, how are you?" he said, speaking low.

"I'm fine. You?" she said in the same tone.

"We're okay about what happened, right?" he asked, as if they'd shared wild sex, not two brief kisses.

"Sure. It was just…spontaneous."

"As in combustion? Then yeah."

"Yeah," she whispered and watched his pupils explode with desire. His throat worked over a swallow.

She ducked her gaze to the roses. "So beautiful."

"Yeah." But he was looking at her, not the flowers.

The heady scent of Seth's leather-coconut-spice combined with the roses to make her feel dizzy. "You have questions?" she reminded them both.

"I do." About what was going on between them, she could see on his face. He looked as though he'd awakened from hypnosis with everyone laughing at something he'd done while under the spell.

That made her want him desperately. Having a guy as restrained as Seth practically shaking with desire was incredibly thrilling. Oh, it was heaven.

And absolutely pointless. Because she knew how it would turn out—she'd get hooked and he'd leave.

"You need more photos? How about at my desk?" She moved, relieved to break the magnetic pull, and went to her chair.

He remained standing in a daze for a second, then joined her. This time he took his time with the shot, considering her entire body, his eyes taking a slow ride over her form so that she could hardly sit still. She crossed her legs to keep her aching sex in check.

He made the photograph feel as intimate as a kiss, which made her shiver. Then he suggested a different expression, a new angle, a tilt of her head, a lifted hand. Shot after shot after shot. More than he could possibly use. He photographed her pretending to talk on the phone, staring meditatively off in the distance. Each time, he arranged her body with tender care, crossing her hands, placing one at her cheek, clearly needing just to touch her. Their breath mingled in uneven waves, harsh and shaky.

There was sexual energy in what he was doing, but also close attention, the incredible, skillful focus of an artist. No quiver of her body or flicker of feeling in her face escaped his notice. It was so intimate—his soft touch, his breath and heat on her exposed skin, but also reaching her through her clothes, making her feel raw.

She was hyperaware of his body, the flex and release of his muscles, his strong fingers, the crinkles around his startling blue eyes, their intelligence and wit. And how blasted good he smelled. She almost moaned with frustration.

Finally, he quit with the camera and sat beside her desk for more questions. This time he didn't sit back or act casual. He leaned forward, digging in, wanting to *know*. Everything. This time the questions weren't so much about Personal Touch, but about her. As if he were her biographer. He asked about starting the business, her psychology background and her philosophy, but also about her family, her childhood, her hobbies, her favorite movies and music.

Overwhelmed and in self-defense, she asked about him and learned he was working for his uncle on the magazine for now, but hoped to move to the newspaper. He told her about a fishing trip with his uncle's stepkids, their interest in journalism and his own love of the work. He talked about winning a Pulitzer for a story series in Florida, minimizing his role, and explained in murky terms his reasons for leaving the state. Which meant it had something to do with Ana, the woman who'd broken his heart.

He sounded restless, uncertain of where he wanted to be, but he never let his eyes waver from her face and that made him seem steady and dependable. And raised a dangerous hope in her heart.

"I can't believe some guy hasn't snapped you up," he said finally.

She laughed. "When the time is right, I'll look for someone."

"And you'll do the compatibility chart and all that? Probably chase the guy away."

"Not if he's the right guy," she said slowly.

He searched her face. How had she ever thought he was laid-back? "I guess the right guy wouldn't let anything stand in his way. He wouldn't take no for an answer."

And what if Seth were that guy?

"Come here," he said, leaning toward her. He wanted to kiss her and she wanted to kiss him. Didn't she owe it to herself? Maybe those kisses had been anomalies. She tilted her mouth, slid closer, closer, a breath a way, almost there, and—

"Deborah Ramsdale, line one!" Gail's voice through the intercom smashed the moment like a glass flung against a wall.

Janie froze in place, her mouth close to Seth's. "Can you take a message?" she said to Gail.

"She wants to renegotiate her membership fee, can you believe that?" Gail said, not picking up the tension. Seth's eyes, so close, twinkled with amusement.

"No, I'm with someone now, Gail, and—"

"She hasn't even met Cole and she wants six months off," Gail continued in her chatty tone. "What does the woman expect?"

"Tell her I'll call her back, Gail."

"London, hon. Big bucks for the call."

"It'll be fine. Really." She knew Deborah had been delighted by the phone call. That and the flowers from Cole convinced her that the match-up was on track.

"And can you watch the phones for a bit? My nail tech ditched her loser fiancé and I just happen to have snapped an acrylic... Prepare for a new client."

"Just hurry back." She rolled her eyes for Seth's benefit. He sat back in his chair, giving up on the kiss, and grinned.

"Oh, and be warned. Harry Hand Job may call."

"Harry Hand Jo— Gail!"

"Don't worry. I'm talking him out of the habit. Byeee."

"Bye." Jane looked at Seth in the silence that followed. The urge to kiss had been whisked away by the silly conversation like smoke beneath a fan. This was a gift, she told herself. A chance to be smart, so she would explain it to Seth, keep it in perspective. "I know what's going on here. For you, it's the hunt factor—it's a male drive. You see me as a challenge."

"And how do you feel about that?"

Desperately aroused. "I'm flattered."

"That's all?" His eyes flared.

"No. It's not all. But it will pass."

"What if we don't want it to?"

"In your heart of hearts, you do. Remember the story you're writing? That's why we're here."

"Yeah." A shadow crossed his face and settled into a frown. "And you shouldn't have to remind me. Right." He pushed himself slowly to his feet, looking down at her the whole time. "Guess I'll leave you to your sex calls."

She stood, too, forcing herself to think of Personal Touch and her own heart, which couldn't take another blow. "Thanks for the flowers and the plant. And for doing so much work on my story. And if you have any more questions—" *Like, what am I doing for the rest of my life?* "—don't hesitate to call."

"I won't." He held her gaze. "Could you possibly be as good as you seem?"

"I hope so."

"I believe you." He looked at her as though that were a bad thing. A chill shivered down her spine again. What did he really think? There was something about him that didn't add up.

Then he touched her cheek and gave her a last regretful look before he turned and left.

She sank into her chair, her eyes on the tattered banana plant he'd brought her. How sweet. And hokey.

She'd done the right thing, hadn't she? Seth was probably a Stubborn Single—the dangerous kind who didn't know he was one. Maybe she'd cured herself of her bad-boy fixation.

Except he didn't quite match that profile. He seemed tender and sweet and steady. Or she could be fooling herself. How could she find out?

QUIT SCREWING AROUND *and write the damn story,* Seth told himself, riding away from Jane Falls's office. He was losing his edge—no, his mind. Thank God for Mr. Hairy Palms or he would have kissed her again. He'd gone to see her to get an angle for the story—his aborted drafts ranged from lame description to puffy praise—but the truth was that he'd fixated on her.

She was hot, of course, with a long, lovely body, arresting eyes and a butter-soft mouth, and he liked her voice—firm and serious—and her laugh, which was solid as though she really knew what was funny. It delighted him to earn one.

Maybe it was the hunt factor, as she'd said. Maybe he just wanted into her *Saturday* panties.

But it was more than physical. Her warmth, her relentless hope, her spunky tenderness drew him like the moon tugged the tide, made him want to promise things he didn't dare promise.

Or did he? It wasn't as if he never wanted to settle down. Hell, he'd tried to buy a house to live in with Ana. Did he want a lifetime with someone else? Someone like Janie?

Just write the freakin' story. He kept letting himself get sidetracked from the work at hand. Was she as good as she seemed? He felt as if he was waiting for a shoe to drop. Was it an innocent little marabou-lined glass slipper or a big, dirty boot?

The receptionist had said Deborah Ramsdale wanted to cancel her membership. Something about Cole Sullivan, who'd been strange on the phone when Seth had called him. Maybe something was amok. And he still hadn't checked on the sex calls.

What he wanted to do was write something as sweet as Jane and be done with it. So he could see her? Figure out if they belonged together?

There was something wrong with his thinking, but he couldn't quite figure out what. He'd have to come back... for more background, more questions, more something. He wasn't even going to think about it.

A LITTLE AFTER ten on Sunday morning, Kylie strode into the Terminal Four baggage claim after her return from L.A. feeling weary, but satisfied after the S-Mickey-B retreat. Three solid days and nights, including dinners and late drinks, of working to make a good impression on everyone, while absorbing every detail about the S-Mickey-B team—styles, interests, personalities and conflicts—had taken immense energy. She'd liked everyone. Spending time with Gina, whom she saw as a kindred spirit, had been especially good.

The only disappointment had been the work. The year's agency plan, the main product of the retreat, had been...well...mundane. She'd expected to be awed by the combined brain power and brilliance of the group, but figured she'd get the full dazzle at next week's meetings. They'd be talking about her Home Town Suites concept, too, so she intended to polish her ideas to a shimmer.

Now her plan was to nab a power nap and work on the concept for a few hours before Janie arrived at five with Thai takeout so they could go over the new Personal Touch business plan Kylie had scored as a trade-out with a client.

At least things were settling down for Personal Touch. The magazine story would be out soon, the Web site was fixed, she'd already placed some promotions and made modest ad buys. Only the lawsuit loomed large and if the meeting with Marlon Brandon went well, even that would be resolved and Kylie could move to L.A. with a clear conscience and no lingering worries.

She waited for relief and excitement to hit—she was about to get her fondest wish. But instead, her stomach felt empty and her chest tight.

She was tired and hungry, right? And all she'd eaten this morning were a handful of peanuts on the plane. *I don't want to leave.* She pushed away that thought. Just last-minute doubts.

She reached the carousel where her flight's luggage circled and her cell phone sounded the unknown caller music. She grabbed it out of her purse. She didn't recognize the number.

"Hello?" she said into the phone, watching her black traveler tumble down the chute, the red-checked ribbon she'd tied to recognize it by fluttering against the handle.

"Got your bag?"

"Cole?" Glorious warmth flowed through her, filling the emptiness in her stomach and relaxing the tension in her chest. "Almost. How did you…?"

"Roll it out to the north curb. Radar and I will drive you home."

"Why did you come?" She laughed, so happy about the surprise. Their goodbye after the all-nighter had been brief—both were late for meetings—but they knew without saying the words that it would be the last sex. She'd expected they'd plan the Brandon meeting over the phone.

"Because cabs are pricey and SuperShuttle's slow. Because we need to work out the Marlon Brandon strategy.

Because Radar waits for you at the front door, glaring at me like it's my fault you never arrive. And because I missed you." He said the last low and soft.

"I missed you, too." Blush burned her cheeks and she grabbed her bag and half ran toward the exit doors, the bag tilting, tipping and swinging behind her, not even on its wheels. She felt like dancing and singing and shouting with joy. She felt as if she'd come home for the first time ever.

She ran through the automatic doors to the curb, glanced to the left and there they were, Radar in the passenger window of Cole's Acura, Cole on the driver's side, grinning a huge grin. At the sight of her, Radar's body seemed to throb with pleasure—a considerable amount of emotion for such a subtle little dog.

Her heart throbbed, too.

Cole came around the car and grabbed her into his arms. Her suitcase tipped over at her feet. "I don't want to stop," Cole said. "Not yet."

"What about Deborah?"

"I know." He got an agonized look on his face.

"We have two weeks, though, don't we? Until she gets here?"

"Almost two weeks."

"Why not enjoy the time that's left?"

He looked into her face, considered the idea, struggled with it, then said, "Let's say ten days."

"Okay. Ten days it is." She threw her arms around him. *Ten more days.* Why not? They'd given themselves a deadline, a time limit. That made sense.

Not exactly, but she didn't want to stop and figure out why. Not while they were kissing like this, arms wrapped tight like long-lost lovers at last reunited. Cars swished by, people called to each other, someone whistled for a cab, carts and people moved past them.

"It's, uh, pick up and drop off, not make out." An airport security woman spoke near their ears and they broke apart, apologizing in a daze. "Take it indoors," she said with a wink.

"We will." They headed to Kylie's house with a plan: make love, work, make love again if time allowed, then send Cole home before Janie arrived to work on her business plan. It was ten-thirty. Plenty of time to do it all. She might even have time to work on the Home Town Suites project. They were being so very sensible, Kylie was proud of them both. And Radar let her scratch his tummy all the way home.

JANIE PULLED into her sister's town house complex two hours early and sans Thai food. She needed distraction from her thoughts about Seth. She couldn't get him out of her mind.

He'd been so *there*. Asking so many questions, studying her so closely. She realized that it hadn't been like that with any of the men she'd dated. They'd enjoyed each other, the sex, various activities, but they'd never really connected.

With Seth, she felt an odd recognition. *Here you are at last.*

Their Mate Check profiles weren't too far off….

Holy Hannah in July, who was she kidding? She'd erased and rewritten the damn charts to give them an above fifty match score. Hadn't she learned anything?

She was definitely not cured.

Someone had parked in Kylie's guest spot—a presumptuous neighbor, no doubt, since Kylie was too busy for guests—so Janie had to park in a distant visitor space.

Soon, Kylie would be gone altogether, Janie realized. Her lungs tightened a little. She'd put off acknowledging this painful reality as long as possible. She would miss her sister terribly. The one good thing about the Personal Touch troubles was that they'd spent more time together.

Her intense focus on Personal Touch over the past year had kept her too busy to insist they get together regularly and she hadn't done her usual bit to keep Kylie from obsessing about work.

Anything too easy made Kylie suspicious. She thought she had to keep managing, planning, organizing, working, or life would fly out of control.

She'd been that way since they were kids. As soon as they moved somewhere, Kylie had to scope out the place. Find the park, the library, the places kids hung. *Let's ride our bikes to the mall and meet people.* It was exhausting, but it helped Kylie, so Janie was game. Her sister's assertiveness was helpful because Janie was a little shy. Still, she couldn't help wanting to ask Kylie why the rush, the constant push, the go-go-go?

She'd sensed the reason as a child, but her psychology training confirmed it: fear of intimacy. Kylie was unnaturally queasy about emotional attachments, and ran from sadness as if it might break her in pieces.

In quiet ways, Janie had tried to get Kylie to slow down, to feel what she felt, but she was only the little sister and Kylie discounted her wisdom, opting instead to overprotect Janie. So Janie let her second-guess her decisions as cheerfully as she could, then did what she knew was best in her life.

Including trying to help Kylie recognize that what mattered most was family, friends and a meaningful life. Rewarding work was part of that, but not the whole story.

In the past couple of weeks Kylie seemed to have lost all focus except on work. She was frazzled and sluggish—not her usual self at all.

Her overwork was partly Janie's fault because of Personal Touch, but she'd bet Kylie was also using work to duck her grief over leaving Phoenix, her business and her sister.

Janie took the sidewalk to Kylie's door. At least the Personal Touch problems were easing up. The business plan was drafted and Kylie had arranged for an attorney to help them. Her sister was a whiz at solving problems. For that, Janie was eternally grateful.

Maybe Janie should get Kylie's opinion about Seth. Her sister was no-nonsense when it came to matters of the heart. She'd tell her to forget it, move on, be strong.

Janie sighed, knowing she'd keep Seth to herself. Which, of course, was a bad sign.

She tapped at Kylie's door.

A dog yipped.

A dog?

There was rustling, whispering, then something—a body?—thumped to the floor.

"Just a minute…hang on," Kylie called breathlessly.

Good grief, what was going on? Kylie had company? She'd only returned this morning from L.A.

Kylie flung open the door, looking messy and sheepish as hell. "You're early!" A fair-haired terrier looked up from the floor beside her, trying to act innocent. "It's only…um…three-thirty."

Inside, the air swirled with energy…. "Are you busy?"

Janie asked. Then she noticed a man sitting on the floor at the cocktail table. Cole Sullivan, of all people, pretending to write on a piece of paper that was upside down. He looked rumpled and chagrined and his face was bright red.

Sex. That's what the air swirled with. Janie's heart filled with dread. At least it wasn't her fault Kylie was in a sluggish daze. It was Cole. And whatever they were doing together.

"We were…strategizing…for the Marlon Brandon meeting," Kylie said brightly.

The dog emitted a cross between a snort and a sneeze—*oh, please.* Janie couldn't agree more.

"Cole offered to help us with the legal issues," Kylie said. "We wanted to surprise you."

"Oh, you surprised me, all right," Janie said drolly.

"I had time," Cole said. "No big deal."

An awkward silence fell. Kylie and Cole jumped on it at once, their voices colliding like butting heads.

"What we were thinking about doing—"

"We can fill you in on the plan—"

They looked at each other, blushed, then smiled.

"I'm early and you two are obviously busy," Janie said, trying not to roll her eyes. "I'll come back with dinner—" Then she noticed that kitchen counter was littered with take-away boxes. The smell reached her nose. "Mexican food?" she asked, amazed. "But you swore off lard."

"It's…a special occasion. You can eat with us. We can discuss our…strategy, right, Cole?" She nodded at him. He'd stood and was approaching, nodding, too. They looked like a pair of blushing bobble dolls. Discombobulated bobble dolls. Kylie's blouse was misbuttoned and Cole's T-shirt was inside out and back to front—the tag a wagging tongue at his throat. So *not* the outfit of the work-aholic attorney who'd done his Close-Up with one eye on his watch.

She noticed the TV was on, too—muted on Comedy Central, Kylie's favorite. "You're watching television?" she asked Kylie. *What does this mean?*

"Just in the background," Kylie said. *I can explain.* "Did you want to borrow that…book?"

"That book?"

"About the…thing." Kylie motioned toward the hall, clearly wanting to duck into her office.

"Yeah, the thing. Sure."

"Do you mind, Cole?" Kylie asked.

"Take your time," he said and gave her a look filled with stars—no, an entire meteor shower. Holy Hannah, Mary Mackerel, Cole was smitten. And it was Janie's own fault. She'd practically begged Kylie to date the man.

Janie's dearest hope was for Kylie to find true love, of course, but this was a life-transition fling. Textbook. Obvious in the desperate looks they shot each other, in their dazed expressions, in the fact that they'd just let themselves get caught in the act.

Janie should have seen it coming, but she'd been too harried with Personal Touch and preoccupied with Seth.

This was trouble. This could jeopardize the Cole and Deborah match. She wanted the best for her sister, but a fling was just a distraction and Cole's future was at stake here.

Janie had to do something to stop it.

11

KYLIE LED Janie into her office, mortified that Janie had caught her and Cole *strategizing*. Her usual vivid sense of every ticking minute had gone wacky. With Cole, she slipped into a freakish time warp.

She shut the door and turned to face her sister's stern expression, her hand up to stop the lecture. "I know what you're going to say, but we have a plan, so you don't have to worry."

"A plan? To ruin Cole's future?"

"We're just blowing off steam until Deborah gets back. We *were* working, too." Except that they kept getting distracted. Her by Cole's lips when he was explaining something, the ripple of his forearm when he held the pen, the gleam in his espresso eyes when he made a point. And Cole by the pulse at Kylie's throat...her laugh...her plump toes, especially the pinky ones, which he'd named *Pinky* and *Plumpy*. Not clever, but who cared?

They'd had enough sex to leave every muscle aching, but they couldn't leave each other alone. They couldn't even watch *Last Comic Standing* very well. It turned out to be impossible to laugh and kiss at the same time. You banged teeth or bit each other's tongue.

"Cole is mad for you, Kylie," Janie said. "He's got the entire Milky Way in his eyes. And your feet don't touch the ground."

She looked down to ensure that her bare soles were indeed planted firmly on gray berber. "We're just in lust. We're both stressed at work and being together is a relief. It's like a vacation. No strings. No worries. Simple sex."

"Sex is never simple, Kylie."

"It has to be. I'm leaving town and Cole's hooking up with Deborah. There's a definite bookend to this thing. It'll be fine." Except for the hitch in her breathing and that empty stomach pain again.

"This is a life-transition fling for you, but it's risky for Cole. If he's still mooning over you, he won't be open to Deborah and she's skittish about men. She needs a guy like Cole, who's emotionally steady. She's exactly what he wants in a wife."

"I know. We both know." She fought the stab of jealousy and loss she felt listening to Janie describe Cole's future with another woman. Of course it was right and good and she wanted him to have the perfect wife. Still. Her stomach was really bothering her. Maybe she should try one of those major antacids….

"You need to end it now, Kylie Rachel Falls. Today."

"Jeez. Do I sound that bossy when I tell you what to do?"

"More."

"Sorry." She was uneasily aware that Janie might be right about ending this sooner rather than later. She was feeling pretty floaty, even with her toes digging into designer wool beneath her. *I don't want to quit, damn it.* She felt like stamping her tootsies hard. Another bad sign.

"Don't apologize for caring." Her sister abruptly sighed

and stopped pushing the issue. "Maybe I need you to tell me what to do sometimes."

Kylie noticed for the first time how odd Janie looked. Her eyes were shiny, her face pink. Was she ill? Did she have a fever? "Are you okay?" she asked, alarmed.

"No, I'm not. I feel terrible." She sank onto the futon-sofa.

Kylie sat beside her and placed the back of her hand against Janie's forehead. "You *are* warm."

Janie pushed her hand away. "Not that kind of terrible. It's a guy."

"Oh." Kylie relaxed a little, though the new worry whirred to life inside her—this one not about her sister's lungs, but about her heart. "Who is he?"

"Promise you won't yell?"

"Of course. I'm your sister. I love and fully support you."

"It's Seth Taylor. The reporter from *Inside Phoenix*."

"Are you nuts?"

"What happened to 'I love and fully support you'?"

"You can't date a reporter writing a story about you. And how did that happen anyway? You tried to get him kicked off the assignment."

"We worked it out. He went to the skating party, returned to ask more questions and take more pictures. He's tuned in to Personal Touch now."

"And to you, you seem to think. Look, reporters have to act tuned in. It's a technique. He needs you to trust him, to relax and confide juicy tidbits. And we've got a few right now."

"Seth's not like that. He's really very tenderhearted. Peanut brittle crust, soft caramel center."

"Uh-oh. When you start with the candy metaphors,

Janie Marie, I know we're in trouble." Janie tended to idealize the men she fell for. "You're too trusting. I don't want you to get hurt."

"I don't intend to get hurt." But she sounded absolutely bereft and looked pale as glue.

"You want me to talk you out of it?"

"When I'm around him, I feel alive and so hopeful."

"That's lust and adrenaline. You've felt this way before."

"Not like this. Liam never really paid that much attention to me. Even before he went to Peru. And I knew Richard wouldn't stay past the gig. Seth is *there*. Present. Focused."

"It's infatuation, it's wishful thinking, it's…"

It was awful to see Janie grow to need these guys, then be crushed when they left. If only she were more self-sufficient, less vulnerable. Janie's misery with men had made Kylie even more committed to not get serious about anyone until she was absolutely ready, careerwise, and then she would go slow, slow, slow.

"Now he seems a bit unsettled, but I think that's his job situation. I've figured out that he's a Scared Single. There was a heartbreak he doesn't want to talk about."

"Sounds like Mountain Climber Derrick. What did you call him? A Wounded Loner? You can't fix these guys. Remember your plan. You're waiting until you're ready and then you'll find an appropriate match. Work up a Mate Check profile and do the math."

"I did a profile," Janie said sheepishly.

"You did?"

"It turned out…decent."

"You cheated, didn't you?"

"A little." She shrugged, looking miserable and hopeful at the same time. "It's not all in a profile, you know. There are other considerations."

"What would you tell a client who said that?" Kylie spoke as gently as she could. She'd never seen Janie quite so overwrought over a guy.

"Know yourself. Know your partner. Dream dreams anchored in reality." She looked down.

"And what counts is compatibility, right? Not the twinkle in his eye or the way he says your name like his life depends on it."

"Yeah…the twinkle and the name thing."

She sounded so sad that Kylie's heart ached. "If I thought it would help, I'd tell you to just sleep with him. After the story is out, of course. But would it help?"

"I'm not sure."

"It's risky to get close to a reporter. They're always on duty. You get cozy, mention the lawsuit or the money troubles, and he'd have to look into it. Then where would we be?"

"You're right, I guess." Janie shook her head, as if coming to her senses. "And for all those reasons. He's a reporter, he could be a Wounded Loner, I cheated on our profiles. I'm probably deluding myself. I'm as smitten as Cole." She gave a watery smile. "I'll let it go." She sounded determined, but she looked as though she'd accepted a life sentence of grief.

Kylie leaned over to hug her. "You'll find the right guy when the time is right, sweetie. I know you will."

"Thanks for being here for me." Janie looked her over with newly sad eyes. "What am I going to do when you move?"

The words hit like a punch in Kylie's already upset stomach.

"I'll miss you, Kylie Rachel. So much."

"I'll miss you, too." Tears burned, but she fought them down. No point in getting hysterical. "I'll just boss you around long-distance. Easy."

Janie barely smiled.

"But that's not happening yet. I'm still here for a while." *Only a couple more weeks.* Kylie forced steadiness in her voice. "We've got a lawsuit to nix. And there are business details to settle. Who knows, I may never be able to leave." The words gave her an odd spurt of hope. *Don't leave. Never leave. Stay right here.* She forced away that thought.

"I know why you're joking, Kylie, but it's okay to feel sad about saying goodbye. You love me and Phoenix and your clients and your life. Leaving is hard."

She felt that desperate long-ago pain again from deep inside—the Patti pain that she'd felt with Cole—and she fought against it like mad. It made her feel exposed against her will, open to any passing hurt.

"It's only for a while, really, so don't get too upset," she said. "I'll start my company again in a few years. Maybe I'll come back to Phoenix."

"I'd like that," Janie said, cheering slightly.

Being practical, though, the business contacts she'd make through S-Mickey-B would make it far more lucrative and challenging to stay in L.A. Coming back to Phoenix would be a step backward. Looking into her sister's sorrowful face, though, she almost didn't care.

"I want what's best for you," Janie said.

"I know you do." Kylie hugged her again, so filled with love she had to blink madly to clear her vision. She wished she could hug away the hurt, the way she used to do when they were kids. How could Janie allow herself to feel so much pain? Kylie was lucky to have more self-control.

She released her sister. "So how about Cole and I fill you in on the Brandon meeting?"

"Not today," Janie sighed, swiping at her eyes and sniffing. "I'm kind of worn-out now. Let's meet on Monday. We can do the business plan then, too. Besides, you need to talk to Cole." Her look was stern, then something she must have seen on Kylie's face made her say, "Unless there's something else going on? Something more I should know about?"

"Of course not." Kylie gave a dismissive snort and her heart stalled on a beat, but she rose and went to the door so her intuitive sister wouldn't pin her down and make her confess the feelings roiling inside her, cruelly refusing to behave.

They walked into the living room, where Janie said goodbye, and left.

Then Kylie turned to Cole, going to him, his features otherworldly in the blue glow of the TV. He was so dear to her. He looked so right there on her sofa with his temporary dog at his side.

She curled up beside him, loving how perfectly she fit the hollow of his body, and how warm he was and how good he smelled. Radar jumped over Cole's lap to snuggle into hers, completing the picture of domestic bliss.

Why couldn't they stick with the till-Deborah-returns plan? What difference would a few more days make?

Cole kissed her hair and shifted to look into her eyes. "Janie forgot her book."

"What book?"

"The one she went into your office with you to get."

"Oh, that. We were just talking."

"About what? She looked pretty deflated when she left."

"She's sad about me leaving." She didn't want to tell him that Janie had demanded Kylie stop seeing him.

"Oh. Yeah. Me, too."

Her heart swelled and ached with agony. Cole would miss her. That was a good thing and a bad thing at the same time. How did Janie stand all this pain? "Cole, I…" Kylie didn't know what to say to him.

He seemed uncomfortable that he'd revealed that reaction. "At least L.A.'s not far away. You'll visit each other."

"Of course. The fact is we weren't seeing as much of each other as we should, considering how close we live. We go for Christmas with our parents in Chicago, so we'll still have that."

Though it sounded far from enough right now, as she rested against Cole's warm chest, a dog curled cozily in her lap, her sister's hug still on her skin. In fact, Janie was the one who hounded Kylie for dinners and lunches and movies together. Janie bore the burden of their relationship. And that was wrong. "I'll just have to come home a lot," Kylie said, promising herself she would. "Gotta look out for my little sister, right?"

"Of course."

"Especially now. She's hot for the wrong guy."

"Janie's very wise about relationships." He kissed the top of her head. "She's an expert, remember?"

"Not for herself, I'm afraid." She sighed, feeling as though her brain was about to explode. "I wish she could do what we're doing," she said, not sure she even meant that.

"And what are we doing?" he asked, something flaring

in his eyes. She couldn't tell if he wanted her to minimize this or make it bigger than it was.

"Having sex and letting it be enough." She held her breath, waiting for him to respond, her heart pounding some crazy Morse code of helpless hope.

He hesitated, but finally said, "Yeah."

"We're lucky, aren't we, Cole?"

He ducked her gaze. "Yeah, lucky." But there was sadness in his voice. He wanted more. It wasn't so simple for him, either. Were she to ask him if he wanted to stop now, he'd say no. It was as plain as the way she'd tightened her arms around his ribs.

"Kinda cutting off my breathing there." He patted her hand.

"Sorry." She loosened her grip on him.

"Nah, I liked it. Just didn't want to lose consciousness."

"Sure. I can understand that."

They knew what they were doing, right? They could quit anytime. Just not in the middle of *Last Comic Standing*.

JANIE FINISHED the client's Close-Up, then led him out so Gail could do the last of the paperwork. Janie then returned to the video room and Seth, who'd observed the entire process from the love seat, making her jumpy as hell. The client hadn't seemed to notice the peculiar energy in the room, what with his tension over his dating video, but she'd been twitchy as hell.

Now she sat beside Seth on the upholstered bench. There was just room enough for two.

He looked up from his notebook and smiled his cocky grin, stretched a little wider just for her. The stinging blue of his eyes took her breath away and his scent made her dizzy. She wanted to lean close, tuck against his body. She wanted his arm around her, his kiss on her lips, his voice in her ear.

He'd come for more atmosphere, he'd said, but his gaze clung to her like polyester socks in a dryer and every word he said to her was soft with longing. The heat between them made the air thicken and time slow.

He's at least a Wounded Loner, possibly a Stubborn Single, she reminded herself sternly. He was a reporter. He had to make her think he was tuned in. Their profiles were impossible.

But he was looking at her as though she was his sun, his religion, something he had to commit to memory from top to bottom and inside out. This had to mean something, didn't it?

She struggled to focus on helping him with the story. "So, you can see how the Close-Up gives character insights, right?"

"I'd say it was utterly mortifying. That poor guy had sweat rings on his sweat rings."

"Everyone shows tension, but the videos give Potentials a better sense of the person."

"At least talk them out of clichés. 'I enjoy quiet evenings with a good book and the woman I love'? Sounds like a bad personal ad."

"That's what Gail says. When she does the videos, she tells the client to 'be fresh' and 'go deep.' Except those come out kind of…raw."

"Better raw than canned."

"I suppose you could do better," she teased, then realized what a good idea that was. "Why don't you show me? Just as a for instance?"

"You mean…sit *there*…and do *that?*" He pointed at the set.

"Sure. Show me how it should be done."

He wanted to decline, she could see, but he shot her a piece-of-cake grin and headed to the stool.

He leaned on it, half-sitting, legs crossed at the ankle, arms folded, but she could tell he was uneasy. He glanced at the camera, then away, and a muscle ticked in his cheek.

She loaded a tape, then peered through the viewfinder at him. "Okay. You look good."

He looked straight at her then, warming her from all those feet away.

"Ready…? You're…on."

"I should say up front that I'm not the easiest guy to be with." He flashed his teeth in a wicked grin. Essential bad boy. "I'm a journalist, which makes me curious…and… skeptical. No bullshit, I guess. I can be…opinionated." Then he paused and she felt his eyes bore through the lens straight to her soul. "But spend time with me and I promise I'll make it interesting."

"How will you do that?"

"By keeping my eyes open—yours, too, if you'll let me. Even a stint at the DMV can be fun. Say you conduct a poll of what people would be doing if they weren't standing in line. Or take bets on which line will move faster. The losers pay the winners' fees."

"So, you'd take a date to get license plates?"

"We'd work up to that. Maybe we'd start at the airport—baggage claim…make up stories about the arriving passengers. Who's in love? Who's leaving home for good? What's in the pink flowered bag? The long skinny case? If that's too dull, we'd wander over to the shoe-shine guy and let him tell us stories he's heard polishing wingtips over the years."

She found herself smiling. "Not bad."

Now his words seemed aimed straight at her. "This is the deal…I'm not much for roses and sunsets and cognac by the fire, but I promise my favorite view will be your face."

She took a shaky breath that made the camera jiggle.

"You interested, Janie?" he asked softly.

Her ears burned at the way he'd said her name…as if his life depended on it. *What matters is compatibility,* Kylie had correctly reminded her. But look at his eyes… only for Janie…as if his mission were to learn how she ticked…his expression so steady, so there.

She straightened to face him. "Very," she said and found herself moving toward him. Slowly, not entirely sure of what she was doing, but making a beeline all the same.

And he was coming at her dead-on, too.

They met halfway and wrapped their arms around each other so hard they swayed. His lips took hers and she opened to him, tasting coffee and mint and man and so much heat. They held each other as if for dear life.

This kiss was so much better than the first two. It was deliberate and solid and real and all of him was in it. Along with all of her.

Janie's heart flip-flopped in her chest like a frog escaping a child's grasping fingers. Her blood rushed downward, making her heavy and achy below the waist. She was desperately aroused, but at the same time, she wanted to release a big belly laugh. Lust and laughter at the same time? This was new. It scared her and she liked it.

They kissed for long, lovely minutes. The room slipped

away, her doubts faded, until all she was aware of was this man who wanted her so much he was shaking with it.

Then Seth stilled. She felt him pull back a barely detectable bit. A warning trickle of ice water eased down Janie's neck and she knew the truth. Seth would leave. This hello kiss held the seeds of farewell. There would be a goodbye as painful as this embrace was glorious. And she was too strong and too smart to go through that again.

What the hell was he doing? Seth asked himself. He wanted this woman as much as he'd ever wanted anyone. Which was insane. Even if he'd finished the story, Jane Falls would want the whole megillah—a relationship, a future, something concrete with a mortgage. He couldn't commit to anything now. Not with so much of his life up in the air.

He forced himself to break it off. Janie jerked away at the same time, so that they both rocked into thin air and back, nearly banging their heads together.

"Whoa," he said. He tried for a grin, but ended up with something as foolishly lopsided as he felt.

"This could be trouble," she said. She was trying to joke, but her eyes burned with desire. At the same time panic flickered like a TV about to turn off.

He cupped her cheek with one hand and wanted to kiss her mouth, bruised-looking from the kiss they'd just shared. "I'd better write the damn story."

"Sure," she said, kissing his palm, fighting sadness. "Make me look good?" There was a whisper of worry in her voice.

He stopped himself before he promised exactly that. "I'll write the best story I can."

"But it will be positive, right?"

He wanted to reassure her, but he couldn't and be the kind of reporter he prided himself on being. The kind who swore impartiality, accuracy, fairness. Period.

Even a puff piece demanded integrity.

"I'll write the best story I can," he repeated flatly. He wanted to make her happy, though, wanted to promise her whatever she wanted or needed. What was going on? He felt soft and confused and not himself. He had to get out and clear his head.

Except his thoughts grew muddier than the Blue Mountain Jamaican he was soon sucking down in the nearby coffee shop. He wanted her in his life. Jane was a butterfly with a steel spine and he just felt better around her. The bitter thoughts about Ana blew away like smoke and he felt different. Hopeful.

Maybe it was her faith in love. Or that bite to her eyes that said she had fire and dreams. She was different from Ana, who was as cynical as he was, truth be told. Janie was easier on the world. And he found that relaxing—life-affirming, which sounded hokey as hell.

Hokey wasn't all bad, was it?

Could he be what Jane needed? He wasn't so sure. He had to talk to her. And grab that video, now that he thought about it. Talk about feeling naked. He wasn't even sure she'd shut it off before the kiss. That was a perfect example of how he lost his sense of himself around her. That made him uneasy.

He headed back for the video. And to talk to Janie. He'd write his story, file it and they'd take it from there. By the time he pushed through the Personal Touch door, he was shaking like a leaf. Too much caffeine, no doubt.

No receptionist again. Gail was a ghost who made her

presence known only by the occasional clank of a brace-
let. Janie's office was open, but empty, so he headed down
the hall to the video room. He could hear voices as he approached, including Janie's distinctive laugh. The video
room was empty—Janie was in the room just beyond talking to at least two people. He paused between the doors,
just to get a sense of whether the meeting was ending. He
burned to talk to Janie.

"I have to say your client agreement invites legal action," a man said. "Frankly, I'm surprised you haven't been
sued before now."

Sued? Janie was being sued? Seth's neck hairs stood up
like a short forest. He backed silently away from the door,
unseen by the group, and into the video room, moving
close to the thin wall to listen in.

"Not to mention using me—your own sister—as a dating shill," a woman said, sounding amused. "The worst
were the married ones."

The man laughed. His voice was familiar to Seth.

"It's not funny, Cole. It was a Web site glitch," Janie said.

Cole? Had to be Cole Sullivan. That was why he
sounded familiar. Seth kept listening, his attention sharp
as razor wire, dread a stone in his chest.

"And you didn't have to *sleep* with them, Kylie," Janie
said in a serious tone. The other two stopped laughing abruptly. Sullivan cleared his throat.

Good God. Janie had her sister sleeping with clients?
Was this an escort service after all?

"The point is, we should be grateful for this lawsuit,"
Janie's sister said. "Now Cole's helping us cover your ass.
Thank you, Marlon Brandon." No wonder Sullivan had
been so cagey on the phone. He was their *attorney*.

"How could his parents do that to him? Name him Marlon? I bet he gets called Brando all the time," Janie's sister said.

"He's a little sensitive about it. He goes by Brandon as a first name sometimes. Though that might be because his business is Brandon Remodeling." Janie sounded pretty calm for someone in big legal trouble. Had she been coolly lying to him? Blinking those big eyes and feeding him a fat line of bull? Seth felt chilled to the bone.

"He doesn't sound like the sensitive type," her sister said.

"Trust me. He is. So I kept that in mind when I chose his matches. I try to keep client sensitivities in mind. Like I know you and Deborah Ramsdale both have time-management issues when it comes to relationships."

"That's true," the guy mumbled.

"And you're ready for her return, Cole? You two have this *thing* under control."

"Of course," Janie's sister jumped in. "Just like you have your *thing* under control with the reporter. You do, don't you?"

"Oh. Yes. I…" Her words trailed off and he could practically hear Janie breathe.

"Uh-oh," her sister said. "What?"

"Nothing. He was here this morning, that's all."

"Again? Why?"

"He watched me make a Close-Up."

"The man could have written that story six times over, Janie. What's going on?"

"Nothing. He's writing it now. Don't worry. He's done."

He was back, though. To tell her he cared about her. And find out she *was* too good to be true.

"At least *you* worked *him* instead of the other way

around," the sister said. "And the story will be positive, right?"

"I did my best," she said. The words hit him like a bat across the back. She'd worked him? He couldn't have been that blind or dimwitted. There had been real emotion in her eyes, real heat in her kiss, real longing in the arms she'd wrapped around him.

Meanwhile, she was being sued and her sister was sleeping with clients. Married ones even? His neck prickle intensified and his reporter brain went into crystal focus. Here was the angle. And he'd sensed it all along. She'd been nervous when he'd asked about finances, now that he thought about it, and practically begged him for a good story—even joked about a bribe. He'd yet to check out the sex calls. Phone sex would be fast cash for a strapped business. And an escort service was big money. He'd been an idiot.

He'd been so taken in he'd ignored his instincts. He knew about sociopaths. He'd just never fallen in love with one before.

He listened long enough to learn about a meeting the next day with the remodeler. He would check out the lawsuit with the guy. Track down Deborah Ramsdale, too, through her firm, which the receptionist had mentioned the other day. What would Ms. Ramsdale think about Sullivan sleeping with Janie's sister? His reporter side thrilled with the rush of the hunt. The rest of him was pissed. At Janie for tricking him. And himself for falling for it.

But he wouldn't be sidetracked now. If his guesses proved true, he'd forget the *Inside Phoenix* piece and take the exposé to Eye Out For You. In fact, he'd pitch the idea to the producer right away, just to test the waters. This could be his ticket to local investigative work. This fluff crap had made him soft.

Through the wall, he heard Janie laugh and his heart cramped tight. *She would be so hurt.* He didn't want to get ahead that way. He pictured her face when she talked about her mission. She'd actually had tears in her eyes telling him about the couple naming their kid after her.

She's a sociopath. It's a disorder. But he ached all over at the thought. Maybe he would confront her with his suspicions and let her explain them away.

I did my best. That's what she'd told her sister about working him for a good story. If she was a crook, she'd cover her tracks if she knew he was on to her, and he owed the truth to the lonely slobs who gave her their hard-earned cash to find them mates.

He wanted to be wrong. So much he could taste it. Somehow, Janie had changed him, dulled his reporter instincts, weakened the healthy skepticism that ruled his life. If he wasn't who he thought he was, then he was completely lost.

12

"I'M EARLY," Kylie said to Cole, when he opened his office door. Cole was driving them to Personal Touch for the Marlon Brandon meeting, after which she'd catch the SuperShuttle to the airport, bound for L.A. She was way early. And not by accident.

She wanted to maximize every bit of alone time they had. She'd actually done the math on their possible hours together, factoring in work and her travel time—she'd be back tomorrow, late afternoon. Silly, but here she was, squeezing out every drop of face time. Body time, too, she hoped.

"Good idea." Cole shut the door behind her and trapped her in the corner with his hips. "I won't see you until late tomorrow." He'd done the math, too! Thank God she wasn't being silly all alone. "If we don't go sit, the secretary will wonder what we're doing," he murmured, lazily examining her mouth. "She can't see us in the corner here." There was a glass panel beside his door.

"Should we go sit and talk?" she asked, her heart tripping into high gear with excitement.

"How about we do it right here?" And he didn't mean *talk*.

She dropped her briefcase to the floor and put her arms around him. "When you review my strategy, I'll try not to scream."

He kissed her and his fingers found her under her skirt. "You're wet."

"Just knocking on your door turns me liquid."

"I want you right now," he said roughly.

"Right here? On your big lawyer desk? In front of everyone?"

"Everyone. Secretaries, associates, even the partners. Yeah." Was he just fantasizing? She decided to test him.

"Well…how about…?" Holding his gaze, Kylie deliberately unlatched his belt and slowly lowered his zipper, waiting for his reaction. *Yes or no. Do you dare?*

Cole's dark eyes swirled with emotion. Desire, obviously, but also tension. He glanced toward the glass panel, considering the risk of being seen, no doubt. But then he focused his gaze on her face and determination and desire burned out at her. *Nothing can stop me from having you.*

She loved him for that. For being willing to do the wild thing just a few mahogany inches from all the people he had to impress as sober and steady and about to settle down with a wife.

In that flicker of a second, she realized the truth: *Cole would never bore her.* She'd told herself she'd tire of peanut butter brickle, but a man who would risk this just to be inside her, could never be dull. What was she going to do about that? She had no time to decide because Cole shoved his pants to the floor and hiked up her skirt, slid her panties out of the way and pushed into her, easy and deep and hard.

A gasp tore through her.

He responded with a groan of pleasure that matched her own. "I can't believe we're doing this," he rasped, thrusting in and pulling out again.

"I can't, either." Beyond Cole's shoulder, was a wall of

sober-looking law books and diplomas, reminding her of all he wanted, all he was putting on hold to be with her now. For as long as they could manage it.

"You make me surprise myself." He kissed her neck.

"You, too…surprise me…and I…" She couldn't think, could hardly see, didn't know what she was saying or where she ended and he began. She couldn't even feel her feet and feared she'd faint from sheer ecstasy.

He stroked in, out, then in and in and in. Their arousals rose in the natural wave of two lovers who knew all each other's spots and surges and quaking needs. In seconds they took off together, launched into space, holding each other tight, struggling to breathe the thin air.

Finally, their spasms faded, their movements slowed and Kylie buried her face in Cole's neck. His pulse throbbed against her lips, his chest heaved with fast breaths.

They clung to each other for a few moments, there behind the door, breathing hard, hanging on, eyes closed, sensation returning to her feet in her sensible heels resting firmly on the carpet.

Then someone knocked on the door, the tap vibrating against Kylie's back like a guilty conscience.

Panic flickered in Cole's eyes. He nodded at his guest chair—*go sit*—then quickly yanked up his pants.

She straightened her skirt—as best she could with her underwear still around her knees—grabbed her briefcase and rushed to the chair. She opened the case and pretended to read something inside, her whole body vibrating from the physical strain of the last few minutes.

Cole faced the door, put himself together, then opened it. "Trevor," he said, sounding like he'd run a mile.

Kylie turned her body to greet the newcomer, fighting for calm. Had the door rubbed her hair weird in back?

"I wanted to go over the due-diligence stuff," Trevor said, then he saw her and stopped. "Ah. Looks like you're busy."

"We were going over strategy for a meeting."

"Strategy…sure. You bet. Buzz me when you're… done."

"No problem," he said, holding the door for him.

"You might want to…." The guy glanced at Cole's crotch.

Cole looked down. From her angle, she saw he'd zipped his shirttail into his zipper. He fixed it fast.

She felt on fire with blush for them both.

"Good luck with your *strategy.*" Trevor nudged Cole in the ribs, saluted her and left.

Cole looked completely bereft. "Now he's got something on me. I'm not usually like this." He ran his fingers through his hair, one hand at his waist, elbow bent, head ducked, looking sheepish and confused.

"I know." For her part, she sat with her panties trapped somewhere around her thighs just minutes away from a crucial meeting. She wasn't herself at all. And neither was Cole.

This had gotten out of hand. They were jeopardizing Cole's future—love life and career. Janie had said he was smitten and warned her that might interfere with his connection with Deborah—a woman primed to be the corporate wife Cole needed. Something Kylie could never be, even if she were staying, which she wasn't. Even if she were smitten, too.

Janie was right. They should stop.

Cole went to sit behind his desk and they managed a queasy laugh at what had happened, then walked through the plan for the upcoming meeting. All the while, she felt Cole's uneasiness, his worry. He would probably be relieved when she suggested calling it quits, which she would do when she got back from L.A. Give him a chance to clear his palate before Deborah returned. And she would focus on her future.

On the way to Personal Touch, Kylie studied Cole's profile. She knew every line and bone in his face. Just a glimpse of his face made her heart lift until she wanted to sing.

She would miss him so much.

Was she falling in love?

A life-transition fling. That's what Janie had called it. For Kylie, Cole was a safe raft in an uncertain sea and she was hanging on tight. She hadn't moved in a long time, so her adventure muscles were atrophied. She was clinging to Janie, too, miserable about saying goodbye. Just transition stuff, like Janie had said.

Cole pulled into a parking spot at Personal Touch and turned to Kylie with a reassuring smile, squeezing her knee with a blend of tenderness, ownership and lust that just made her melt. She didn't want to say goodbye. Ever.

"What?" Her expression seemed to worry him.

Sex is never simple. But she couldn't say that. "I guess I just realized that my little sister is a lot wiser than I gave her credit for."

"Better tell her that," Cole said.

Yeah. Janie owed her a big fat, painful *I told you so.*

LORENZO INOCENTE, Brandon's attorney, gave Cole the asshole eye. "I'm flat opposed to this meeting." The guy was pug-jawed, balding and portly and looked exactly like his client. They were twin Danny DeVitos, only taller.

The meeting had started off badly. First thing, Jane had asked the pair to extinguish their cigars and the air was still thick with cheap cigar smoke and tension.

"You two must be related," Kylie said, trying to smooth the moment. She was in charge of the meeting.

Cole fought the urge to stare at her like a moonstruck teen. He had it bad. That had been clear in his office. He'd dropped his guard at work just to get inside her. And that meant something. Something he had to figure out before he shared it with her.

"Cousins," Brandon shot out. "He's my father's baby sister's kid."

"Could we move on?" Inocente said, evidently not liking being called a kid. He flashed a watch that must have made one arm drag when he walked.

"We all want a solution that benefits your client," Cole said. His role was mediator.

"Yeah?" Inocente lowered a brow and locked his underbite. If Kylie could make headway with this guy, she was even better than Cole thought. And Cole thought she walked on water.

Kylie tilted her head at a warm angle, attempting to hold Brandon's beetle-browed gaze. "Why don't you tell us what your expectations were when you signed with us?"

"Like the brochure said, a customized relationship search. Customized to what *I* wanted." He glared at Janie.

"I selected wonderful Potentials for you," Janie said, waving the *Book of the Possibles* under his nose. Yellow stickies flagged key pages. Janie's job was to sound wounded about the failure and to help Marlon see what he'd missed. This was no stretch, since that was how Janie felt and what she wanted.

"Janie." Kylie patted her hand as if to correct her. "We're talking about Mr. Brandon's expectations."

Brandon gave a snort of approval, then chewed on his cigar. He took it out of his mouth to study it, as if annoyed that he wasn't getting any smoke.

"Why don't you go ahead and light up? We can make an exception this once, right, Janie?" The brilliant move launched the good-cop, bad-cop strategy by criticizing Janie, while obtaining a concession for Brandon. At the same time Kylie had soothed Brandon's ego, she'd offered him a needed pacifier.

Inocente watched longingly while Brandon stoked his cigar. When the lighter hit the table, Kylie lifted it, offering to light Inocente's stogie. She made him lean forward, though—the first compromise—and lit it. Subtle and smart.

Once both men were happily sucking nicotine into their lungs, Kylie continued. "How would you describe your perfect match, Marlon?"

"That's easy—a woman with some life to her. Someone who can handle herself on a ski slope and the dance floor. Someone perky. Not a gray-haired, saggy, old…"

"Please!" Janie said sharply. "I won't allow you to insult my clients."

"Sorry." He sounded like a kid whose knuckles had been rapped.

"The women you asked for—the ones willing to date someone of your *stature* were, to put it kindly, looking for a financial resource or a father figure. That's no basis for a relationship."

"Marlon wants what he wants, Janie," Kylie said. "How did you come to choose Personal Touch, if I may ask?"

"I read the ad. I had a friend." He shrugged.

"Many clients come to Janie because of the way she evaluates credit and criminal reports and employment history, as well as compatibility. Was that something you valued?"

Brandon looked to Inocente, who snapped, "My client has explained the services he expected. Move on."

"Had you tried other dating services?"

"Do I have to answer that?" he asked his attorney.

"This is not a deposition," Cole inserted. "We need to understand the whole story if we're to resolve this to everyone's satisfaction."

"Then, yeah, I tried a couple services. So what?"

"And how has that worked out for you?" Kylie pressed. "Have you been able to date the younger women you seek?"

"Yeah, but…" He shrugged.

"But they got bored?" Janie asked. "Or they wanted you to spend, spend, spend?"

"They had other interests, okay?" He glared at her. "You promised me women *I* wanted."

"And that's what I offered you. You wouldn't even try." Janie opened the magazine and tapped at a photo of an attractive woman, early fifties, dressed stylishly. "This woman owns three hair salons and loves to travel. Talk about perky. She rock climbs, for heaven's sake."

"You never showed me her," Brandon said.

"I told you about her, but when you heard her age, you refused to even meet her."

"You should have showed me the picture."

Janie gave a long-suffering sigh. "It doesn't matter now. Another client of mine was thrilled to meet her. And now they're getting serious."

"This woman, as accomplished and attractive as she may be, is not what Marlon had in mind," Kylie chided.

Though Brandon was clearly interested now, Cole saw, watching him push his cigar to the other side of his mouth and shift his bulk in the chair.

Now it was Cole's turn to speak. "So what can we do to make up for our error, Mr. Brandon?"

"Our error?" Janie yelped. "What are you saying? We should be suing him for wasting these wonderful women." She flipped open the book to a few marked pages, tapping each photo, then she slapped the magazine closed. "I can't take any more of this. You'll have to excuse me." She pushed to her feet and dashed out of the room.

"Jeez. So sensitive," Brandon said. He seemed to have bought Janie's act, though Cole thought she'd overdone it a tad.

"She hates when she can't help a client," Kylie sighed, slowly tugging the magazine toward her. Brandon's eyes darted there.

"We're prepared to offer one free year of Personal Touch services," Cole said, swinging into his prepared remarks. "With the proviso that at least two of the first five dates be with women *you* select, whether or not Ms. Falls believes your profiles match. Of course, Personal Touch has no control over the willingness of these women to date you."

"Only two that I choose?"

"You've been damaged, Marlon," Inocente said through gritted teeth. "You deserve compensation."

"But a free year…" He muttered to his cousin.

"It's probably moot," Kylie said. "Janie wants your perfect match. She won't risk someone tempted by your money alone."

"Okay, I'll take it, but five choices, not two." Brandon jutted his jaw.

"Janie will never accept that," Kylie said. "Even two is iffy, but I can at least ask her. Would you excuse us?" As she pushed up from the table, she just happened to shove the magazine closer to Brandon.

Cole accompanied her and they joined Janie outside the door, giving Brandon a few minutes to drool over the flagged clients. Finally, Kylie nodded at him and the two of them returned to the room, leaving Janie outside.

Brandon flapped the magazine shut like he'd been caught with pornography. "Is she all right?"

"She's hurt, but coping," Kylie said as she and Cole sat.

"And the offer?" Inocente asked wearily.

"She'll give you eighteen months, providing she makes all matches," Cole said briskly. "Though she will skew the age range slightly younger."

"*All* the matches?" Brandon frowned.

"We're out of here," Inocente said, starting to rise.

"I'm sorry it didn't work out." Kylie took the magazine and began to remove the yellow stickies, slowly, one by one.

Brandon's eyes were glued to each photo in turn. "Eighteen months you say?"

"Insanely generous," Cole said.

"Good Lord." Inocente plopped heavily back in his chair.

Before long, they were putting it in writing. As they exchanged signatures and went over the details, Cole found himself watching Kylie.

He realized he couldn't take his eyes off her. Deborah was headed home to him in no time, but he wanted Kylie.

He'd talked with Deborah several times and gotten numerous messages from her over the past week. She was bright and ambitious and she'd support him in his career. In fact, she'd already hooked up a client of her firm with BL&T, which made Cole look even more like partner material. Sure she was a little neurotic and kind of bossy, and, God, she called him twice a day, but no one was perfect. He should give her a chance. Meet her in person, at least.

But he was in love with Kylie. He loved everything about her. The way she hurried and pushed and worked too hard and did too much. He loved the quick tilt of her head when she was really listening to him. He loved the impatient tap of her fingers on the table, the cute way she pursed her lips. Every little gesture shot yearning through him.

He never stopped thinking about her. The instant they parted, he started planning their next moment together. Every store held something he wanted to buy for her. Love songs played in his head constantly. This morning he'd been so caught up listening to the Muzak version of "You Are So Beautiful," he'd taken the elevator to the top of his building and down again just to hear it all the way through.

Because of Kylie he was completely at sea at work. McKay had handled far more of the Littlefield case than he should have and the secretaries had smirked at him when they left for this meeting. But he didn't care.

Kylie made him want more than work. He wanted her and plenty of time to spend with her. Not squeezed-in Sunday morning newspaper readings before work, but long, luxurious weekends in bed, feeding each other homemade strawberry waffles stark naked. With whipped cream.

He was in love with Kylie.

Was she in love with him? Possibly. But she was leaving for L.A. Could hardly wait, as a matter of fact. She considered them *lucky* to be able to have just sex. Now what?

He didn't want Deborah, but he couldn't have Kylie.

The meeting over, Janie walked the DeVito twins out, leaving him and Kylie alone in the video room. He didn't know what to say or how to start.

"I can't believe that worked," Kylie said, her cheeks pink with triumph, her eyes gleaming with pride. Definitely the shiniest eyes he'd ever seen.

"You were brilliant, Kylie."

"It was both of us."

"I was a mere supporting player. You should teach this stuff to lawyers. We tend to be an uncreative lot."

"That was an obvious strategy." She seemed startled by his compliment. "Believe me, I'm not that creative."

"I hope you're just being modest."

"Not really. Creativity's my weakness," she said, flushing with color.

"How can you say that? I've seen your projects. That gun-guard, that shoe store ad series and all that stuff for the hotels. Just inspired."

"Come on. It's good, not brilliant. I'm organized and dogged and thorough and I know my craft, but I'm not innovative or fresh. S-Mickey-B will be good for me that way—build my skills."

For all he thought he knew her, he realized for the first time that Kylie was insecure about her abilities. "I'm no marketing whiz, but I'm not blind. You have a definite flair."

"You think so? Really?"

She seemed so touched by his praise he wanted to blurt out more, babble all he felt about her talent. But he held back and stayed professional. "Let me put it this way. If you're going to L.A. to confirm your brilliance, Kylie, you're wasting your time."

He watched his words hit home. She blinked, tried to smile, but it faded into a grave expression.

"Is that the reason you're going?"

"For the challenge, of course. And the prestige. It's an honor to be asked…." Her words faded and he could feel that he'd hit on it. She didn't think she was good enough.

Don't go. You're great. We're great together.

That was selfish of him. Even if she loved him, she had an amazing opportunity before her. How could he ask her to give it up? He sure wouldn't leave BL&T to chase her to L.A., would he?

How could he? He'd put everything he had into making partner here. He didn't want to lose that. And she'd expressed nothing but passion for her work. She considered settling down an *if*, not a *when*. They were in different places entirely. Unless she'd changed?

He opened his mouth to say something, he wasn't sure what, when his PDA chimed, reminding him of a meeting in twenty minutes. "Kylie, listen…"

"I know. You have to go and I have a shuttle to catch," she said, her eyes jumpy, as if she feared his next words. Or her own. "We'll talk when I get back."

"Sure," he said, and left.

What exactly would they say?

He had no right to ask her to stay. He didn't want to be the cause of her passing up the career chance of a lifetime.

And he wasn't exactly himself lately. Entertaining the thought of leaving BL&T for a woman—even one as remarkable as Kylie—was pretty bizarre. So, what did he want to tell her?

He had thirty-some hours to figure it out before she returned. Maybe while she was gone, his feelings would fade.

Or grow. Then what.

KYLIE WAS SO GLAD Cole had to take off. Her mind was exploding with ideas to ponder. *If you're going to L.A. to confirm your brilliance, Kylie, you're wasting your time.*

He'd nailed it, just like that. As usual, she realized. And told her at the same time he didn't want her to go. They spoke to each other in longtime lovers' shorthand—telegraphing secret messages with gestures and looks and tone, as if they had years of shared experiences and mutual understanding.

She *was* heading to L.A. to confirm her abilities—to wipe out that gut-level fear that she was a hack about to be found out.

What if Cole was right? What if she was creative, after all? Maybe she could grow K. Falls PR right now, without a boost from S-Mickey-B. Stay right here and keep doing what she was doing. She'd had to turn down several new projects already. What if she stayed?

Her heart raced. She'd be letting down Garrett and that could hurt her reputation. But she could work out a short-term contract with them. But would she be staying for K. Falls PR or for Cole? Was she looking for any excuse to stay?

And what was that about? Even if she wanted to settle down, she'd never be the corporate wife Cole wanted. She didn't have time to make a garden, let alone a marriage. Later—much later—after she left S-Mickey-B, started her own firm at a higher level, got settled at a comfortable plateau, then she'd get married, have a child, maybe two. Family was important.

Though, the truth was, for someone who lived to make plans and set goals, this home and hearth stuff was a nebulous swirl of maybes and kinda-sortas and one-day-sures. Maybe she didn't want that at all.

But Cole did. And right now. Maybe with her?

But what kind of marriage could they have? They'd be high-powered roommates, leaving notes for each other about who needed to buy milk and who should pick up the dry cleaning. That was not the way to blend your lives. Besides, Deborah was waiting for him. His perfect match.

But was Deborah really perfect? Kylie looked at the wall of Personal Touch videos. Deborah had one here, somewhere. Cole, too. Maybe she'd just take a peek. Just to be sure she was leaving Cole in good hands. She grabbed the binder directory and in a few seconds she had both Close-Ups in her grip.

First Cole's. It flickered black, then there he was on the stool, in front of that goofy forest scenery, his white shirt open at the collar, his hair adorably mussed, sleeves rolled unevenly.

"Cole Sullivan here," he said, beginning with a darling Hugh Grant hesitancy. "I'm a lawyer and I love my work. I'd better, since I spend so much time at it, right? Heh, heh."

There was a pause, while he listened to something Janie said. Then he forced a smile and continued about his readiness to get serious, wanting a woman as a partner.

Then the video crackled and she heard a muffled voice—Gail's?—before Cole started talking again, saying he wanted a woman who was "self-sufficient, a self-starter and a team player." So cute. As though he were rattling off a job ad. Her throat squeezed tight. She couldn't listen to one more lovable word.

She clicked Cole off and clicked Deborah on. She was

decent-looking and smart. Too nervous, though, like some twitchy bird. That wasn't fair. Videos made people tense, she knew, and maybe it was the fact that her eyebrows were plucked too thin and high.

The truth, she saw as the woman spoke, was that Deborah couldn't have been more perfect for Cole if he'd written her script. "I'm ready to reduce my travel and settle into a life with someone special." They would fit like a key in lock, a hand in glove, tab A into slot—never mind.

Kylie turned off the video, aching with jealousy. So stupid. She didn't want what Cole wanted. Not now. She didn't want to give up her ambition. She didn't want to disappoint him either working so many hours.

There was another problem, another fear, she couldn't quite put her finger on, but she didn't have to because Janie bounded through the door. She hit rewind on Deborah's tape.

"I can't believe that's over," Janie said, rushing to give her a hug, then plop into the chair beside her. "What a relief."

Kylie was grateful for the distraction and held on a little longer than normal to her sister, squeezing her eyes tight, taking in the powder-sweet smell and all that warm love.

"I can't thank you enough, Kylie," Janie said. "You and Cole were incredible."

"We were glad to help."

"With this handled, it's all coming together. The new ads are working, the Web site's bringing in more calls, and I think the business plan will help me prioritize." Janie's color was a happy pink and her inhalations were full and deep.

"That was the idea. After the *Inside Phoenix* story shows, you should get another surge in membership."

"Which should get me over the hump…and, minimum,

keep me out of bankruptcy court. All thanks to you." Her eyes glowed with gratitude and relief.

"I'm your sister and I love and fully support you," she said, mocking herself. "Even when I'm too bossy."

"Even then." Janie laughed. "I know how to breathe, Kylie. And don't forget I have an inhaler for emergencies."

"I just worry about you. It's an old habit."

"I know. That's not all bad. In fact, if I thought it would make you stay, I'd stage a case of pneumonia."

Her heart pinched with pain. "Janie."

"I'll miss you."

"I'll miss you, too."

Janie grabbed her into another hug, this one so tight her own lungs seemed to collapse. What if she stayed?

Janie leaned back, brushing tears from her cheeks. "Look, I'll come visit every three months, how's that? I've got that airline credit card for business now—great idea, by the way—so I'll have frequent-flyer tickets up the ying-yang."

"I'll come to see you, too, as soon as it's feasible." What if she never left?

"You can be obsessive about your work. I'll be getting on your case, you know."

"Sounds good," she said. Very good.

The VCR clicked, signaling it had reached the beginning of Deborah's tape.

Janie's brows lifted. "You were watching a tape?"

"Just checking out Cole's and Deborah's Close-Ups." She popped out Deborah's tape and handed it to Janie, embarrassed. "She's perfect for him, isn't she?"

"I wouldn't have matched them otherwise," Janie said gently, sliding the tape into its case.

"I just wanted to be sure." She sighed. "You were right. Sex isn't simple."

"Are you in love with him?"

"No," she said sharply. "I mean, I don't know. What's the point? It's a transition thing, right?"

Janie studied her face. "I'm sorry, Kylie."

"Don't be. It's for the best."

"The best?" She sighed. "I don't know what's best anymore." Her face took on a faraway look. "I have a…situation."

"With the reporter? We agreed that was a bad idea."

"I know. But we've spent some time together. And… he's just…well…he really sees me. I can't explain it, but I'm thinking that after the story comes out maybe we could…date."

"Date? You don't date, Janie. You fall in love. Too soon and all wrong. He's a Stubborn Loner or a Wounded Stubborn or something, isn't he?"

"I don't know what he is. But I want to find out."

Not again. She couldn't leave Janie with another heartbreak in the works. "Don't do it, Janie. Don't risk it."

But there was a mulish glint in her sister's eyes that told her she was wasting her words. Janie's heart was in line for another bruising and there wasn't a thing Kylie could do about it. Except stay. And how could she do that?

13

JANIE POPPED Deborah's video back on the shelf. It snicked into place between its neighbors. The video had showed Kylie the truth. That was the value of the Close-Up. Seeing was believing. There were rows upon rows of truths right there to be perused, stilled, fast-forwarded and rewound to study and ponder. *Snick, snick, snick.* Tape after tape of truth.

Maybe she should look at Seth's Close-Up. Watching his video, maybe she'd see whether or not he was her usual escape artist. She needed an objective view of him. A rational opinion to override her impulse—which was to throw caution to the wind and be with him.

Except where was the tape? She hadn't boxed or labeled it—she'd spaced that. It wasn't still in the camcorder. Had Gail accidentally taped over it? For sure Gail hadn't seen it. One look at that kiss and she'd have been all over Janie with "I told you so," and "you're in love," and "just another Personal Touch miracle."

"Marlon Brandon, line one," Gail shouted down the hall—what did she have against the intercom? "I'm off to my gyno. Wish me luck and watch the phones."

Janie took the call in her office, certain the man wanted to get started dating the women she'd yellow-stickied.

"Listen, Jane, I got a strange call you should know about…from a reporter. Asking about the lawsuit."

"A reporter? Was it Seth Taylor?" She held her breath.

"That's him. He said he'd heard about our meeting and wondered about the outcome. I told him it all worked out good, but I don't get why you'd tell him about the, um, misunderstanding."

"I didn't." Her lungs pinched tight and she fought for air.

"Then who did?" He gave an awkward laugh. "The guy asked me, get this, if you'd ever offered me sex for a fee."

"Sex for a…? You've got to be kidding."

"You don't, um, do that, do you? Because I—"

"Of course not."

"I figured. So, weird call. Anyway…the thing is I'm thinking hair plugs. To look younger? What do you think?"

"I think you look just fine as you are. I have several Potentials in mind for you…." She managed to dissuade him from that procedure and a stomach staple, while her mind reeled. How had Seth heard about the lawsuit? Gail wouldn't have said anything, though Seth and she had chatted a few times, for sure.

Then both lines rang at once. She put Marlon on hold and took the second call.

"Hey, beautiful, guess what I'm holding?" Harry Hand Job again. Good Lord. Gail was close to getting him to see a therapist, so Janie didn't want to hang up on him. "Keep holding it then." She pushed the button for the third line, but it disappeared. The caller had either hung up or was leaving a message. Darn. She returned to Marlon and scheduled a new Close-Up, then convinced Harry to redirect his energy. When she hung up, she found the third caller had indeed left a voice mail.

"This is Deborah Ramsdale, Jane." The woman's voice shook with rage. "What the hell is going on? A reporter called me with some outrageous story about your sister being a dating...*shill*. And sleeping with Cole. I've left Cole a message. *Another* message. Don't you people take calls, for God's sake?" *Click.*

Holy heavens, what in the...? Seth had called Deborah? And Marlon. How had he even known about them? And why hadn't he asked her these bizarre questions? Hinting at prostitution? And knowing about Kylie and Cole? Surely Gail hadn't blabbed....

Abruptly, she remembered where the word *shill* had come from. Kylie had joked during the pre-Marlon consult with Cole. Right after Seth left. Had he returned for some reason? And eavesdropped?

Her mind reeled and she fumbled in her drawer for her inhaler, sucking in medicated mist, forcing herself to breathe slowly and exhale completely. Not easy when shock sent icy panic along her nerves. Seth had convinced her he believed her—worse, that he cared about her—and meanwhile he'd been investigating her like she was a criminal.

Her gaze fell on the ratty banana plant, then flew to the window, where Seth's roses still gleamed. Hokey gifts. Trojan horses hiding his perfidy. She'd told herself he was different than her usual bad boy. He was different, all right. He was a master manipulator. And she'd fallen for it, hook, line and clearance-priced banana plant.

She wanted to cry, but she didn't have time. She had to call Deborah and straighten her out and she had to stop *Inside Phoenix* from printing whatever trash Seth had—

"Jane?"

She looked up to see the man himself in her doorway.

If she'd been standing, she'd have tossed his plant and his roses at his adorably tousled head. "I just talked to Marlon and Deborah Ramsdale left me a message. What the hell are you doing?"

"Checking out what I heard."

"You eavesdropped on a private conversation? Why didn't you talk to me?"

"I had to get the facts straight first."

"The facts? What facts? You jumped to bad conclusions based on misunderstandings."

"I wanted too much to believe you, Janie. I had to verify things. Now I'm here to get your side."

"My side? *Now?* After you've freaked out my clients?" She was so angry she could hardly speak, but she had to defend herself. "Personal Touch is not an escort service. Nobody gets paid to date anyone, let alone sleep with them." Her voice shook. "My sister is no *shill.* Gail got overly ambitious with the bookings and Kylie stood in…to be polite. The married matches had to do with a Web site snafu and as for the phone sex—"

"A mix-up, I know," he said softly. "I checked with the classified ad rep. Gail explained about the Web site error. Marlon Brandon thinks you're a saint, by the way."

"Despite your efforts to convince him I'm a hooker?"

"I believe you mean *madam,* and I was just doing my job. I do need you to explain the joke about your sister sleeping with Cole Sullivan."

She caught her breath.

"What?" He honed in on her, his eyes a sparkling blue "gotcha." How had she thought he was tenderhearted, or vulnerable, or even hokey? He was a cynic. He expected the worst from people, including her.

"They slept together, not that it's any of your business, but it's over." She would hold back nothing. "Deborah was out of town and I asked Kylie to meet Cole to apologize and they hit it off. That's no crime, though I'm sure you intend to make it sound like one."

"I just want the truth, Jane."

"No. You want to make me look bad."

"That's how the game is played. You put your best foot forward and I look under the carpet for your dirt."

"There was no dirt. There were a couple of mix-ups."

"That you should have told me about."

"Oh, yeah? And when I didn't tell you anything racy, you decided to kiss me? To loosen me up? And all that stuff about my face being your favorite view…" Her voice wobbled, so she swallowed.

"Was true. I had feelings for you. I still do."

"How am I supposed to believe that?"

"Look at me." He stepped closer, dismayingly sincere and steady. Like a man she could love.

But she didn't dare. He'd suspected her of terrible things and shared those suspicions with her clients. She shook her head, feeling betrayed and sick and so sad. "If you could believe for one second that I was capable of the things you accused me of, then we have nothing to say to each other."

"You're upset and I understand that, but this is who I am. I'm a reporter. I have to prove things to myself." His blue eyes glittered with determination, with emotion. He was asking her to accept him, love him anyway.

But it wasn't enough, she told herself. All her charts, everything she'd studied before starting Personal Touch told her not to believe his eyes, his face, his words. She'd spent the past year determining what made couples bond and re-

lationships work. It was time she applied what she'
learned to her own life. This was one bad relationship sh
would not start.

"I don't want someone who doesn't believe the trut
when he hears it from me."

He looked at her, opened his mouth to object, the
closed it again and the light in his eyes disappeared like
blown match. "Makes sense."

Fight me, argue with me, insist. Hell, kiss me.

"You confirmed what I'd learned. Thanks. I guess I'
better hit it. Keep the candles away from the trash. Wa
ter this maybe." He fingered one tattered banana leaf. "I
it can be saved." He shot her a shadow of his mock
ing smile. "Don't worry about the story, Janie. You'll b
happy with it."

And then he left. Just like that. Took his gorgeous back
side in those well-worn jeans right out the door. He wa
done with the story and she was done with him.

She hurt, of course—throbbed inside—but nothing lik
how she'd feel if she'd let him into her life and then he lef
At least she'd learned that much.

And now she had to get Deborah on the phone and ex
plain what had happened, try to rescue the match wit
Cole. Compatibility won out every time, she knew. She ha
the facts and Deborah was a rational woman—practical, ef
ficient and determined to settle down. Just like Cole. If sh
just wouldn't panic.

Except it turned out that that Deborah had checked ou
of her London hotel. Abruptly. With many meetings sti
pending, according to her flummoxed secretary. It looke
as though Janie might be too late. Deborah seemed to hav
already panicked.

KYLIE DROVE to Cole's house after the shuttle had dropped her off from the airport, mixed emotions swirling through her like smoke from competing fires. She'd been energized by the meetings with S-Mickey-B. Everyone had fawned over her Home Town Suites campaign, which included an edgy competitor comparison and a promotion that invited viewers to report their experiences to a "Bad Bed Hotline." The team had softened her concept a bit, which was a major glitch in her mind. She'd decided not to object yet. No point getting argumentative so early. Compromise was essential when you were part of an agency—especially a powerhouse like S-Mickey-B. She'd work around it somehow.

She'd also enjoyed the visit to Gina's town house for margaritas. Kylie had seen the darling room she would live in until she found a place of her own. That made the move more real in her mind. She had a job, an office and a home, however temporary.

All she had to do was finalize the Personal Touch details and the last work for K. Falls PR, give S-Mickey-B a start date, and she'd be cleared for landing in her new life.

Except for the goodbyes. To her assistant Candee, her favorite clients, to Janie. And, of course, Cole. She would stay in touch with Candee and Janie and she'd start K. Falls PR again in the future, probably in L.A., but she'd never see Cole again.

That was the hard part.

So now, as she exited the freeway in the direction of his apartment, her heart felt like a giant knot of twine around a stone—tightly twisted and heavy in her chest. The plan was to walk in, say goodbye and leave. It was the only way. If they kissed, they'd want sex and if they had sex, they'd want more sex and that was just plain sad. Deborah was arriving soon. They had to let go. Hanging on was just childish.

In brief minutes, she pulled into Cole's complex and forced a smile for the security guard who knew her by now. She wound through the narrow streets to Cole's unit, feeling her heart race. She'd spent her entire flight gearing up for the farewell and she was as ready as she'd ever be.

At his door, she knocked, braced for a quick hug—no all-body connection this time, no siree. She still wore a suit to remind herself how serious she was. Except she realized abruptly it was the one she'd worn when they'd met, sans ice cream stain and with a new zipper, thanks to her dry cleaner. And that made her hurt all over.

The door flew open, interrupting her nostalgia, and there was Cole, making it worse.

"Kylie!" His face lit from inside at the sight of her. He seemed to want to embrace her, but her expression made him lurch back to let her in.

She turned to close the door behind her, aware that normally he'd have slammed her against it, ripped a jacket button, retorn the zipper maybe, in his frantic need to get at her. A sad shiver rippled through her.

Radar yipped for attention at her feet, so she bent to pat him, then stood on the entry tile, suddenly shy.

Cole seemed uncertain, too. They jolted forward at the same time for an awkward hug—wooden marionettes slapped together, then jerked apart.

"How was your trip?" Cole asked, running his hands down his sides, nervous, and clearly wanting to touch her.

"Good. Productive. Very good."

"I taped *Last Comic Standing* for you. I figured you'd

be too busy in L.A. to catch it." He fisted and released his fingers again and again.

"We worked late that night, yeah, so thanks. You're so thoughtful…. I—" Get off the subject, stay clear. "We were launching a new e-music company. Web site, major media, big splash, national stuff. Very exciting." She kept talking about work, standing there in the entryway, because it always helped to share ideas with Cole and because she didn't know what else to do. Her words tasted like cardboard in her mouth.

"Sounds like you're excited to get out there." He managed a half smile that didn't light his dark eyes. *Are you? Are you leaving me?* That was what he wanted to know and her heart throbbed.

She forced herself to stay strong. He had to give Deborah of the overtweezed eyebrows a fair chance. She was what he wanted. Kylie was clinging to him out of selfishness, scared of her future. Which was totally unfair to Cole.

"Oh, yeah. I'm totally jazzed." *Totally? Jazzed?* She sounded like a cheerleader. "They truly are on the cutting edge. And they loved my presentation."

"How could they not? Your stuff is great. Creative and fresh and strong… You underestimate your talent, Kylie, but they won't. Or they better not or they'll have me to answer to."

She held up her hand, smiling at his encouragement, soaking it in like lotion on chapped skin. "Enough. You're overdoing it." How did he know she needed this boost for the courage to leave? "I am nervous, though. I feel like I'm jumping into the ocean from the kiddie pool."

"Nah. You belong with the big PR sharks."

She loved hearing that from him. Cole got it. He got her.

Knew how she ticked. Her usual men found her ambition either mystifying or annoying. And she'd never felt safe enough to share her doubts with them.

Cole's praise was honest, if overstated. Coming from a man who knew professional competence it was balm to her jittery self-esteem. In short, she believed him. She made a mental note to expect that from the man she settled down with. Eventually. In that nebulous swirl of a future life of hers.

"Your confidence in me means a lot," she said. "It helps."

"You don't need me for that, Kylie," he said seriously, as if this was a vital point. "You've earned what you've been offered. S-Mickey-B is stealing you away." *From me?* Is that what he was telling her?

He moved closer, keeping his arms at his sides like a soldier with a grim duty to perform.

"I missed you," he blurted finally, as if the words were ripped from his throat. His dark eyes flared and she fought the desire to melt into his arms.

"Oh, I missed you, too." She couldn't risk a closer step. Not if she expected to walk away. She stayed rooted in place, swaying in the hot breeze of what they wanted from each other, but didn't dare take. They couldn't give in. They had to end this now. They both spoke at once.

"We should stop—"

"We have to quit—"

"Sorry," she said, "You go ahead."

"We should stop seeing each other."

"My exact thought," she said, half relieved, half sad, that he knew it, too. "Being with you has been, well, wonderful. The sex, of course, and…other things."

"For me, too, Kylie. It's been…"

"Wild," she added quickly, afraid he'd say something touching and she'd get all emotional and not be able to bear the pain swelling in her, reaching up like a bruised balloon into her throat. "I embarrassed you at your office, for God's sake. Got us both behind on our work, took us off course. *Waaay* off course. Distracted you..."

From Deborah. Jealousy burned in Kylie's veins at that thought, startling her. That woman better appreciate what she was about to get.

"We did it together. All the way."

"And had so much fun doing it." Kylie was trying to stay light, but her voice quavered.

"All that exercise." His voice shook, too, and the joke seemed so lame. "That sense of well-being."

"Right." The words echoed over their heads, even though the ceiling wasn't high. There was so much they weren't saying, but what was the point? She couldn't change anything. Even though she felt as if she was giving something up that she really, really wanted. No, needed.

Had to have to be all right in the world.

Stop it. Stop it.

They stared at each other. The silence swelled and beat the air like a pulse or a drum.

"I should go," she said.

He nodded. Then his eyes lit with a new idea. "But wait. Did they feed you on the plane? Are you hungry?"

"Starving! It was just crackers. Stale ones. Can you believe how little sustenance they give you these days?" *What are you doing? Are you crazy? Get out now.*

"How about Mexican?" he said. "This is a special occasion, right?"

"Our last lard together?" Jeez, there were tears in her

eyes. Over animal fat. She should run, not walk, this instant, but instead, she said, "Sure," and followed him to the kitchen, where he grabbed his very own copy of her favorite take-out menu. Now it was *their* place.

She looked over his shoulder at the choices, distracted by the sight of his fingers sliding down the columns, remembering them sliding over her skin, finding her softest spot and not moving until she was gasping and twitching in ecstasy.

"Remember that first order?" He caught her eye.

"Every second of every minute," she whispered.

He stilled, the phone at his ear, dial tone sounding in the air between them, his breathing as ragged as hers. She'd bet his heart was pounding out a rib just as hers was doing.

"Then we ate in the bathtub. And made love."

"Splashing the leftovers to mush."

"But the sopaipillas were in the kitchen. For later."

"With the honey."

"Yeah. The honey."

She could hardly contain herself. She itched for him, ached for him. They were inches apart. All she had to do was lean a little closer.

"Do you know what you want?" Cole asked, unconsciously licking his lips, his pupils flaring. He meant from the restaurant, of course, but she was too far gone to care.

"Absolutely." She grabbed him.

He let go of the phone and grabbed back. They kissed deeply, sweeping tongues, massaging lips, then shifting to kiss cheeks, ears, necks, smearing their mouths everywhere, wanting it all, not getting enough. They squeezed forearms, rubbed pelvises, pressed bodies, struggling for balance, banging into the wall, then the counter, finally knocking over a stool.

"What are we doing?" Cole gasped, looking at her, eyes glazed.

She didn't want to figure it out. She just wanted to put out this heat, feed this hunger. "Having one last time?" she gasped. "It's…a…special…"

"Occasion?" he breathed, yanking at her jacket. This time the button didn't fly off—darn that dry cleaner.

She had to unbutton it, frantic, then dropped the jacket at her feet. She went at his belt, unlatching it.

"We might as well order some food, huh?" he said, undoing her blouse.

"That would be efficient." She bent and retrieved the fallen phone and while Cole placed the order, she stripped him of his clothes and took hers off, too. He fumbled the order, watching, taking in her body with greed and delight. *I'll have that…mmm, and that… Oooh, that, too. I want it all.*

Finally, he thanked the clerk and hung up the phone. "Come here, you." He yanked her to him, then swept her up into his arms, naked against his bare chest. His erection brushed her stomach as he moved. She wrapped her arms around his neck and looked into his dear face, feeling secure in his arms. *I could rest here. I could breathe.* It was so delicious and so right.

Radar trotted behind them, her bra strap between his teeth. Oh, she would miss this.

Cole settled her on cool sheets—the new ones he'd bought for her—and climbed into bed beside her, twining his legs with hers. Now that they'd decided to make love, time slowed.

She ran her fingers across his chest, studying his nipples, the swelling and ripple of muscle, the swirl of hair, brown and gold, committing every delicious inch of him to memory.

He ran his finger over the tops of her breasts, one after the other, delicately, tickling her, his eyes intent on his finger's journey. "I'll always remember this."

"Good." Even when he started with Deborah? Kylie closed her eyes against the jealousy that throbbed through her like a toothache. Would Deborah be good in bed? Better than Kylie? More in synch with Cole? That wasn't possible. And did the woman even like comedy?

"This has been good for me," Cole was saying, drawing her back to the delicious moment. "You've been good for me."

"When I wasn't getting you in trouble, you mean."

"You've got me thinking about taking it easier. There's more to life than work."

"I *have* been a bad influence on you."

"You've been a kindred spirit. You've made me see myself differently. You've made me feel…better." He seemed to want to say more, but stopped himself. "I hope when you get to L.A. you won't push yourself so hard you don't have any fun."

"Not to worry. I always make time for Comedy Central."

"Plant a garden, though. Right away. Go out for drinks with your colleagues. Find a man. Ouch." He grimaced. "Forget that. I don't want to think of you with anyone else. Is that bad?"

"No. I know how you feel." Kylie swallowed a knot the size of a golf ball in her throat. *Forget Deborah. At least get the woman an eyebrow pencil and some Valium. Oh, hell. Forget her. Be with me.*

Fearing she'd blurt those very words, she shifted to pull Cole over her, and wrapped her legs across his back.

"Mmm," he said, instantly getting the idea. In seconds, he slid inside, smooth and easy, with a groan of rich pleasure. Like he was finally home after a long, long trip.

She lifted her hips to get all of him inside her. They rocked together, smooth and sweet, holding each other's gazes as they climbed the familiar peak, their bodies knowing every move, every nuance of reaction. They stared at each other freely, filling up, fixing in their minds the way they were together. Did it get any better than this? Could it?

Maybe it was because of their sexual connection, or because it was the last time, but each stroke felt more familiar and more right, as if Cole belonged inside her. Always.

An odd light came into his eyes as his pace quickened. An odd light she recognized. *Don't go. Never go.*

If they both felt that way…

But then her orgasm caught her sharply and she buried her face in Cole's neck.

"What am I going to do without you?" Cole whispered and pulsed into her.

"I don't know." She nearly cried the words, and blinked back the water in her eyes. She looked into his face. It could be so easy with him. *I could just be.*

No work, no struggle, no worry. Feel whatever I feel. Not hurry past, not move on. Just be myself. Be here.

But there was something scary about that. A big, deep hole of expectation and need. What if it wasn't enough? What if things changed? What if it didn't work? Then where would she be?

She pushed away that thought. She was overreacting. Some of this was probably jealousy. Another woman wanted

him, after all. There were still her fears about leaving to
blame this on.

She seemed to have one excuse after another. Meanwhile, there was so much emotion in Cole's face. Desire
and longing and something he wanted to say. Something
that would make things right—

Then the doorbell rang.

"Food!" she said. "I'll get it. Just stay naked."

She leaped out of the bed, grateful for the reprieve, and
rushed to the kitchen where their clothes lay scattered. Radar ran with her, his tags jingling merrily. He thought this
was a game, not the end of everything.

"Just a minute!" she called toward the door, throwing
on her skirt, buttoning her blouse quickly. Realizing her
nipples showed through the fabric—what had Radar done
with her bra?—she threw on her jacket, then slid her bare
feet into her shoes, hoping to hide the fact she'd just had
sex by looking put together.

She yanked open the door…to a woman in a pinstriped
business suit. No delivery person, this one.

Her eyes went wide, her eyebrows shot up. Her thin and
jumpy eyebrows. Kylie would have recognized them anywhere. Oh. My. God. It was Deborah. "Is Cole Sullivan
home?" she asked.

"Uh, yes. Of course. Come in." What the hell was Deborah doing here? Worse, what was Kylie's excuse? Janie
would kill her for this. "I'm…here to…" She spotted Radar heading toward the hall. "Get the dog. I'm Cole's
friend…the one with the dog. Radar, let's go. Cole, you
have company!"

"He'll be right out," she said to Deborah. "I think I, um,
woke him up coming for the dog."

She glanced at Deborah, who was staring at her, wanting to believe her, Kylie could tell, but not quite able to. Two dots of red—alarm or anger—popped onto her pale cheeks and began to grow.

"Radar, come on. Let's go." She grabbed the leash from the entry table, then realized Deborah was staring past her toward the floor. She turned and saw Radar trot her way, her bra in his teeth. Good Lord.

Deborah stared at the dog as though he'd taken a dump in the living room. Her eyes jumped up to Kylie's.

"That silly dog. It's his favorite toy, can you believe it? My old bra and he carries it around like a chew toy."

Then Cole appeared, his shirt open over his chest, pants barely zipped, hair disheveled. When he saw Deborah, his jaw dropped.

"Cole?" she said in a quavery voice.

"Deborah! You're early," he said lamely, looking sheepish and guilty as hell.

In the silence, Radar trotted the bra to Kylie and dropped it at her feet, sitting back on his haunches. *Did I do good?*

Deborah's gaze zipped from the bra to the dog, to Kylie, and finally settled on Cole's face. "No," she said bitterly. "It looks like I'm too late."

14

IT MUST HAVE BEEN in Deborah's voice mail message, Cole realized with sick dread, watching her put the obvious two-and-two together about him and Kylie. He'd ignored the cell phone beep from the night before, figuring it was Deborah dissecting her latest meeting. He'd found the chitchat very awkward, with her acting cozier and cozier and him pulling away more and more. He'd planned to take her to dinner at T. Cook's the day after she returned and break it to her as gently as he could. He hoped that physical proximity would show her there was no chemistry, too.

But here she was. In a room alive with chemistry. None of it involving her. He felt like a complete jerk.

"I'll just get Radar and his chew toy out of your way," Kylie said and lunged for the dog, who galloped away. What the hell was Kylie doing? Pretending to be a dog sitter? And her bra was a chew toy? No one would believe that.

"There was a window in my schedule..." Deborah said faintly, sounding stunned. "I left you a message. Your office said you'd gone home early, so I came straight here. All the way from London. To surprise you."

"I'm surprised. You bet." Horrified was more like it.

"Radar, dammit, come to Mommy," Kylie said through

gritted teeth, bounding after the dog who seemed to be playing tag with her.

"What's going on, Cole?" Deborah demanded, her eyebrows doing jumping jacks on her forehead. They were strangely thin, almost invisible.

"Deborah, listen, I—"

"Nothing's going on," Kylie blurted, ceasing the chase. "Really. Let me just get the dog out of here and you two can talk. I know Cole's been dying for you to arrive, Deborah. Just let me get out of your hair." She shot him a frantic look.

He hadn't told Kylie Deborah was no longer a possibility, and now she was madly trying to salvage a relationship that was dead before it started.

Radar emerged from the kitchen at that moment. With Kylie's panties in his teeth.

"Oh!" Kylie yelped and lunged for them, but Deborah, of course, had seen. She had the quick eyes and head movements of a nervous bird.

"So it's true. You are sleeping with her."

What did she mean by that? She'd suspected? How?

"It's not what you think," Kylie said to her, scooping up her panties and wadding them in a ball. "This is all a big, fat mistake." She shot him an apologetic look. "Just erase this from your mind like it never happened."

"Kylie…" he warned, not wanting to hear the most beautiful experience of his life described as a mistake, even to save hurt feelings.

"You lied to me." Deborah's voice went high and sharp as a blade. "We talked and talked and you never said a word. We agreed—no games, be honest, be direct."

"I should have said something, I know, but you and I were just a possibility and—"

"And you and her?"

He looked at Kylie and his heart flipped over. *We were heaven on earth. Pure joy.*

"We were killing time," Kylie said, her voice jagged with emotion. "Just until you got here and I left town. Consider me gone already. Forget this terrible moment. Please."

He felt her words like blows. He couldn't let her go. Not now. Making love to her before the doorbell, he'd known it in his soul. Maybe she wouldn't stay, but they could visit. They had to do something, work something out.

She turned to him. "I wish you every happiness, Cole." Her face was sad and embarrassed and scared. "I'm sorry. I knew better. I should have just said goodbye like a sensible person." She blinked quickly, bit her lip, then rushed off, pausing to scoop her bra off the floor and blast out the door.

"What about her dog?" Deborah demanded of him. "She left her dog. And, who knows. Maybe a slip?"

"Radar's not Kylie's dog. That was…"

"Another lie?"

"Yes, but…"

"Is that hers?" Deborah pointed at Kylie's purse on the floor where she'd flung it when they threw themselves at each other while ordering food.

"Yes, it is. That's Kylie's purse." He grabbed it and headed for the door, hoping for a private moment in the parking lot to explain everything, but Kylie had returned and stood on his landing.

"Hard to stomp off without my keys," she said, taking her purse from him.

"I'll call you," he murmured. As soon as he talked this through with Deborah, to whom he'd been unfair.

"Don't. I can't handle it. I have to leave and you have to fix this."

"You don't understand. I—"

"I do understand. Just fix it." And then she was gone.

But it was Kylie he wanted to fix things with. He wanted her in his arms, his heart, his life.

He turned to face Deborah, who stared at him, arms folded, her eyes red, lips tight and thin with fury. "How long has this been going on?" she demanded.

"Just a few weeks."

"And you're in love with her!"

It sounded ridiculous, but it was true. He was in love. Desperately. Wildly. Head over heels. "Look, Kylie is—"

"Stop saying her name like that. Like a wish or a sigh. It's irritating."

"I'm sorry, Deborah. I know it's ridiculous. And I'm as surprised as you are really."

"Oh, please." Deborah's hard eyes swam in soft tears. A few weeks ago, he would have been willing to give this a try, despite his misgivings. But not now. Not after he'd been with Kylie and felt what he'd begun to feel. His settled life with an appropriate wife wasn't working out the way he'd planned.

"I'm sure Jane will have a number of other Potentials for you and—"

"Don't you dare pity me, Cole Sullivan." Her face seemed stung with red, as if from a slap. "I paid Janie Falls one thousand dollars so this kind of thing would not happen again. I didn't want to compete with other women. That's why I chose Personal Touch. Jane Falls stole my money."

"She sent Kylie to meet me so I wouldn't quit the service before I met you. Her intentions were completely honorable. She was trying to help you."

"Please. If that woman had a clue what she was doing, she would never have put you two in the same room. You look at each other like…dessert or a dream or a jackpot. It's sickening. Jane Falls is a fraud."

"Be angry at me, not Jane."

"Oh, I am angry at you, but how does that help? Compatibility scores mean zip when you're in love with someone else. This has been a complete waste of time and…" Her lip trembled. "Just a waste." She spun on her heels and marched out the door.

"I'm—" He started to apologize, but knew she'd think he pitied her. He'd call her later, take her to lunch, urge her to stay with Personal Touch, help her however he could.

Radar gave a low growl as she passed him. Poor Deborah.

Except then the dog growled at him, too. For hurting Kylie, no doubt. He had to talk to her, too. Tell her how he felt, see if she felt the same and figure out what they could do about it.

KYLIE BLINKED back tears and pushed send on her cell, making the call to S-Mickey-B. She was breaking her own rule again—talking on the phone while driving—but this was an emergency. She had to tell her new boss she would start next week. Make it official so she could forget about Cole. She was headed to her office, where she would bury her angst in work.

She couldn't believe she hadn't had the sense to end it at the doorway the way she'd planned. Now Cole and Deborah would start their relationship with a big, terrible fight. That was so wrong. That poor woman had been so shocked and hurt—her frayed little eyebrows twitching like cat whiskers. Kylie felt like some evil home wrecker. Which was practically what she was.

"Garrett McGrath, please… Yes, I'll hold."

In a way it was good, though. The shock showed her how far she'd strayed from who she really was. She was acting like Janie, who got so lost and sad after each breakup—and every move when they were kids. She would lose her appetite, pore over the photo album she kept of each place, dropping tears of desolation on the plastic cover sheets. Each drop stung like acid when Kylie watched. She hated, hated, hated seeing her little sister suffer. Her stomach would be tight with nausea.

Kylie had wished that Janie would handle it like she did—by holding back a little. That way moving became an adventure. New people. New places. New fun. She always did her damnedest to help Janie see it that way, but when they trekked through the new neighborhood Kylie often had the sense that Janie was just pretending to cheer up.

And now she understood Janie's reaction. Kylie had never felt this much misery. She even had tears dripping onto her navy-blue lap.

She loved Cole. She wanted Cole. She missed Cole.

Which was ridiculous. Hell, the man had evidently been having long-distance heart-to-hearts with Deborah. Hopefully they could straighten it out. Deborah was what he needed, bad eyebrows or not, and Kylie couldn't stand it if she'd ruined the match Janie had made for him.

The whole thing was bad timing. Bad timing to be having a farewell boff when his perfect match dropped in. Bad timing to fall in love with a man who was already taken…or at least promised.

She had to put it all in perspective. She wanted to roll into a ball and cry for hours. But she had steps to take, work to do, a future to step into. The S-Mickey-B hold music was Paul Simon's "Still Crazy After All These Years." She gritted her teeth. She would come through this fine. This was all for the better. She'd been playing with fire. And escaped with just the whiff of singed hair. Make that eyebrows.

"Hey, girl, Gina here. Garrett's golfing somewhere. Can I help?"

She smiled at the sound of the friendly voice. Keeping her tone level, Kylie explained her plan to move over the weekend. She could handle the final Phoenix details from L.A.

"God, don't hurry," Gina said, surprising her. "We need to suck every bit of creativity out of you."

"What does that mean?"

"You know, before group-think sets in."

"Group-think?"

"Yeah. You start out with your own unique vision and fresh voice, but gradually the team grinds you down until you see and sound just like us."

"You're kidding."

"I wish. Two years ago I was hot and new. Garrett hired me and now I'm hopelessly derivative." Her tone was lightly ironic, but Kylie could feel there was honest worry in her words.

"That's not true. You're very good."

"Maybe I'm being neurotic. Or maybe I was always derivative. Oh, and I should warn you that Garrett thinks the Home Town Suites stuff is, quote, 'a mite confrontational.'"

"But that was the whole point."

"Exactly. We have *got* to get Garrett to golf more. He's a buzz kill in account meetings."

"But Garrett is brilliant."

"He's the talent scout—sees it, reels it in. Just stick to your guns, Kylie. Push us out of our rut. No one wants to take chances or buck the partners. You'll be good for us."

While Gina's words sank in, Kylie stared at a couple making out in the front seat of the car ahead of her, part of her wishing she could just escape into love like that. With Cole.

Group-think? Great. Something else to worry about. She'd thought the edges of the Home Town stuff were already rounded too much and now she'd have to convince Garrett not to squeeze it to pap? She'd barely accepted the fact she had ideas and now she had to do battle to use them?

Maybe she should delay her departure. Gina sure wanted her to. What about not going at all? She could help Janie with the final turnaround of Personal Touch, spend more time with her, ease the inevitable misery with the reporter she'd fallen for.

Oh, who was Kylie kidding? She wanted to see Cole, despite how impossible it was. He could be falling in love with Deborah this very minute. Kylie wasn't herself.

Forget that. Now. She told Gina she'd think about her move date a little longer, and said goodbye just as she pulled into the parking lot of her office building. If only she could talk to Cole about this—the move, what it might be like at S-Mickey-B. Did she really want to give up her *own unique vision,* as Gina had called it? But she couldn't talk to him. They'd broken up. Oh, this was agony.

And then, there he was, waiting in her lobby, sitting beside Candee's desk, flipping through a magazine.

"Cole, what are you...?"

"I had to see you," Cole said, rising. He let the magazine drop to the table. It slid to the floor.

Simply Sex

"Well," Candee said, looking from one to the other. "I've got class, I guess…in a while anyway." She turned to Cole and said, "Good luck," as if she thought he'd need it.

Then they were alone. In her office. Which Cole had never visited. Kylie's heart heaved in her chest and her face grew hot. She wanted to run into his arms. *I love you…. Do you love me? Help me figure out what to do.* Instead, she said, "Everything straightened out with Deborah?"

"There was nothing to straighten out."

"But you talked to her before? While we were…?"

"She called from London and we talked a couple of times. She seemed to feel more strongly about it than I did."

"This is all my fault," Kylie said, feeling despair and desperate hope. "Janie warned me I was distracting you. You have to give it a chance. You were counting on this. She's perfect for you." She fought like crazy to hide her real feelings, not even certain what they were. Her thudding heart and shaky breaths were her only clues.

"No, she's not." He stepped closer.

She stepped back. "Yes, she is. I saw her video."

"You saw her video?"

She nodded, feeling miserable and foolish.

"You're who I want." He reached for her, but she froze. Everything inside her went still and scared.

"Deborah pointed out that I say your name like a sigh or a wish."

"She did?"

"Kylie…" he said, as if trying out the tone. "How does that sound to you?"

Like heaven. "Like my name. What do you want me to say?" She swallowed, crazy hope filling her chest. Deborah was out of the picture. Cole wanted her. And she was terrified.

"I can't stand the thought of not being with you. I feel better when I'm around you. Not so much like a hamster on a wheel. You make me laugh. You make me want to slow down and, I don't know, plant a garden."

Her heart felt as though it might explode. Cole loved her. Or at least he thought he did. She loved him, too, if she was capable of that in her current confused state.

Part of her wanted to sink into this feeling forever and the rest of her froze with terror. Cole mattered too much to her. It just wasn't right.

"Say something, Kylie. Don't leave me hanging…"

"I don't mean to. It's just a shock. And, well, maybe we're making too big a deal of all this. Like a vacation we don't want to end. Too much peanut butter brickle gets old."

"Peanut butter brickle?" He shook his head, puzzled.

"Never mind. The point is that we're having what Janie calls a 'life-transition fling.' You want a wife and I'm leaving town so we're clinging to what feels good and safe." The words hurt her throat coming out.

"Do you really believe that?"

She wasn't sure, but she watched the possibility flicker in his dark eyes. "It makes sense," she said. "Don't you think? I'm not what you want. Maybe you don't want Deborah, but you want someone like her. Someone not pushing so hard on her career."

"When you love someone you compromise."

"Not on your dreams. You know that. I can't give up on mine, either. We care about each other, we had a wonderful time together, but now we have to move on."

Keep moving. Keep your distance. New adventures

around the corner. New friends. Otherwise you could get hurt. Bad.

"How do you feel about me?" he demanded. He was stubborn, of course, the way she was.

"I'm not sure."

"Do you love me?"

"I don't know. I care about you. But it's too soon and it's not—" she swallowed a lump the size of a grapefruit "—enough."

"Not enough. You don't love me. I see."

She fought like hell to not react.

He bought it and his whole demeanor went flat and still.

The lines of connection between them dropped like cut string and she felt abruptly alone and wobbly. Tears stung, but she blinked them back.

"I'm sorry, Cole. Maybe it's not too late to give Deborah a chance."

He shook his head. It was too late. "Goodbye, Kylie," he said, and this time her name on his lips sounded just plain sad.

SETH WAITED for his printer to spit out the Personal Touch story. He'd written the most saccharine tripe of his entire career, but he was almost happy about it. He'd described Janie's dedication and her romantic practicality, included her bubbly absentee receptionist, even mentioned the fat, bald guy who'd sued over the lack of bimbos in his date book.

His suspicions had been groundless, thank God. He'd been so thrown by Janie. First, wanting too much to believe in her, he'd ignored the weird issues. Then, when he thought Janie had lied to him, he'd overreacted. He'd pitched the story to Phil Verde, the producer at TV 7 before he had enough facts together. But he'd nixed it in time. When he couldn't get Verde in person, he'd explained the situation to an assistant.

He stapled the print-warm pages, then folded the story into his bomber jacket pocket to take to Janie. He owed her some peace of mind after grinding her through the mill of his skepticism…and his own career doubts.

The truth was that he hadn't been himself since Miami. Being around Jane was the first time he'd felt good in two years. She showed him how wrapped up in himself he'd been, how lonely and downright bitter.

When she read the story, she would forgive him and they could take it from there. He couldn't wait to see her face when she read the part about her being a starry-eyed romantic with a steel spine of practicality. She'd love that. That said it all.

He was still grinning when he pulled into the Personal Touch parking lot and spotted the Eye Out For You SUV with its garish eyeball logo. What the hell was going on?

He parked beside the van and hopped off his bike.

"You don't get it!" Gail shouted from the front door at two guys headed his way—one in a blazer, the other with a camera on his shoulder. "And furthermore, if I can give some poor slob a better way to spend his Friday afternoons than chokin' the chicken, I'm a saint, not a pervert."

Seth loped closer. "What's going on?" Seth asked them.

"Just doing our job," the guy in the blazer said.

"You're working on a tip about a dating scam?" he asked, backing up to keep even with the guy. He was aware of Gail watching him from the doorway.

The reporter stopped to look him over.

"Because it's a mistake. This place is legitimate."

"Tell that to the pissed-off woman I interviewed yesterday. Former client." He started moving again.

The camera guy had opened the back of the truck and was detaching and twining cords.

"Listen, this is my story. I called it in to Phil," he said, catching the guy on the passenger side of the vehicle.

"And Phil assigned it to me. Sorry."

"No. You don't get it. There's no story. I told Phil's assistant it didn't pan out."

"We taped a woman last night who got cheated out of her money, and just now in there the owner went white as a sheet when I told her about it." He shrugged. "I'd say that's a story. It runs tonight at ten. Check it out."

The guy pulled the door shut with a firm click. The camera guy had taken the driver's seat and they pulled away, leaving Seth furious and frustrated. They'd ambushed Janie, no doubt, and who wouldn't freak at that? Pretty scummy technique, now that he thought about it.

Seth galloped toward the office to get to Janie, but Gail blocked his way, arms crossed. "Come to see the devastation you wrought, Mr. *Inside Phoenix*?"

"What happened?"

"Exactly what you intended. They treated us like pimps and perverts and liars. Janie's in tears. You should be ashamed of yourself."

"I told the producer there was no story. This is a mistake. Let me talk to her."

She blocked him. "You're the last person she wants to see right now. Really." There was a flicker of sympathy in her face.

He had to make this right. The thought of Janie crying her eyes out because of him made him sick. He fished his piece out of his pocket. "I'll fix it for her. Give her this."

"Promise me you're not a Wounded Loner." She took the story with reluctance. "Or a Stubborn Single."

"Not if I can have Janie in my life."

"That's what I want to hear." She surprised him by yanking him into her generous bosom. "Now ride like the wind and kill that story, Mr. Hot Shot Journalist. The light of your life is counting on you."

He couldn't believe that he knew exactly what she meant and it didn't even make him cringe.

15

"JESUS, SULLIVAN, you look like something even the cat wouldn't drag in. Let's get a brew across the street," Trevor McKay said the day after Cole had broken up with two women. Quite a feat for a guy who hadn't had a date for two years before that.

It was 9:00 p.m., they still had tons to do, and he was bleary-eyed and dull-witted from lack of sleep and depression. He missed Kylie. So did Radar, who'd kept him awake whining at the door, Kylie's stockings at his feet. The dog had it almost as bad as he did.

"Sounds great," he said, though he knew it was a mercy beer. McKay, his chief rival, felt sorry for him. More bad news.

They walked to the hotel across the street and entered the bistro to order a pair of Coronas with lime.

"So, Tuttleman asked me on the golf weekend with the execs from Valley Rentals," Trevor said, shoving the green wedge into the neck of the bottle. "You're the golden boy he usually takes. What gives?"

He shrugged. "I'm not so golden these days. I've been distracted."

"The hot thing from the other day?"

He nodded miserably.

"If you're going to run with the big horn dogs, Sullivan, you gotta pace yourself."

"How do you do it, anyway?"

"I have my rules."

"Like what?"

"Never two weekends with the same woman. Never date her friends. Watch the alcohol. When I start dozing at my desk on a Monday, take a week breather."

"Don't you want to settle down? The partners look for stability." He found himself wanting to help the guy. This was new and it felt good. It was a relief not to be angling for an advantage. Since Kylie, he'd been thinking more about what really made for happiness.

"Me settle down? No thanks. I need my edge. Look at Trisha. She'd be nose-to-nose with us for partner, except she's mommy track. She's got a uterus, so she's kicked to the curb. Sad."

"She's happy. She only stays late three nights a week." He and Trisha had met to go over what he'd done for her in her absence and he'd probed her approach more carefully—curious and a little envious of her determination to keep balance in her life.

"Yeah, and the partners bitch about it."

"She cranks out the billables, working through lunch, never stops to bullshit. She gets more out of sixty hours than lots of us get from eighty."

"But perception is everything." Trevor shrugged. "I guess she makes her life work for her. We all do. You make your choices and take your chances. Hey, that's damned philosophical." He lifted his beer to clink against Cole's.

He liked the guy, Cole realized, now that he wasn't looking at him only as a bump on the road to becoming partner. Maybe when he hung out his shingle he'd talk to Trevor, too. Trevor was thorough, for all his playful ways, and dogged.

If he hung out a shingle, he reminded himself. Odd how he was thinking more about that way lately. Wanting to carve out his own spot on his own terms, not get pushed around by someone else's idea of what mattered.

"As long as I have to work for it, I'm good," Trevor continued. "Which is where you come in, my friend. You're making it too easy on me."

"Don't worry. I blew it with the woman, so I'll be living through my work again." At least until he was ready to move on.

"Glad to hear it."

He wasn't giving up on making partner, but he didn't regret the ground he'd lost at BL&T by leaving early to be with Kylie, letting Trevor take the lead on the Littlefield case. Kylie had enriched his life. Without her now, the hollow sound was back. And it would get bigger and louder once Radar and his opinions went home in two days.

Did he still want a wife? He wanted Kylie. Period. Though that was impossible. She either didn't love him, or she didn't love him enough, or she was afraid to love him, and that made him feel like shit.

This love stuff was hard enough to figure out without having to drag someone into it, kicking and screaming. She didn't want what he wanted. And he was just now figuring out what that was.

He'd want a wife eventually, right? And he'd be ready this time, because he'd have his life in balance. Maybe he'd get a Cairn terrier of his own. Maybe he'd learn to cook. Mexican food. Flautas, guacamole, chile relleno…

First, he had to stop thinking about Kylie.

"Shall we head back?" Trevor said.

"How about a game of pool? It'll clear our heads." He hadn't played in years. He intended to take it up again. Along with photography. And bike riding. He wasn't giving up what he'd learned with Kylie. He wanted a life. A full one with pleasure and fun. No more would he mete out the pleasures in guilty increments watching Comedy Central.

He hoped Kylie had learned that lesson, too.

They were heading for the pool table when his gaze snagged on the television over the bar, which was showing a teaser for the 10:00 p.m. news. He was shocked to recognize a frightened, pale Janie Falls trying to block the camera. "Your Eye Out For You team follows the story of a dating service under fire," the voice-over said. Then a shadowed woman spoke in a disguised voice. "She sent a woman to pretend to be me who slept with my supposedly perfect match." Deborah. No question. Deborah had called a television station? She'd blamed Janie, he knew, but he never imagined she'd go this far.

"What are the warning signs that your dating service is ripping you off?" the voice-over continued. "We'll tell you that and more in our Eye Out For You report tonight at ten."

Damn, damn, damn. This was his fault. He grabbed his phone and dialed Kylie's number.

"Hello?" Just hearing her voice sent a charge through him.

"It's Cole."

"Cole?" She sighed with soft longing and he had this flicker of hope that she would come around, want to work things out.

"I just saw a news thing about Personal Touch and—"

"I know. We get our rebuttal tomorrow. The magazine

reporter—the one who called you?—convinced them to do a follow-up."

"That's good. Can I help, Kylie? They could interview me." Lord, what was he saying? That would really fix him with the firm.

"The reporter has agreed to do it, but thanks, anyway."

"I'd like to support you," he said, trying again.

"Please don't," she said shakily. "I'm fine. Really. And we're here together—Janie and Gail and me—to watch the piece and be sure we're prepared for tomorrow."

"Can I apologize to Jane then?"

"She doesn't blame you. I'll tell her, though. And I appreciate your call. Really."

I don't need you. I don't want you.

He got the message loud and clear, but still he said, "If you change your mind…"

"I won't," she almost snapped at him. "I need time, Cole. Time to remember who I am."

"I know who you are."

"I know. But…"

"But it's not enough. Yeah. I got that." And it hurt like hell. So what else could he do but say goodbye?

SETH PULLED INTO the Personal Touch parking lot, his palms sweaty, his gut knotted. He'd scored another interview for Janie—burning the bridge to a Channel 7 job in the process, but he didn't give a damn. Besides, the shabby bunch of half truths and unsubstantiated rumors they'd aired was worse journalism than his puff piece on Personal Touch. At least his tripe was true.

He'd fix the Eye Out For You piece in person. On camera. He gulped, feeling sweat pour from his body. He'd bas ically be making a commercial for a dating service. Way out of his realm, but he'd do his level best. He'd bought a dress shirt and gotten a haircut so he'd look respectable.

He climbed off his bike, scratched under his collar where bits of cut hair itched like hell, then grabbed the bunch of yellow roses he'd strapped to his seat. Yellow for apology, the florist said. He headed for the door, holding the flowers out like a shield. Hokey, but hell.

The TV truck wasn't here yet, he was glad to see. Kylie, who'd prepped him over the phone, had asked him to come a little early to touch base. Besides, he wanted to talk to Janie. He hoped his story had convinced her to forgive him, but he had his doubts, since she'd ducked all his calls.

This snafu had made him realize a few things, like the fact that his uncle was right. He'd been living off old glories, at least in his mind, and acting superior to the job he'd agreed to do. So it wasn't investigative work or even news analysis. It was worthy of his best efforts. And he had to stop living in limbo. This was his life, not a way station until something bigger showed up.

He had to start fresh in his heart, not just on paper.

And his fresh start had everything to do with Janie Falls.

Inside Personal Touch, he confirmed a few details with Kylie, then veered off to Janie's office, taking in the faint smell of her perfume mixed with roses.

No Janie, but he took a slow turn in the utter pinkness of the room. It was so her, though she was more than rosy dreams. She was a butterfly with a steel spine and a snappy gaze. She was romantic and pragmatic and stubborn as hell. A mix that could keep him interested for a long time. Unlike Ana, who'd been too much like him to kick him out of his natural gloom. When he was with Janie, he'd felt lifted up…open…fresh as the roses shaking in his hands. And he wanted more of that. A lifetime of it maybe.

"Seth?"

He turned and found Janie standing there. She looked so different. She wore a body-hugging suit, not a loose, fairy outfit and her wavy hair was pulled back and tight. She looked so serious. And pale and nervous. Her smile was polite and there was no light in her eyes for him.

"These are for you," he said, handing her the flowers.

She took them. "I still have the others." He looked with her at the window table, where the red flowers seemed to droop. Was it a good sign she hadn't tossed them?

"These are to say I'm sorry."

Hurt sprang into her eyes, but she blinked it away and smiled. "I know you're sorry. And you've intervened for us, so thank you. Being interviewed is probably the last thing you want to do."

"I'm the best one to set them straight. Did you read my story?" That would tell her what she needed to know about what he believed about her.

"No." Her gaze slid toward her wastebasket. She'd tossed it? "But Kylie and Gail told me it was positive. Thank you." She clearly hadn't forgiven him.

"It's not the kind of story I usually write, but it had to be done." That made it sound like a grim task. He didn't really know what to say. *Forgive me. Don't shut me out.* Then he noticed the tree he'd brought for the burned rug. "The tree's sure grown." He was an idiot.

"It's only been a week, Seth." A smile lit her face for a instant, making him want to make her smile again and again. For years.

"Everything grows fast around you." *Good God, wh*

eeds you? "Listen, Janie, I've been doing some thinking about us—"

She held up her hand. "Please don't. I have the most important interview of my life coming up. I can't think about anything else."

"I understand. Sure. We'll talk later."

"We've said everything there is to say, Seth."

"We'll see." He wouldn't push, but he wouldn't quit. He'd talk and talk and talk until he got through to her. He wasn't sure what he was going to do with his life from here on out, but he knew he wanted Janie in it.

JANIE WAS ALMOST relieved when the TV crew arrived. Seth looked so good to her she wanted to run into his arms. He wanted to talk about them. But they were all wrong for each other. Love could alter your perceptions, but it didn't change who you were. She would have to explain it to Seth.

But first she had to save Personal Touch. The cameraman was setting up the lights. She felt as if she was waiting for the dentist to give her the injection, jumpy, breathless, her heart in her throat.

She looked at Seth, who smiled bravely at her, trying to encourage her, though he was plainly nervous himself. He kept clearing his throat and fidgeting and he sat on the very edge of his chair. His hair was newly cut and his shirt had fresh-from-the-package creases in it. And he was going to defend a dating service on television. Very against his nature. He was doing this because he cared for her.

How could she believe anything she wanted this much?

The cameraman gave her the mic cord to slide down her blouse, so she did that, her fingers trembling, her heart pounding so loud she was sure the man could feel it against

his fingers as he clipped the device to her collar. She was
so sweaty she felt as if she'd walked through a car wash.

"You'll be fine," he said, stepping back.

"She'll be great," Seth said, sounding annoyed the guy
thought she needed reassurance.

She smiled at him. He could be so sweet.

"All set?" The reporter—a different one from the day
before—smiled his fake smile at her.

Stay relaxed, speak warmly, be honest. That's what Kylie had advised her. Stay relaxed? With a light so bright it
hurt her eyes shining down on her, a huge camera lens ze-
roing in on her every flaw, a smarmy reporter primed to trip
her up? But she would do it. She had to. For Personal
Touch. For herself. She took a deep breath from her dia-
phragm, sat up straight, smiled and said, "Ready when
you are."

The interview went like lightning and her practice paid
off. One by one, she neutralized the loaded questions and
delivered her message: The Personal Touch system works
and no one tries harder to find love matches than Janie
Falls. By the end, the reporter seemed almost annoyed. She
hoped it was because she hadn't given him anything to ex-
ploit. Kylie shot her a secret thumbs-up.

"That's it, I guess," the reporter said. "Who's next?"

Seth, of course, who wiped his forehead with his sleeve.
They shifted the lights, arranged his chair and set him up
with the mic. As she waited, Janie's gaze fell to the trash
where she'd tossed his magazine story. What had he written exactly? She scooted her chair to the edge of her desk,
found the folded pages and began to read.

*The heart and soul of Personal Touch is owner Janie
Falls, who tempers her starry-eyed romance with a steel-*

spined practicality.... That was nice. She kept reading. Seth wrote about her inventory and screening process and people skills, even the skating party, listing her descriptions of the couples and predictions about their futures. He even described her reaction to the Jensens naming their little girl after her. He called her a marvel.

She read further. *Of course, a service this ambitious experiences setbacks—a disgruntled client who wants women all wrong for him, and a client base slow to build because of its careful screening requirements.*

She looked up from the page as the interview started. Seth explained to the reporter how each of his suspicions about her business practices had been wrong. He even made a joke about Gail either making sex callers into clients or sending them to therapy.

Then he turned to the reporter and spoke dead-on. "Sure, there are scams and overpriced services and even hookers masquerading as dates, but Personal Touch is for real. Janie Falls, too." He glanced at her, then stared back at the reporter. "She should be granted sainthood, not maligned by reporters too cynical to believe in love…myself included."

"Okay. I get it," the reporter said with a frustrated sigh. "That's it." He made a cut gesture at the cameraman and practically rolled his eyes. That sound bite, delicious as it was, would never make airtime, but she didn't care.

Seth believed in her. And he wanted to be with her. Was that enough?

Sure, his face was warm and open, not skeptical and gloomy, but she could be under a spell, deluding herself again. Like always.

She was so troubled she was almost relieved when the

TV crew stayed around, keeping her from her moment of truth with Seth. The camera guy had a newly divorced sister and needed an info packet. The reporter took her aside to inquire how many women "of his caliber" belonged to Personal Touch, and he, too, took a packet. In the lobby, she heard Gail handing out flyers for upcoming socials to post at the television station.

But finally she was alone with Seth in her office. "Thank you for what you did," she said, her heart so full it hurt.

"I meant every word. And more." He took a step closer. "Janie…I was so wrong."

"I don't know what to say, Seth. We're a terrible match. I, um, did an inventory on us."

"You did?" He blinked at her.

She nodded miserably. "And it's a mess. I had to cheat like crazy to get us even on speaking terms, let alone in a relationship."

"But you only guessed at my answers. Maybe it's not as bad as you think. Show me what you've got."

"I don't know…." But her heart rose with new hope, and she led him to the video library and pulled their profiles out of the file cabinet where she'd stuffed them in despair.

She handed Seth the printout she'd filled in by hand, and he sat at the table to study the pages, his brow furrowed.

"Here's your problem. I can be more positive than that." He grabbed a pencil out of the holder, erased a mark, and bubbled in something higher.

"Seth, that's not you. That's Mr. Sunshine."

"Or me when I'm around you." He looked up at her, absolutely sincere. Was she seeing things? He bent his head and read through the next section. "Conformity is not my thing, true, but I'd consider some traditional options. A

ranch house and an SUV, say, if it mattered a lot to you."
He glanced up at her, more convincing than ever, then
down again.

She noticed the fresh red prickles on the back of his neck
from where the barber had shaved him. A plastic price-tag
holder stuck up from the collar of the brand-new shirt he'd
bought to wear while he humiliated himself on television
to help her. She felt such a rush of tenderness she wanted
to cry. "You don't have to do this," she said, covering his
hand to stop the pencil.

"I want you to believe in us," he said, giving her a shot
of his blue eyes. There was no shard of cynicism in their
depths, just fire and commitment and…love. "I guess I
lost faith in myself, but you brought it back. Sounds hokey, but…"

"Seth…I—I'm just not sure…."

"I thought you might say that. So I brought proof." He
reached into his jacket pocket and pulled out a VHS tape,
which he slid into the VCR across the table. He pressed
play and there he was on the monitor, saying how hard he
was to get along with, his grin belying his words.

"*You* took the tape," she said.

"I had to. Too incriminating." His smile was teasing.

She watched as he explained that his favorite view
would be her face. Again she saw how he seemed to stare
right into her soul. The picture wobbled, then went slightly
out of focus. Then she saw her back as she stumbled into
Seth's arms. And there it was—the kiss. They held each
other tight, Seth's fingers digging into her back as though
he never wanted to let go. He pulled away to look into her
eyes, then dug in for more of her mouth. It was impressive,
but it could still just be lust and adrenaline.

Seth pushed pause, freezing them in each other's arms. "See what I mean?"

She saw...and she didn't see. The answer wasn't in the fuzzy video really. Or in the mismatched inventory. She looked down at it and saw the answer—in the shreds of eraser, the twice-rewritten numbers—their frantic efforts to prove that what they felt in their hearts was enough. She looked up to Seth's face. More answers...in the fiery determination in his eyes, in the stubborn set of his jaw, in the hope that softened the hard planes of his face.

Where was the inventory of this? Fire, determination, hope? The intangibles that held people together in love? She knew about them, counted on it with clients. That was why she interviewed them. For the extra intuitive leaps she needed to find the right matches.

She picked up the papers and, holding Seth's gaze, slowly tore them in pieces. "Not everything fits on a chart."

"Oh, yeah?" He smiled that darling half smile.

"I've been wrong so many times in my own life...I was afraid to trust myself."

"Come on, Janie. You've got a crusty cynic wanting two kids and how-was-your-day blather over meat loaf on Tuesdays. And cognac in front of the fire and moonlit walks and frickin' calico cats."

She laughed and knew he was right.

"Oh, and you in your Saturday panties." He said the words low and leaned over to kiss her, soft and slow. "We never got to the sex attitudes on your profile. How did they come out?"

"Synchronicity," she breathed.

"Are you sure?" He kissed her again and every instinct in her soul told her this was right. She'd never before given her heart. Not all of it. She'd held back. Maybe she'd chosen men she knew weren't really available to her. But Seth was here—all of him—for her. This was the compatibility of hearts. The compatibility that counted.

THEY WENT to Janie's place. Normally, she would offer him something to eat, put on some soft music, light some candles, don a sexy teddy and generally set the scene. But neither of them needed anything but each other. Seth took her in his arms and kissed her, and all she wanted was him and her together.

She didn't need to fuss or fix or primp or hold in her stomach or turn the lights low. She was enough, just as she was, and she knew it, through and through.

"Are you okay?" he asked her, kissing her before she could answer.

"Fine," she managed to mumble into his mouth. She broke away, took his hand and tugged him straight to her bedroom.

When they got there, he froze. "Condoms." He patted his pocket. "I don't have any."

"I do, but I'm on the pill…"

"And I'm healthy as a horse."

"Hung like one, too," she said, surprising herself, but she felt so free with him that she could say anything.

"Flattery will get you laid," he said, kissing her again, sliding down to her neck and working magic there for a few seconds. He held her backside in both broad palms. Oh, he did have the best hands.

Smiling into each other's faces, they undressed each other, kissing every few seconds, as if for strength. Seth examined every inch of her as he uncovered it, studying her breasts like they were works of art, just the way he'd looked at her when he took her photographs. His looks were like touches, so intense, so vivid, she thought she might climax from that alone.

He squeezed her shoulders, then slid his grip down her arms. "I can't believe I have you," he said. He cupped both breasts in his fabulous hands.

"Oh, you have me," she said, her legs turning to water. "Every inch of me." She'd never felt this way making love to a man. She was offering up her entire being—body, heart, mind—and it was safe. Maybe because he was giving himself fully to her, too. *I'm yours. Take good care of me.* What could possibly be sexier than that?

He hugged her tight, wrapping his arms fully around her so she was completely enveloped in his embrace. The hard velvet of his erection was there, showing how much he wanted her, making her liquid with want. She slid her hips against him and he groaned, leveling his gaze, seething with new heat.

She backed up to her bed, threw back the covers and pulled him down with her. They lay face-to-face and explored each other's bodies. This felt so new. Every inch of his skin, muscular and firm, seemed like a miracle. Every brush of his fingers set her on fire. He stroked her nipples, watching as they beaded with arousal. She rotated her hips toward him.

He reached down to cover her pubic area with his hot palm, sending a shudder through her. She ached for him, for all of him.

She grasped his penis and he pushed into her palm. Looking into each other's eyes, they worked each other with their hands.

"I love how you feel," she said.

"You, too. You're soft and strong. I love that you're both. Everywhere."

She smiled, trying to focus on his words while his fingers were doing breath-stopping things to her sex. It confused her to feel so hot and so tender at the same time.

"I'm in love with you, Janie."

"Me, too. With you." That was all she could manage, with arousal prickling through her, rising in her brain like a hot tide. She wanted him inside her, wanted their bodies as close as bodies could be.

She shifted, put her leg over his, allowing space for him to enter her while they lay on their sides.

Seth eased slowly into her, watching her face, pushing in inch by inch, and she welcomed each tiny movement, which seemed like the gift of himself. The slick space she opened to him was her acceptance, the squeeze and release of her internal muscles her gift back. They clung to each other, arms wrapped tightly as they rocked their hips gently back and forth.

Wordlessly, they climbed the peak at a steadily building pace, their eyes fixed on each other's, the blue of Seth's smoky with desire…and love. Her orgasm warned her with a tingling rush.

"I'm about to…"

"I know," he said and smiled that cocky smile. He watched until she had to close her eyes and cry out her pleasure.

"Janie," he breathed in her ear and then he let go, too.

She'd had sex before, but not like this. Sex with love made all the difference in the world.

KYLIE GLANCED at Janie, smiling dreamily at the television set, her face glowing brighter than the screen. They were in the video room, Gail on Janie's other side munching noisily on caramel corn, her bracelets clicking against the edge of the bowl. The newscast would start in a half hour. Seth was due soon.

Seth and Janie had fallen in love like one of Janie's Close-Ups on fast-forward. In fact, it had something to do with Seth's video and a kiss. And Kylie was sick with worry. These things tended to end badly, and with Kylie in L.A., Janie would be all alone with her broken heart.

Again, she considered the possibility of staying in Phoenix, keeping K. Falls PR going. She could work on contract with S-Mickey-B, discount her rate to compensate for any inconvenience she'd cause….

She became aware that Janie was looking at her.

"Something wrong?" Janie asked.

"No," she said, trying to smile. "I'm just worrying."

"It'll be fine. You said yourself we nailed the interviews."

"It's not the news piece."

"Oh, no." She groaned loudly. "You're worrying about Seth and me. Just stop, Kylie Rachel. I'm happy. Really. This is different. I know it is."

"Take things slow, okay? Don't do anything drastic."

Janie put her arms around Kylie and delivered a bruising hug. "I know what I'm doing."

It was true that she'd never seen Janie look so sure before, but it was too soon to tell. And she'd be too far away to help.

The phone rang and Gail left the sofa to grab it. "Personal Touch, can I help you…? Marco? Hon, get outside, get some air. You're spending a fortune on these calls. Sign with Personal Touch and you'll bank cash. I swear…

What? No, you don't have to lose fifty pounds. We have zaftig women. You prefer what? Now, now. We don't discriminate based on weight, so neither should you."

Kylie smiled at Janie. Gail was a great saleswoman. If things went well, Janie would have her do sales full-time.

"I wish Seth would get here. I miss him already. Can you believe that? I never *missed* a guy before."

This was bad. Dangerous. She'd really get hurt this time. "Just be careful. Please."

"Oh, relax. I should have invited Cole—given you something to do besides worry about me. He's called three times to check on you."

"I'm fine. It's over. Why drag it out?" Because Kylie was dying to see him. Each time he'd called, she'd itched to say, *Yes,* please *come over. Support me, comfort me, hold my hand, make me feel better about every little thing.* Pure weakness on her part.

"What are you afraid of, Kylie?" Janie asked gently.

"Everything," Kylie said on a moan. "Half the time I think I'll just stay in Phoenix."

"Really? You're considering that? Oh, that would be great!"

"I'm scared it's for the wrong reasons."

"Because of Cole? Would that be so bad?"

"It would be terrible. It's not healthy to need anyone that much. You of all people should understand that."

"You think that was my problem? Needing the guy too much?" Janie shook her head. "I chose the wrong guys to need. I picked the ones who weren't really there. People who love each other need each other, Kylie. Not for survival, of course, and not to the point of losing their identity, but that's what it's about—sharing it all—the blues, the wins, all that for-better-for-worse jazz. You don't get a medal for doing it on your own. Life's a team sport."

"You say that now because it's new and exciting. You're forgetting how miserable you get. Lost and so very sad. I hate seeing you that way." She felt the knot of fear, the bubble of nausea rise up. *Please don't get hurt.*

"I know you do and I appreciate your concern. Maybe it won't work out, but it's worth it to see. Sometimes life hurts. I know you want to save me from every toe stub, but I can handle it, I promise. I do know how to breathe."

"I guess," she said. She let Janie's words sink in. Maybe she had been too much of a big sister to Janie. Kylie thought about that photo Cole had admired on her window ledge where she'd practically choked poor Janie with her protective death grip. "I remember when you were so shy in fifth grade and you squeezed my hand looking up at me with eyes big as moons, asking me to make it all right."

Janie chuckled. "Hon, that's not what I was thinking. I was thinking, 'You love me so much.' I didn't need you to make it right. I just needed you to love me. I could handle my life and the pain when it came."

Kylie stared at her sister, reframing the moment in light of what she'd said. Maybe Kylie should have trusted her sister more to be okay on her own. Certainly now. She was a grown woman. Mature and sensible…and madly in love. But was she safe?

"The person who needs you is Cole," Gail said abruptly. She'd finished with Marco the Masturbator and was back on the bench.

"Why do you say that?"

"Here." She thrust the bowl of caramel corn at Kylie and bounded over to the video racks, where she grabbed a tape and popped it into the VCR. "See for yourself." She pushed play and Kylie watched as Cole flickered into view in his Close-Up, with his crookedly rolled-up sleeves, his awkward posture and nervous smile.

Before she could point out she'd already seen it, Gail pushed fast forward and stopped at a spot Kylie hadn't seen. Here the camera showed a much sweatier, more miserable Cole slumped on the stool.

"Go deeper," came Gail's muffled voice.

Cole wiped his brow with an extended arm, then blew out a breath. "Deeper? Okay…I guess sometimes I feel a little…empty. I wonder what I'm working so hard for. I want to help the clients and the firm, I want financial security and prestige, but at some point it's just money. I want to be working *for* something—some*one,* I guess." He shrugged, then seemed to sit up straighter.

"Here's what I want—to open my eyes Sunday mornings smiling into the face of the woman I love. I want to read interesting bits out of the paper to her and sing songs to her in the shower, get her opinion on everything from what tie goes with what shirt to global economics.

"I want a woman who'll help me sort it out and do it right. Someone I can laugh with…hell, someone I can just stare at the TV with. This sounds stupid. Stop the tape, please."

Gail complained, then the tape went black.

"Holy Hannah," Janie said. "Why didn't you show me this, Gail? I might have thought twice about Deborah with Cole. She's not soft enough for him."

Kylie took a bite of crunchy corn and chewed slowly, the sweet warmth filling her mouth the way Cole's words eased through her thoughts. He needed her. He'd said as much when he told her he loved her. And she'd blown him off in a panic, not heard, not listened.

The picture of them together on Sunday with twin papers rose in her head, Comedy Central in the background. *You can rest here. Just be.* The idea was so glorious it took her breath away. She'd closed her eyes to the possibility, thrown up barriers—the ghost of Deborah, Cole's laundry list of corporate wife characteristics, her move to L.A., her relentless ambition.

But it was all just smoke, she realized, looking at his dear face on the video. This was real. This was what counted. Cole needing her. And her needing him.

"What are you afraid of, Kylie Rachel?" Janie asked softly.

Tears sprang to her eyes and for once she just let them roll. "I don't know. My own heart, I think."

Janie put her arms around her with a sad smile, new authority in her eyes. "It's the hurt, sweetie. You've always been scared of it. You used to drag me all over town whenever we moved to exorcise the pain, remember? The minute I'd pull out the photo album to remember my friends, to just feel my love for them—and my grief—you'd whip me out of there to a water park or a bike ride or to a movie. *New adventures, new fun, new friends.* That was your mantra."

Janie was right. Her sister was much wiser than Kylie had ever given her credit for.

"But it made you feel better, didn't it?"

"Not really. You made me feel better by loving me, by being there for me, by looking at me like you'd rather die than see me hurt or sad."

"Oh, Janie," she said and hugged her back harder than she'd ever done before, really feeling it now—her love, the old worry for Janie and her health and her heart. It hurt like hell. But it also made her feel fully alive.

"You have to change, Kylie Rachel." Janie leaned back to look into her eyes.

In the background, she heard Gail sniff. Her bracelets rattled as she reached across Janie to grab some corn.

"You can't run away from love because you might get hurt," Janie continued. "That's my lesson, too. All my analyses and inventories can't guarantee a relationship will succeed. Only the people involved can do that. With faith and work and love."

Janie looked at her and Kylie looked back, the words reverberating inside her, reaching deep to her very soul.

"Kylie? You okay?" Janie asked. "You look like you broke a tooth."

"That's just me seeing the light. It hurts a little."

"Thank goodness."

"If you need a dentist, though, I have a good one," Gail said. "Divorced sister you could maybe talk into becoming a client."

Kylie and Janie just laughed, looking into each other's eyes. Love hurt, Kylie knew, but it also healed. And it was what mattered most in the world. She loved her sister. She loved her life and her work. And she loved Cole.

So much she'd scared herself away. But no more. She had to talk to him. Judging from her sister, love was worth the risk.

It would have to wait for the news, which was about to start. And maybe she had a better idea for how to do this….

"YOU WANT ME to go on a date?" Cole said to Janie. It was a mere two weeks since his breakup with Kylie and Janie had called him out of the blue.

"It'll be good for you."

He couldn't imagine anything worse. "Thanks, but you'd better deactivate my file for a year or so. I'm not ready." He wondered if he ever would be.

"Listen, the truth is, Cole, I need a favor. We've been swamped since the news story aired and the new receptionist misbooked somebody. We need you to stand in for a guy…just this once."

He'd seen the follow-up newscast, which had made Personal Touch look like the answer to every dating dilemma. The kiss-ass piece screamed, *Please don't sue us!* to his attorney mind, but he'd been relieved for Janie, since he'd been partly the cause of the scandal.

"You want me as a stand-in date? The last time you did this, all hell broke loose." He'd fallen in love with his stand-in and gotten his heart broken so hard it seemed permanently wrecked.

"This is an emergency. Besides, if I know you, you've been working too hard all week and you need a break. It's Friday night, Cole."

The truth was that lately, he'd been pretty balanced, leaving the office most nights by seven. He and Trisha had agreed to work as a team, bent on proving they could be successful and still have lives. But that didn't mean he wanted a Friday night date.

"I have a dog waiting for me," he said. He'd gone straight from returning Radar to his neighbor to a Cairn breeder and gotten Lulu, a sweet ball of furry energy that soothed his pain.

"I'm sure your dog wouldn't begrudge you a few laughs over a quick dinner. Can't a neighbor watch it?"

She could. "I'd rather not ask."

"It's just a dinner. I swear you won't be sorry."

"Janie…"

"Consider it a personal favor to me. Which you owe me after you almost lost me my company, remember? You don't want me to burst into tears, do you?"

"No, I don't." She was laying it on thick, but he did owe her. His affair with Kylie had taught him the importance of balance. And the power of love.

He wanted to ask about Kylie…was she liking L.A.? Was she happy? But that would only hurt. Instead, he gave in and said, "Where and when and what's her name?"

"You'll be glad you went. Trust me."

He did trust her. She knew what she was doing. The woman she'd selected for him—Deborah—had been his perfect match. She just hadn't been Kylie.

In an hour, he sat at the same restaurant where he'd met Kylie—a painful irony—waiting for a medium-height brunette named Kay. For old time's sake, he'd sat at the same table and ordered a martini. He half expected to see Kylie dash in, rumpled and ink-smeared and dripping with chocolate mint.

And Kay was late, which annoyed him more. He wanted to get back to Lulu…and moping.

"Sorry I'm late."

At the familiar voice, his gaze shot up to find Kylie looking down at him. He lunged to his feet, making his chair scrape against the floor. "Kay" was obviously "K." Jane was something else.

Air crackled around her and men watched her like the first time, but she only had eyes for him. A loose dress danced around her body like the mischief dancing in her eyes, still the shiniest he'd ever seen. Mischief and something else that stopped his heart.

Love.

"No problem," he said, struggling to control his voice and his hopes. "In my experience, the best dates start a little late."

"I'm sorry to inform you that your date couldn't make it tonight," Kylie said, moving closer. "Will I do?"

"Absolutely." She was the song in his heart, the light in his life, just as Gail had described her husband. He hauled her close and kissed her deeply, surprised at how fiercely she returned the embrace. This was new. This was strong. He realized with happy relief that she'd been holding back all along. Right now she was squeezing him so tightly she might have a cracked rib.

She broke off the kiss and looked at him with eyes hot with love. "Cole." She seemed to taste the word on her tongue. "How did that sound?"

"Like you love me." She'd said his name as if her life depended on him. He wanted it to.

"I want to wake up Sunday mornings smiling into your eyes."

Where had she got that...? From his video. "Hell, I thought I told Gail to erase that part."

"I loved it, Cole. Every desperate and embarrassing word."

"Then I guess I made that tape for you."

"We need each other," she said. "To do it right. To know when it's time for *Friday Night Stand-Up* or at least to tape it for watching later. To know when to order Mexican food."

"Whenever I smell frying lard, I long for you." He was so happy he wanted to whoop out loud.

"I was thinking maybe we could get a dog?"

"Already done. Lulu. She could be Radar's twin. I'm training her to deposit her opinions outside, however. What about L.A., Kylie?"

"I'm staying here. Keeping K. Falls PR. I'll do contract work for S-Mickey-B, but I don't need some big firm to validate my abilities. You helped me see that. I'll still have travel and I won't have much time for charity balls or volunteer boards of directors or—"

"Who cares? I'll be too busy planting your garden. How do you feel about decorative cabbage? And you'll be taking more baths. Long, long, hot baths. And not alone."

Kylie looked into Cole's eyes and for the first time let herself accept his love. She didn't shut down after a few scary seconds. She took it in and let it swirl through her, despite the fear, the risk, the worry.

Since her talk with Janie, Kylie had let herself slow down, let in the world and her reactions to it. It wasn't easy and it involved some pain, but it also made life more vivid. And nothing was more vivid to her than the love she felt for Cole.

"I was scared to love you, scared it wouldn't work out. Janie helped me see that."

"I told you she was wise."

"Yeah." She'd begun to see Janie's business through new eyes, too, and had some innovative promotion ideas to go with it. Though Janie hardly needed help. The rebuttal news piece had gone so well, the phone was ringing off the hook with new clients.

She no longer saw Personal Touch as silly and desperate and sickeningly romantic. It was sweet and serious and sturdy with hope. For every sappy song playing overhead, Janie had a sensible file folder with compatibility scores. Head in the clouds, feet on the ground. That was how Janie approached love. And it was how Kylie would approach it, too.

"Help me be brave, okay?" she said to Cole.

"I'll consider it my life's quest," he said, his eyes twinkling. "Along with making you happy. And making you the best chile relleno you've ever tasted."

"Are you sure?"

"You're a self-starter and a team player, right?"

They laughed together, the sound like magic, like heaven. There were no guarantees, as Janie said, but they had faith and work and love. Tons of that.

Then they kissed and she became vaguely aware of applause. They separated and found three waiters clustered around their table with the small candlelit cake she'd requested.

"What's this?" Cole said, his eyes shining with love and surprise.

"Our anniversary—one-month to the day that we had our mistake date."

"Best mistake I ever made," Cole said.

Together they leaned over and blew out the candle. And Kylie knew without guessing that their wishes were a perfect match.

* * * * *

Watch for TEASE ME
by Dawn Atkins coming in November 2005
from Harlequin Blaze.

HARLEQUIN®

Blaze™

COMING NEXT MONTH

www.eHarlequin.com